WHEN HE DESIRES

A DARK MAFIA ROMANCE

FALLEN GOD DUET
BOOK 1

GABRIELLE SANDS

To everyone who's ever felt like they don't belong: You don't need them. You just need a possessive mobster who will love you exactly as you are.

CHAPTER 1

In that book which is my memory,
on the first page of the chapter that is the day when I first met
you, appear the words,
"Here begins a new life."

- Dante, La Vita Nuova

NERO

Three days after we leave the bodies in New York, Sandro and I cross the border into Missouri.

"You been to the Ozarks before?" the kid asks, his hands relaxed on the wheel and his voice chipper enough to make me think he's forgotten how we ended up here. "I've heard it's beautiful."

Outside the car window is a sea of green. July in southern Missouri looks like nature threw up all over the winding roads, the canopy lush and overflowing. Every now and then, the midday sun reflects off a river hidden somewhere in the valleys. When I roll down the window, I can hear it gurgling.

"I'm more of a big-city guy." I prop my elbow on the window ledge and drag my closed fist over my lips.

Places like this are too quiet. They make my thoughts too loud.

I've always been a gangster. My stepdad was a gangster. My mom came from a long line of gangsters. If there's a gene for crime, there's no doubt I've got it.

Imagine a truck stopped on the side of the road with a flat tire, the driver trying to get enough signal to call Triple-A.

You see a man in need.

I see an opportunity.

I see crates of merchandise inside the aluminum body. I see the empty stretch of road where other drivers know better than to stop after dark. I see the bags under the driver's eyes and know he won't put up a fight.

Depending on what's inside the truck, there's anywhere from ten to fifty grand to be made in fifteen minutes. All I've got to do is load up whatever I can into my own vehicle, destroy the driver's phone so that he can't call the cops, and drive the merchandise over to one of our warehouses.

Show me another job where you can make that kind of dough that quickly.

Now imagine you do this for a few years, and you have ten or twenty guys doing it on your behalf and giving you seventy percent of what they get just because you've worked your way up the food chain.

It's beautiful. There's nothing else like it.

I've always *loved* being a gangster.

But as of three days ago, I can't be one anymore.

I reach inside my jacket pocket and take out the ID again. Staring at my fake name is a new habit. Reading it over and over. Hoping that it'll feel real any minute now.

"My name is Rowan Miller," I say under my breath.

Sandro glances over. "Trying it on?"

"Something like that." I tilt the plastic card against the light, watching the laser engraving shimmer. If only the ID came with instructions...

Who the fuck is Rowan Miller?

I've been Nero for thirty years, but now I'm *him*.

"It's better than Sam fucking Wilkins." Sandro huffs. "Sounds like the name of a kid who got his head shoved in the toilet in grade school. Just my luck."

I give him a look. If I were him, and I had to pick one thing to complain about, it wouldn't be my new name. I don't get him. Rafe told him he had to leave with me, and he just went with it, as if he's happy to play babysitter.

Guess he didn't have much to leave behind.

I did.

"We need to iron out our backstories," I tell him gruffly.

He nods. "Over lunch? I could eat."

We're far enough from New York that we can stop for good, but where? Kansas City, Columbia, and Springfield form a triangle, and we're driving somewhere in the middle of it. I zoom in on my phone's GPS and a plethora of tiny towns appear as dots on the map.

When I search for "lunch," the first place that pops up—Frostbite Tavern—is in a nearby town called Darkwater Hollow. In the photos, it looks like the kind of bar-slash-restaurant-slash-coffee shop you find in places that don't have enough demand for any of those businesses to exist on their own.

"There's a spot ten minutes away." I type the address into the car's navigation system. "Let's stop there."

"Works for me." Sandro turns up the stereo, and I see a falcon circling the field next to us as it hunts for prey.

For a moment back in New York, I was prey. Gino Ferraro's prey. Maybe I still am. I'm playing dead, aren't I? Pretending to be someone I'm not just so the fucking Ferraros don't come after me.

I clench my jaw. Over the last three days while driving in this car, sleeping in raggedy hotel rooms, and eating shitty gas-station food, I've been going through the five stages of grief.

Denial. Anger. Bargaining. Depression. Acceptance.

I'm stuck in between the last two.

Yeah, I've accepted that I'm a nobody now, but it's still depressing as fuck. I can never go back home. Sandro's the only person left in my life who knows who I really am.

My life's work—my legacy—was destroyed in one day. I spent my life following my don's orders, and this is where I ended up.

No wonder every time I swallow, there's a bitter aftertaste.

IT's past noon when we get to Frostbite Tavern—a log cabin with a big front porch, square windows, and a sloping roof. Its name is written in cursive lettering on a hanging sign just above the entrance. The parking lot's nearly full.

"It's busy," Sandro says.

"It's probably the only place to eat around here."

Inside, something smells really good. I glance around the bustling dining room, taking in the black-and-white photographs on wood-paneled walls and the bar at the back. The atmosphere is cheerful. Welcoming.

So is the thirty-something-year-old hostess. She gives me a wide smile as she leads us to a table in the corner, her eyes skating down my body with a flicker of interest.

I smile back. At least some things never change.

"Your waitress will be with you in a minute." Two plastic-covered menus appear on the table in front of us. She taps against them once with red nails and walks away.

Sandro picks up one of the menus and sighs. "You know, it's not fair."

"What?"

He tips his head in the direction of the hostess. "*That.* The way you just exist, and they can't get enough of it."

"Don't know what you're talking about," I say just to annoy him.

"I guess I get it. You look like a super-sized version of one of those Greek statues. What are you, six-four?"

"Six-five."

He rolls his eyes. "Of course you are. If I ever want to get laid, no fucking way am I bringing you as my wingman."

I chuckle. "Get laid? Aren't you too young for that?"

He huffs. "I'm twenty-two. Don't tell me you were a virgin when you were my age."

I drag my thumb over my bottom lip. Mary from down the street was the first woman I slept with. I was fifteen and past my growth spurt. She was three years older than me and had tits you could drown in. "Definitely not."

"There you go." He glances around, taking stock of the tables around us, and then he leans in, his voice dropping into a low whisper. "So? What are we going to do?"

"We've got to find something to occupy us in retirement." That last word feels all wrong. Didn't think I was ever going to retire, let alone do it at thirty.

Sandro gives me an assessing look. "I've got to admit, I'm having a hard time seeing you answer to anyone other than Rafe."

The mention of my old boss's name ignites a ball of fury in the pit of my stomach. So maybe I'm still in the anger stage.

He wasn't just a boss. He was a friend. And he told me to play dead and never come back to the city that's been home my whole life.

I did what he fucking told me to do. I saved his wife.

But Rafe fucked up that night. His mistake kicked off a sequence of events that ended in my ruin. It was an accident, but a part of me resents that I ended up being the only one paying the consequences.

I run my fist over my lips. "You couldn't fucking pay me enough to work for anyone ever again." I'm done giving people that much power over me. "We need to start our own business."

"Yeah, but no funny business, right? We've got a second chance here, Ne—"

"Rowan."

"Fuck, right. Rowan." Sandro scratches at his brow and sits back in his seat. "It's going to take me a moment to get used to calling you that."

A waitress stops by the table and pours coffee into the white mugs in front of us. "Are you ready to order?"

"Sure, doll. I'd like a—"

"I'm not your doll."

My gaze snaps up.

Our waitress is a tiny blond. Her hair's pulled back in a ponytail, and she's got a pair of striking blue eyes that are giving me a hell of a glare. I feel like a belligerent schoolboy being chastised by the sexy teacher for trying to flirt with her. It's a ridiculous thought because she can't be much older than Sandro, and she's definitely younger than me.

But she is sexy. Beautiful, in an unconventional way. It sneaks up on you the longer you look at her. The pursed lips and air of hostility somehow only make her more attractive.

7

I scan her up and down. This makes her glare at me even harder, but it's worth it, because beneath that uniform is a body that could cause a traffic accident.

My lips curve into a smile—the one that makes women turn to putty in my hands. "I apologize, miss. Didn't mean to offend you."

Her gaze lingers on my lips for a moment, but her expression doesn't soften. She places—more like slams—the coffee jug on the table, pulls a notepad from her trousers, and fishes out a black pen from behind her ear. "What can I get you?"

"What do you recommend?"

Her eyes jump back to my face. I'm still smiling, and by this point, most women would start smiling back.

But her?

She's giving me nothing.

Actually, she's glowering like she still hasn't forgiven me for calling her doll. You'd think I committed a felony with that word.

"The special today is chicken cacciatore with crispy roast potatoes and asparagus. It's good." Her tone is clipped.

"I'll take it."

She scribbles my order in the notepad and turns to Sandro. "And you?"

"Same for me."

"Great." The waitress snatches the menus off the table and turns to leave.

"Wait."

She stops. Her shoulders rise and fall on a deep breath. When she turns, her expression is more guarded than a top-security prison. "Yes?"

"You got a newspaper lying around here?"

She brings over a paper someone left behind on one of the nearby tables. "Here you go. Anything else?" Her eyes are the same kind of mesmerizing blue as the lake we drove past on the way here.

"Thank you. That's all."

She walks away and disappears around a corner.

Sandro laughs. "You should have seen your face. Now you know how it is for the rest of us mortals."

It's my turn to roll my eyes. It's not like I've never encountered a woman who didn't like me. It just doesn't happen often. "Whatever."

I open the paper on the table and turn to the classifieds, looking for a lead. Job openings, used cars for sale, nanny for hire...

"Look." Sandro reaches over and points at one of the listings. "Handy Heroes. Home renovation business for sale. Think that could work? We know a bit about construction."

"We know how to shake down concrete companies for a percentage of their contracts. Not sure that's all that relevant."

"I helped one of the other drivers back home renovate his apartment last year."

"You did?"

"Yeah. It was fun. I'd have to learn some stuff, but I think I could manage the projects. And you can handle the sales. You're good at shit like talking to people."

He's not wrong. I read over the listing again. Is this going to be enough to keep me from blowing my brains out from boredom?

Guess there's only one way to find out.

"Let's give them a call."

Sandro pulls out his cellphone, and by the time the blond returns with our plates, we've got a meeting scheduled with the owner.

The chicken cacciatore smells incredible. Sandro's no better than a starved animal, digging into his meal as soon as it appears in front of him. The blond looks at him for a moment before sliding her gaze to me.

That blue really is magnificent.

I open my mouth to ask her for her name, but she turns on her heel and struts away before I get the words out.

"So if this Handy Heroes thing works out," Sandro says, his mouth half full, "you want to find a place to stay somewhere in this town?"

I drag my gaze away from the retreating girl. "Yeah. I think Darkwater Hollow could grow on me."

CHAPTER 2

4 MONTHS LATER

BLAKE

I'm just getting to the good part of my book—the heroine's stranded at an inn during a snowstorm, and the morally gray fae prince walks in—when headlights flood through my window. I sit up against the fortress of pillows I've piled into the window seat and squint.

Who is that?

That massive truck definitely doesn't belong to any of my neighbors, and Landhorne Lane isn't the kind of street that gets a lot of random visitors.

There are only four houses on the lane, two on each side. My house is the smallest, but it's also the cutest with white shutters, a cozy front porch, and a cornflower-blue front door. I spent all morning painting it in time for the viewing tomorrow. I'm hoping the splash of color will be enough to distract the potential buyers from looking at the monstrosity next door.

The Jackson house.

The truck with the blinding headlights turns onto their driveway.

I slip my finger between the pages of the book so I don't lose my place and clamber up to my knees to get a better look. Who's going over there at six p.m. on a Saturday?

It's not the Jacksons. They never visit anymore. As far as I can tell, they've left the place to rot after Earl Jackson became some kind of a confectionary mogul in Kansas City.

The door of the truck swings open, and a long jean-clad leg appears.

I press the book against my chest.

Is that...

Hold on a sec.

Rowan Miller?

The man himself climbs out of the truck in a leather jacket that fits his broad shoulders so well it should be criminal.

My lips tighten in disapproval.

It's been four months since Rowan came to Darkwater Hollow with his business partner, and in those *four freaking months*, he's managed to sleep with half the town's female population. Okay, that may be a slight exaggeration, but my point stands—the guy's a womanizer.

As far as I'm concerned, there are few things worse than a handsome man who knows he's handsome, and Rowan *definitely* knows.

He walks around town with that insufferable swagger and a permanent cocky smirk on his face. His attitude reminds me a bit of Brett—my ex—another tall, handsome guy, who turned out to be a liar and a cheat.

I frown at Rowan's silhouette. Did the Jacksons hire him to fix their place up?

My gaze drifts over the dead plants, the overgrown path that leads to the creaky front porch, and the sagging boxes filled with God knows what stacked haphazardly by the front door.

That property is a freaking nightmare. No wonder I haven't gotten any offers on my own home. Who wants to live next to a place that looks haunted? It really does, complete with a steeply pitched roof, peeling black exterior, and a turret.

Rowan shuts the truck and rakes his fingers through his slightly wavy dark hair. He glances around the yard and then moves toward the front door, a set of keys jingling in his hand.

It's late for an appointment, isn't it?

Wait a sec.

There is a mattress in the back of his truck...and a bunch of cardboard boxes...

Is he...*moving in*?

My eyes widen as he unlocks the front door and steps inside.

What the hell?

The book falls out of my hands, nearly knocking over the full mug of tea that's beside my empty one on the windowsill.

This is bad.

I snatch my phone up and press one on speed dial.

Del picks up on the first ring. "Aw, do you miss me already?" Wind crackles over the line. "It's only been like five hours since we last spoke."

"I always miss you, but that's not why I'm calling. Do you have a few minutes?"

"Yeah, I'm just sitting in Golden Gate Park and watching hot, shirtless dudes do calisthenics." She sighs. "God, I love San Francisco."

"Living your best life, huh?"

"You know it, babe. What's up?"

Del left Darkwater Hollow two years ago, but she's better than me at staying on top of all the town gossip. And right now, I need all the intel I can get.

"Did Aunt Lottie mention anything to you about Rowan Miller moving someplace new?"

"Mr. Handy Hero?" Del giggles at the name of Rowan's construction company. "Based on what Aunt Lottie tells me, I wouldn't mind if he got those hands on me."

"Gross. God knows where they've been. What exactly did she tell you?"

"Why the sudden interest in the newest local eye candy? Have you finally decided to heed my advice and start dating again?"

"Definitely not." After what happened with Brett, the thought of dating makes me want to hurl. "I think Rowan is moving in next door."

Del gasps. "Into that dump? *Why?*"

"That's what I want to know. No sane person would choose to live there." The last tenants the Jacksons had were definitely *not* sane. They were the worst. They kept my mom and me up all night with their loud parties, left beer bottles and litter all over their front yard, and they even broke the fence between our properties. Of course, the Jacksons still haven't gotten around to repairing it, and I'm not holding my breath they ever will.

I don't need a repeat of that, especially now that I'm trying to sell my house. The neighbor across from me, the one who blasts heavy metal early in the morning while I'm trying to sleep, is bad enough. When my agent came by last week, we could barely speak over the racket.

"The rent must be cheap, but I heard Rowan is doing well for himself. Did I tell you Aunt Lottie's thinking of renovating her whole kitchen now? This is after Rowan promised he'd come and check on things himself."

I roll my eyes again. "Of course he did. What else has she told you about him?"

"She mostly fawned about how handsome he is. Want me to call her for some real info?"

"Yes, please."

"Okay, I'll call you back in five. Actually, make that fifteen. You know she loves to talk."

We hang up. Aunt Lottie is Del's aunt in name only. She's an eighty-something-year-old gossip who taught Del and me all through grade school, and the two of them have kept in touch.

I glance back out the window. Rowan left the front door cracked open. Maybe once he sees the state of the place, he'll change his mind about renting it. The Jacksons haven't done anything to it in decades.

When he doesn't come out for a few minutes, I pick my book back up, but I'm so rattled that I just reread the same two sentences over and over again.

Books have always been an escape for me, a reliable way to forget about my problems for a few blissful hours. But apparently, even a good story is no match for this level of disturbance.

Ugh. There goes my plan of a nice, peaceful evening. I won't be able to focus until Del calls me back.

My phone buzzes five minutes later. "Aunt Lottie confirmed he's slept with Gina Hardy, Penelope Nott, and Casey Smith," Del says. "All give him glowing reviews in the bedroom."

I wrinkle my nose. "Ugh." Why would anyone with an ounce of self-respect want to hook up with a guy the rest of the town's slept with? Just to be another notch on the bedpost? It defies comprehension.

"And there's a shocking rumor going around that even Aunt Lottie was reluctant to share."

"But you got it out of her."

"Of course I did," Del says gleefully. "Apparently, two weeks ago, Rowan slept with Abigail MacDonald."

"Abigail MacDonald... Isn't she married to the owner of the bakery?"

"Yes! That's why it's so hush-hush. Apparently, someone saw them getting very cozy at a bar."

My stomach curdles. "That's awful. Her poor husband."

A beat passes. "Oh, babe, I'm sorry. I didn't mean to make your mind go there."

"It's okay." For a town as small as Darkwater Hollow, there sure seem to be a lot of cheaters. "Did Lottie know anything about why he's moving in here?"

"Nope. Actually, she knew surprisingly little about his personal life beyond his bed partners."

"How is that possible? She can get a fish to talk."

"She said he has this way of answering questions without telling you anything."

"That's a *handy* skill."

Del snorts. "Nice one. Look, I'm sorry, but she really had no idea when I told her he was moving in next door to you. She said he's a gentleman. He gives her a frequent-customer discount now."

I rub my index finger between my brows. "That's a sure way to her heart, but I think she and I have different definitions for the word gentleman."

"I doubt he'll give you any trouble like the last neighbors did."

I shake my head, skeptical. "If he does something to that house to lower my chance of getting a damn offer, I swear..."

Del blows out a breath. "Still no luck? I forgot to ask how it's going with that fancy Kansas City realtor. You met with her again last week, right?"

"Yeah, Nicole. She came by." Her commission is higher than anyone else I've talked to, but at least she's willing to work with me. The two agents from Darkwater Hollow never returned my calls. It didn't surprise me, but it still pissed me off. "We have a viewing tomorrow morning." The only one on the calendar so far.

Del sighs. "Good luck. You've got to get out of that house and that town and that *fucking* restaurant."

"You're preaching to the choir." I'd love to leave Darkwater Hollow, but to start over somewhere new, I need money. Far more money than I make working at Frostbite Tavern. I'm living paycheck to paycheck, saving a tiny bit each month after all my bills are paid.

I tuck my hair behind my ear. "You know, I did the math. If I sell the house at a decent price, I'll make about twenty thousand after paying off my mom's outstanding medical bills. That'll be enough for a fresh start somewhere far from here."

"I'm so proud of you."

"What for?"

"Are you kidding? You're the most selfless person I know. You spent six years taking care of your mom on your own, while he who shall not be named peaced the hell out of town without a care in the world."

I snort. "Okay, I know you hate my brother, but comparing him to Voldemort is a bit low."

"The fact that you're defending him proves my point."

"I did what I had to do."

"Yes, and now it's time to put yourself first. No more making sacrifices for other people. You deserve a fresh start, and most importantly, you need to leave that toxic asshole behind."

My laugh is bitter. "Yeah. I should get an award for Dark-water Hollow's biggest idiot."

"Hey, don't say that," Del says with reproach.

"It's true. I should have seen it coming."

Rowan emerges out of the house sans leather jacket and with a bunch of stuff in his thick arms.

Broken stuff.

A chair, some rotten planks of wood, a plastic garbage bag...

Wait. What in the hell is he doing? I'm glued to the window. "Hold on a sec," I mutter to Del.

And then my new neighbor unceremoniously dumps everything right on his front lawn.

"Oh, hell no," I hiss. Nicole is going to kill me if that's there when she comes tomorrow with the potential buyers.

"What's happening?"

"He's making a goddamn mess."

"Go yell at him!"

"On it. I'll call you later." I hang up and jump to my feet.

There was a time when I wouldn't have said a word, but four months ago, I decided I was done acting small.

Rowan Miller is about to learn that if he's going to live there, he's going to have to deal with me.

And unlike the rest of the people in this town, I'm not going to let him get away with *anything*.

CHAPTER 3

BLAKE

I slide on my Vans, throw on a cardigan, and tumble out the front door, fists clenched and heart pumping.

Rowan's back is to me. I march toward his hulking frame, ready for a fight. "What on *earth* do you think you're doing?"

He pauses mid-step, all six-foot-something of him, and turns around.

I've seen him plenty of times. He and his business partner have dinner at Frostbite every few weeks, and even though I'm usually behind the bar, sometimes we're short on staff, and I help the servers out. I brought his dinner to him once or twice, so I know exactly what I'm about to encounter.

And still, his face catches me off guard.

It's the face of a seductive villain straight from the pages of one of my books. Tanned skin. Thick brows. Terrific bone structure.

The symmetry of his features is so pronounced that it borders on offensive.

And it doesn't end with his face. Not even close.

I glance up and see the wind ruffling his soft, chestnut hair, blowing a lock across his forehead. He brushes it away with a careless swipe of his tattooed hand.

I glance down and see his body. It's well-built and extravagant. The kind of body meant to be lusted after, obsessed over.

If someone's appearance was the only thing that mattered, I'd say it's no wonder the women in town fall over themselves to climb into his bed.

But looks aren't everything, and I'm convinced that no one that good-looking can possibly be a decent person. When people treat you like you're God's gift to women, eventually you start to believe them.

Rowan blinks at me a few times, apparently confused. "Taking out the trash," he deadpans after a moment. A brow arches on his infuriatingly perfect face. "Is that all right?"

"No, it's not actually. You can't just show up here and turn the Jacksons' front lawn into a dump."

"Who are you? The neighborhood watch?"

I give him a withering look. How nice of him to mock me and remind me exactly who I'm dealing with here.

An arrogant ass.

"You can call me whatever you want, as long as you get rid of *that*." I point at the mess. "If you're renovating the house, you'll need to get a dumpster. I would have expected a general contractor to know that."

A smirk. "You know who I am?"

Of course I know who he is, but his tone makes it sound like if I say yes, I'll be admitting to something illicit. Heat starts to travel over my chest and up my neck.

Then I realize his company name is right on his truck. I jerk my head in its direction. "I can read."

The smirk doesn't budge. "I'm not renovating anything. I'm moving in."

"You sure you got the address right?"

"One Landhorne Lane."

Whelp. That's the confirmation I was dreading. So this is really happening, which means I have to set him straight right away.

I place my fists on my hips. "Here's the deal. I've already got one troublesome idiot living across from me who blasts his damn stereo from seven a.m. each morning. I will not put up with any nonsense from you too."

He looks at the houses behind me. "Number two or number four?"

"I'll let you discover that for yourself tomorrow morning."

His eyes ping back to me.

"If you're really moving in, you have a choice to make," I tell him. "Are you going to be a good neighbor or a bad one? Choose carefully."

"What if I choose wrong?"

"I will make life very unpleasant for you." I sound confident, even though I have no idea what I could do to make things difficult for him. I'll figure it out.

Amusement skates over his features. "And if I choose right?"

"Then I'll walk back inside my house and never bother you again."

He takes a step toward me, as if he wants to get a closer look at me. From here, I see the fine lines on his forehead. They seem to confirm he's at least a few years older than me. Maybe in his thirties? There's no boy left in him. He's all man.

"I don't know." His voice drops lower. "I'm kind of enjoying being bothered by you."

Shock crackles through me. "Are you seriously flirting with me right now?"

The way it takes him just a bit too long to answer tells me he wasn't expecting to be called out. "No."

My God. He really thought that would work. *Flirt with her, and she'll shut right up.*

He's used to everyone falling all over themselves in his presence, isn't he? He thinks that megawatt smile is going to be enough for me to let him off the hook.

No such luck, pal.

"Good. *Don't.* Now listen up. I know you don't know me, but I—"

"I've seen you around. You work at Frostbite. Good to know you're just as hostile off duty as you are at work."

Excuse me? "I'm not hostile," I snap.

He makes a light scoff and takes another step forward. "Oh sure, you're just a ball of sunshine."

Do we really need to be standing this close? We're practically chest to chest. From here, the fact that he's about two heads taller than me is impossible to ignore.

The oxygen inside my lungs thins.

I know what he's doing. He's changing his strategy, moving from flirting to intimidation tactics.

Even with the wind swirling around us, his focused stare right into my eyes makes my cheeks prickle with heat. It would be great if I could back away a few feet, but that would be admitting defeat. And no way am I doing that.

I wave at the pile of trash. "The Jacksons don't care about their place, but I care about mine. I won't let you get away with this."

He drags a palm over his chin, his expression turning thoughtful. "What's the big deal? I'm not planning on leaving it there forever."

"No. You can't leave it there *at all*, okay?" Nicole is going to be here first thing in the morning.

He raises his palms. "Fine. I'll clean it up."

"When?"

"Tonight."

"Good." I flick my hand between his property and mine. "There's history here, and it's not pretty. The last time someone lived in that house, they brought a band of degenerates with them."

"A band of degenerates?" His lips twitch. "Where can I find this band? They sound like a great time."

My eyes narrow. "That's not funny. They broke the fence at the back, and no one's fixed it. They—"

"Why don't you write it all down?"

"Huh?"

"Write down your...list of grievances. Sounds like it might be a long one."

"To what end?"

"So that I don't have to listen to you complain about each little thing. Write 'em down, and I'll take care of them all."

I scowl. "Is this your way of trying to get me off your lawn? An empty promise to solve all my problems?"

He shrugs. "Write the list and see how empty my promises are."

He can't be serious. When something sounds too good to be true, it usually is. But it would be stupid not to take him up on that offer, even if the likelihood of him doing what he says is low. "Fine. I'll go do that. Right now. Stay right here."

"I wouldn't dream of leaving." His gaze bores into me to the point of discomfort. His hazel eyes are dark and thoughtful, and they flicker with the slightest hint of mischief.

I step away from him, and it feels like breaking through a force field. It's easier to breathe, easier to think with some distance between us.

Don't trust him, my gut says. *No matter what promises he makes.*

He huffs a low breath, like he's amused with me. I spin on my heel and march back inside my house, but the whole time, I feel his gaze warming my back.

Inside, I don't bother taking off my shoes. I barrel straight to the kitchen where I keep my notepad and pen, and I write down everything that's bothering me about that damn house, from the broken fence to the banging shutters.

Rowan was right about one thing.

It's a long list.

I'm half expecting him to not be there when I come back out, but he's in the exact spot I left him, arms crossed over his chest and face turned up to the sky.

I pause just on the edge of my porch. What is he doing? Looking at the stars?

The moon has been out since late afternoon, a pale orb in the sky. Now that it's dark out, its full silver glory casts a shadow behind Rowan's imposing form.

The image of him in the moonlight with that old house looming behind him and the dead grass at his feet imprints on my mind. He looks like a dark god coming to rule over his shadowy kingdom.

I shake my head. This is what I get for reading dark fantasy books late into the night.

I walk over to him, and his gaze slowly drops down to me. His expression is unreadable. He plucks the piece of paper out of my hand, unfolds it, and begins to read.

"The most immediate problem is the broken fence between our backyards," I advise while his eyes move back and forth over the paper.

"I gathered as much. You underlined it twice." He squints. "Three times."

I sniff. "I also put a star beside it. Just in case the underlining is unclear."

His eyes snap to mine. "Next time, I suggest you highlight it. It helps orient stupid little men like me."

Little? There's nothing remotely little about him. In fact, if certain rumors are to be believed—

Oh God. Don't go there.

He gives the list a shake. "I'll get everything fixed."

"I'll believe it when I see it."

His chuckle coasts over my skin like a gust of warm wind. "I don't think we've ever been officially introduced. I'm Rowan Miller." He offers me his tanned hand. My gaze momentarily latches onto the tattoos darkening his flesh, letters and designs I can't quite make out in the dark.

I swallow. What's one handshake? It doesn't mean we've made peace. "I'm Blake Wolfe."

One side of his mouth lifts. "Nice to meet you, Blake."

I try to ignore the heat of his touch.

I try to ignore the way his palm completely engulfs mine.

And I definitely try to ignore the way my heart stutters inside my ribcage.

But that night, as I lie in bed, I can't seem to get the memory of it out of my head.

CHAPTER 4

NERO

Blake walks across my lawn, her arms wrapped around her narrow waist, her hair glistening in the moonlight like liquid gold.

She slips inside her house, but her scent lingers in the air. A blend of vanilla and lavender. Her soap? Or maybe her shampoo?

Whatever it is, it makes me want to press my nose into the crook of her neck and see if she tastes as good as she smells.

I recognized her right away, but it took me a moment to get over the shock of having *her* next door to me.

"Don't call me doll."

Whenever Sandro and I go to Frostbite and she's working, he reminds me of that comment. I think he gets a kick out of knowing there's at least one woman in this town who doesn't appear to like me. He'll be fucking thrilled to hear she gave me a scolding on day one as her neighbor.

Yeah, I'm not telling him that.

I turn around and walk back inside my new house.

You know how some people have that little voice inside their head telling them when they're doing something they shouldn't? Not me. The voice in my head is loud as fuck.

You really think buying this house will solve your problems?

That's Nero. The guy I used to be.

You got a better idea?

And that's Rowan. The guy I am now.

Rowan tells Nero he can be happy running a clean business he bought with dirty money. He tells him that one day he'll be able to think of his old life without the urge to trash his surroundings and scream into the void. He tells him it's fine to feel bored and empty sometimes, or most of the time, if that's the price of staying alive.

And he tells him that everything will be fine as long as he finds himself a woman for the night. After all, women always used to make things better.

But it seems like even that's not true anymore.

At least none of the women I've been with over the past few months did the job. As soon as I slip out of bed, that hollow, nauseating emptiness creeps right back in.

So now, I'm trying something else.

I put Blake's list on the dusty counter in the kitchen and wash my hands at the sink just as a firm knock sounds against the front door.

"Come in," I call out.

The door creaks open, and the floor vibrates with the thud of Sandro's footsteps. A second later, he swaggers into my living room wearing a Handy Heroes T-shirt. There's a six-pack dangling from one hand and a cigarette from another. He halts in the middle of the room and looks around. "Holy shit."

He's probably having the same thought I had when I first walked in. This place isn't fit for human habitation. But that's the point. I bought this house to keep myself so busy I'll have zero time to be idle or think about the past.

I tip my head at the cigarette. "Put that out."

He glances around. "You got an ash tray?"

"Use whatever you want." A burn mark isn't going to make a difference.

Sandro winces and puts his cig out against the closest wall. "The fuck, man?"

"It's got potential."

He gives me an incredulous look. "Not that I'm questioning you or anything, but...wasn't there anything else available? Or were you that eager to get away from me?"

I wave him off. Sandro wasn't a bad roommate. The two-bedroom apartment we'd shared since we arrived at Dark-water Hollow is more than big enough for both of us, but I was getting tired of the way he kept looking at me. All concerned and shit. Like he's worried one day I'll bolt.

He walks over to the window and moves a yellowish curtain aside. "That shed looks like it's one rainfall away from disintegrating. What's the rent? They should be paying you to live here."

"Rent? I bought it. It was a good deal."

I got the idea from a client. The guy heard through the grapevine that the Jacksons would sell the house on Landhorne for practically nothing, and he thought I might be interested.

There's a play here—restore the house and flip it for a nice profit. When I drove by and saw the state of this place, I thought it would be a while before I ran out of things to do.

Besides work, there's nothing to do in Darkwater Hollow. It's the world's most boring fucking place.

When Sandro and I first bought Handy Heroes, we had our work cut out for us. It was a three-month crash course in construction and subcontractor management. I learned how to deal with suppliers and clients. Sandro picked up all the rest. The company came with three employees—a project manager, an architect, and an estimator. Somehow, we managed to convince all of them to stay and teach us everything they knew.

But now that we know the ropes, there's more downtime.

I fucking hate downtime.

I walk over to stand at Sandro's side and glance out toward the dark backyard. Through the broken fence, I can see Blake's back porch light is on. Is she outside? Cooling down after our confrontation? Having her chew me out shouldn't have given me a thrill, but it did.

At least it was something new.

Sandro drops his hand away from the curtain and wanders into the kitchen. He spots Blake's list on the counter and picks it up. "What's this?"

"A list of repairs I told the girl next door I'd take care of."

Am I really going to fix all the shit she listed?

Eh. Why not?

"Oh yeah?" He gives me a weary look. "How generous. Let me guess, she's cute? Single?"

Yes and probably, but what I say is, "She's none of your damn business." I take the list from him and tuck it into my back pocket.

"Actually, she might be." Sandro scratches his brow. "Look, I'd hate to tell you how to live your life."

"Then don't."

"I wouldn't if I didn't think your behavior might be affecting our business. You know, the one we've worked our asses off to turn around in record time? The one that's finally getting some good traction?"

"Traction. Isn't that the title of one of the business books I saw you reading last week? Learned a new word, kid?"

He frowns.

Fuck. I'm being an asshole.

Sandro works hard. Really fucking hard. I've lost count of how many business and construction books he's inhaled since we arrived here, and that's on top of working twelve-hour days.

He's earned my respect over the last few months, no doubt about that. The fact that I'm the only reason he's here is something that bothers me more than it seems to bother him. I feel like I owe him, which is why I push my irritation down. "Sorry. All right. What are we talking about?"

He crosses his arms over his chest. "Your body count. Do you know Abigail is married?"

Oh, *that*. "I know *now*. I didn't when…" I rub the back of my neck.

Sandro puts his hands on his hips. "When you fucked her?"

What happened with Abigail was sloppy, I'm not above admitting that. I was drinking that night at Hawk's, a bar not far from here. She sidled up onto the stool next to me, I offered to buy her a drink, and the next thing I knew, we were in the bathroom, and my dick was inside her.

"I didn't know her name until that night, let alone know she was married."

"Well, it doesn't really matter, does it? Her husband appears to have found out, along with a good portion of the town. This is a small place. People talk. And your personal reputation is tied to the reputation of our business whether you like it or not."

A hint of unease prickles inside my chest. "You think this Abigail thing is going to affect us?"

"I think we're going to start losing contracts, because most smart men won't want a guy like you buzzing around their wives."

"I wouldn't have done it if I'd known. I don't make a habit of going after other men's women."

"I don't think anyone is interested in hearing you explain your nuanced code of ethics," Sandro snipes. "Just go easy for a while, okay? Focus on the work."

My temper flares. "Since when did you become my boss?"

Sandro gives me a don't-give-me-that-shit look. "We're part-ners. And partners watch out for one another." He blows out a heavy breath. "Look, are you okay?" He gestures vaguely at the living room. "Is this a cry for help?"

I swipe my knuckle against my nose. "I'm fine." The word "fine" tastes distinctly like a lie.

The dreams have gotten bad the past few weeks. I'm always in a cage in the center of a cold, dark room, hands bound and ankles chained. Things are happening outside the room, a gunfight and scuffles, but I'm isolated from them. I'm useless. Helpless.

Sometimes, the dreams turn absurd. I'm a lion with no claws. I'm an eagle with no eyes. I'm a snake without a tongue.

The symbolism isn't lost on me.

In the dreams, my stepdad walks around the cage, studying and judging. He's silent, but I can guess what he's thinking.

You are not built for this. Men like you can only be happy doing one thing.

Sandro sighs. "I don't know, man. You're different than you were before."

"Of course I'm different. I have to be, don't I? I'm a fucking civilian now." *Just like my useless, piece-of-shit father.*

"That's not what I mean."

"Then what do you mean?"

He clenches his jaw. "You've always been an upbeat kinda guy. But these past few weeks... You seem angry all the time. In your head, you're still fighting this, aren't you?"

I shove my hand inside the pocket of my jeans and feel around for my cufflinks. The steel is cool against my palm.

I *am* fucking angry. I was never supposed to end up like this. I miss the thrill of my old life. I miss the danger and the exhilaration and the power.

It's been four months since we left New York, and you'd think I'd get used to the new normal by now, but it only gets harder with each week that passes.

"I know this has been an adjustment," Sandro says. "But you're a resilient motherfucker. I *know* you are. Ever since you and Rafe took me under your wing, I've looked up to you guys."

His words dig right into me. I look at him and remember how he agreed to come here with me without a second thought.

I owe it to him to keep trying to accept this new life. And at the very least, I owe it to him not to do anything that could jeopardize our business.

I nod. "Okay."

"If you ever want to talk—"

"I heard you about the women. Let's move on."

He stares at me for a long moment, obviously worried, and I hate that he feels the need to worry about me.

I'll figure it out. I have to.

Sandro gestures at the six-pack he brought. "Want a beer?"

Usually, I'd say yes, but I'm not in the mood tonight. "I'm good. Long day. Can you drop off the trash I've got outside at the garbage dump?"

"Sure. I'll see you tomorrow."

Once he's gone, I take the cufflinks out and toss them in my palm.

They've gotten scuffed in the past few months from sharing the same pocket as my change.

My old initials are engraved on the back of each.

NDL.

Besides my gun, they're the only artifacts I have left from my old life, and I can't bring myself to get rid of them.

My stepdad gave them to me when I became made at seventeen. He was so proud of me. It was one of the best moments of my life.

And if he could see me now, he'd be turning in his grave.

CHAPTER 5

NERO

Seven oh five a.m., Sunday morning.

I'm supposed to be asleep. Instead, I'm squinting at my phone and trying to figure out what the fuck is going on. It sounds like someone kidnapped me in the middle of the night and dropped me off at a heavy metal concert.

The fuck? Who's blasting that shit this early?

Then I remember my conversation last night with Blake.

It must be the neighbor across the street she mentioned. She wasn't exaggerating about him being loud.

Yeah, that's not gonna work for me.

I throw the blanket off, get to my feet, and grab my T-shirt and a pair of jeans.

Last night, I slept on a mattress on the floor in the living room because the master bedroom needs to be deep cleaned and repainted before it's fit to be used. I'm not even going to bother with the upstairs until I get the first floor in order. The kitchen cabinetry needs replacing, along with the windows and the doors. The bathrooms are a nightmare. Everything needs a fresh coat of paint, but at least the hardwood floors don't look too bad.

I was up late cataloguing everything I need to do and all the materials I need to get from the store today, so I was really fucking looking forward to sleeping in this morning.

Instead, there's already a headache building behind my eyes. This is criminal, and not in a good way.

I step outside. The racket's coming from house number two. The building looks in better shape than mine, but not by much.

I march across the street and pound on the door.

A movement inside the house next door catches my eye. The curtain in the window moves, and an old female face topped off with a pink bonnet peeks out at me.

If it's loud for me, it must be fucking deafening for her. Imagine reaching retirement age, wanting to live a nice, quiet life, and some neighbor from hell moves in.

My anger burns.

I wave at the granny, and she gives me a sad smile before disappearing behind the curtain.

This fuckery ends now.

I bang on the door again and again, not letting up until the lock turns and a man appears.

The smell of stale beer wafting off him brings me right back to when I used to knock on similar doors back in New York.

Different state, same fucking humans.

The man peers at me from behind suspicious, watery eyes. "Who're you?"

I smile. "I live across the street. Moved in last night. Name's Rowan."

He sniffs. "What do you want?"

"Came to introduce myself. What's your name?"

"Elijah— Hey! I didn't invite you in!"

I shove him forward and slam the door behind me. Slide the chain on for good measure too.

"Get out, or I'm calling the cops," Elijah says, but there's a healthy dose of fear in his eyes. I'm a head taller and in far better shape than he is. I could kill him in three seconds.

But I'm not supposed to do things like that anymore, so I've got to get creative.

"Sit down," I command.

When he just sputters in response, I grab him by his wifebeater and throw him into the closest chair. It creaks under his weight.

The stereo's right here in the living room, two huge speakers, the kind you'd see at a fucking concert. That sound system is likely the most expensive thing in the house.

I walk over to it and turn the music down.

"Elijah, do you have a clock in here?"

He blinks at me, looking simultaneously confused, afraid, and pissed off. "Up on the wall."

Yep, there it is, hanging above the stereo, showing the right time. "So you're aware it's just past seven a.m."

"Yes. What are—"

"Just shut the fuck up for a second and focus on answering my questions," I say to him. "Why are you playing this shit this early?"

He crosses his arms over his chest, his lips curled into a sneer. "I work nights. When I get home, I like to unwind. There's nothing wrong with that."

Oh boy. So he's not a lunatic, like I've been suspecting. He just thinks the world revolves around his needs. "I heard people have already asked you to keep it down."

His sneer turns uglier. "What I do on my own property is my own business."

"Not if your business interferes with my business."

There's a set of noise-cancelling headphones sitting on top of one of the speakers. They look high quality, but they're clearly not getting any use.

A rush goes through me. That familiar feeling of being up to no good and knowing I'm going to get away with it.

I scan the dirty living room for something I can use. A roll of duct tape on the coffee table catches my eye.

"Go fuck yourself," he snarls. "Who the fuck do you think you are?"

I grab the tape.

His eyes flash with worry. He starts trying to get up from the chair. "What are you doing?"

I shove him back down. "Let's go over this again. You like to listen to your music as loudly as you want as early in the day as you want. Yeah?"

He gives a hesitant nod. "That's right."

"Understood. I respect that." I reach for the volume dial on the stereo and turn it back up. Someone's screaming like they're being murdered.

The tape releases from the roll with a crackle. Elijah attempts to rise again, but he's bloated and slow. I punch him in the throat, and while he sputters, I wind the tape around him a few times.

The music drowns out his shouts. I work fast, securing his torso to the chair before I do the same to his legs and arms. All the while, he's kicking at me. It's easy to avoid his hits, but they're still annoying as fuck. If he stopped fighting, maybe I'd use less tape.

When I'm finished, I take a long look at my handiwork.

Not bad.

I crack my knuckles, a smirk on my face. *I've still got it.*

"I'll check back in on you after I get home from work," I shout over the music. "Hopefully, your ears aren't bleeding by then."

"What?! What the fuck! Heya, what do you—"

I slap a piece of tape over his mouth. "That's better."

He blinks at me with wide, terrified eyes, and God if it ain't sweet. My body buzzes. I've missed this.

I turn to the stereo, plug in the headphones, and jack the volume all the way up. It's so loud, they vibrate in my hand.

Grinning darkly at Elijah, I put the headphones over his head. His eyes bulge. He makes a muffled screaming sound against the tape and squirms against the restraints.

I squat down in front of him and mouth, "Isn't this what you wanted?"

He shakes his head, tears leaking out of his panicked eyes.

I give him a thumbs-up. "You got this. I won't be too long." Just long enough for him to sustain some moderate hearing damage.

Ignoring his protests, I walk out of the house and let the door slam shut behind me.

The old lady next door is back at the window. She hesitates and then smiles.

I give her a wink.

If Elijah tries to go to the cops after I free him, he sure as fuck won't find any cooperative witnesses. It'll be his word against mine, and I know how to be convincing.

Maybe this is exactly what I need to do to survive in this place.

Let myself have some innocent fun here and there.

I'm halfway across the street when I spot Blake standing on her porch, staring at me. She's in a pair of jeans and a tight beige T-shirt that's snug around her chest. Her tits look fucking perfect. Does she know how cute she is?

There's a mug in her hands. Another one sits on top of the wooden balustrade. I wonder who she's expecting. Bit early for guests.

When I get closer to her, I give her a wave. "Top of the mornin'."

She takes a sip out of her mug and nods in the direction of Elijah's house. "How did you manage that?"

I grin. "I asked nicely. You should try that sometime."

The scowl that appears on her face is priceless. I kind of get off on how she glares at me like I'm a piece of chewed-up gum on the bottom of her shoe.

"Yeah, right. You're really telling me you just asked him to turn it down, and he listened?"

I stop at the foot of my porch. "Sure did. I know this might come as a surprise, but I tend to get along with most people."

"That's because most people are hopelessly swayed by appearances."

My grin widens. "That's an interesting statement. What exactly are you saying about my appearance?"

Pink spots bloom across her cheeks. "The other day I picked up this book because the cover was eye-catching. It stood out on the shelves. You couldn't miss it, you know?"

I place my hands on my hips. "Uh-huh." Where is she going with this?

"But when I got home and started reading it, the story sucked. Behind that pretty cover, there was no substance."

Oh.

She gives me a thin smile. "In my experience, people are often like that too."

Irritation fans through me. "What can you possibly know about my substance when we've barely spoken to each other?"

She stands up straighter and takes another sip of her drink. "It's a small town, Rowan. I know enough." And then she spins on her heel and goes inside her house, leaving the extra mug on the balustrade.

CHAPTER 6

BLAKE

Here's the thing with getting cheated on—it doesn't just hurt, it pulls the rug out from under you. You start questioning your judgment. Wondering if you can ever really know a person. Suddenly seeing all the signs you missed.

Obvious signs, signs that a smart person would have surely picked up on.

But not you. Because you're a damn idiot. And *everyone* knows it.

Given my family history, you'd think I'd have seen the signs of a liar from a mile away. My deadbeat dad lied every time he said he'd see me on my birthday. My mom lied when she said the doctors told her everything was fine. My brother lied when he said he'd only go to California for a year.

Naively, I thought Brett was different.

Pushing a wisp of hair out of my face, I glance around. We open for lunch in half an hour, so the dining room of Frostbite Tavern is empty now. I wet a sponge and crouch down to clean a spill on the floor that Melissa should have taken care of last night at the end of her shift.

When Brett asked me out three years ago, I couldn't believe it. He was the town's golden boy, the son of our mayor, and he was interested in *me*? I should have known the entire thing was doomed from the start.

Men like Brett don't end up with girls like me.

My mom was born in a nearby trailer park and had me and my brother with a biker gang enforcer. A criminal.

My father never came to any of my recitals or graduations. His idea of quality time was bringing Maxton and me to the annual rally hosted at a nearby campsite by their gang, and leaving us in the care of strange women who smelled like cigarette smoke and bad decisions. The morning after, he'd drop us off at school in dirty, dusty clothes, and the looks I got made me pray the earth would just open up and swallow me whole.

I never felt like I belonged in this town. Growing up, I thought if I just tried hard enough, I could change that. If I got straight As, if I was never late for anything, if I was always flawlessly nice, maybe then the townspeople would see me as more than just white trash.

Brett choosing me felt like the universe had finally granted me my wish. It was so tempting to believe we could have a future together that I let myself be sucked into a fantasy.

The night I walked in on Brett cheating on me, I cried myself to sleep, and when I woke up in the morning, eyes puffy and chest aching, I decided I was done.

Done trusting people. Done putting myself last. Done with this town.

I would *never* be accepted here.

In a perfect world, I'd go no contact with my ex, but I can't do that while I'm still in Darkwater Hollow for a long list of reasons. The most important one being—

"Hey, B. Mel said the Sam Adams keg ran out at the end of her shift last night. Might wanna get a new one in before the lunchtime rush."

Brett comes around the bar, his leather boots appearing in my periphery. I shoot him a glance from where I'm squatting on the floor. Yes, my cheating ex is also my boss. The owner of Frostbite Tavern. Trying to find another job in Darkwater Hollow is hopeless. There are only a handful of other places in town that would hire me, and the only reason they would is if one of their servers died. As far as I know, they're all in good health.

Which is why my number one priority at the moment is selling my house so that I can get the hell out of this town.

"No problem." Changing empty kegs is also something Melissa should have done before clocking out for the night, but I'd rather keep my interactions with Brett to a minimum, so I let it slide.

Just when I'm hoping he'll wander back to his office, he leans against the counter and crosses his arms over his chest, settling in for a conversation I have no interest in having. "Hey, you all right?"

I rub at the dried liquor on the ground. "Fine."

"You sure? You look tired, B."

I finish with the spill and stand up. "I'm good."

He rubs his palm over his cleanly shaved jaw. The concern in his expression is so convincing, I almost believe it.

"I worry about you." He points at my face. "You've got bags under your eyes, and you look like you haven't slept in days. You need to take better care of yourself."

"I said I'm fine, Brett."

He raises his palms in the air. "I'm just worried."

"No need to be."

Reaching into his back pocket, he pulls out a small flat box. "I got this for you. For your birthday."

I blink. *My birthday?*

God, that's today. I'm twenty-three.

I can't believe I forgot. Somewhere between grieving my mom, gluing my heart back together, and now trying to sell the house, it slipped my mind.

Brett gives the box a shake. "Take it."

He's going to keep me here until I do.

I grab it from him and pop open the lid.

It's a silver heart-shaped pendant.

Irritation licks up my spine. "What is this?"

"A pendant."

"No, I mean *what* is this, Brett? We broke up, remember?"

He sighs, like I'm the one being unreasonable. "Blake, don't be like this. It's been like four months since... Well, you know. Don't you think it's time for us to move past it?"

Brett has this annoying habit of minimizing what happened. If you listen to him, you'd think I'm holding something inconsequential over his head, like not taking the garbage out one night.

"Let me remind you," I grind out. "You cheated on me. Right here in this bar. In your office. With Melissa."

I liked Melissa. Sure, she's a bit flighty and harebrained, but she'd always been nice to me. We'd worked together for two years, and I thought she was someone I could trust.

Clearly, my judgment of people's character is seriously impaired.

Just thinking about how the two of them played me for a fool sends a hot wave of rage through me.

Something resembling a pout appears on his face. "I miss you."

I stare at him blankly. Did he hear anything I just said?

When I stay silent, he changes tactics. He rakes his fingers through his flowing, thoroughly conditioned blond hair, and says, "All day and night, I think about you. About how I'd screwed up."

Does he really? I doubt it.

What was he thinking about when he was having sex with Melissa? It sure as hell wasn't me. I walked in on them two months after my mom died. He knew exactly how much I was struggling with grief, and he obviously didn't care enough about me to keep his dick in his pants.

What he did is unforgivable. He lost my trust, and I don't hand out second chances.

I snap the jewelry box closed and hand it back to him. He shakes his head, refusing to take it, so I place it on the counter. There's no way I'm taking it home.

"I've got things to do before we open."

When I move to brush past him, he grabs me by the forearm.

"C'mon. You've punished me enough." His eyes are a perfect shade of baby blue. I used to love those eyes. I'd look inside them and see our future together, all painted in vivid color.

Now all I see is his guilty expression when I caught him with his pants down and Melissa's legs wrapped around his waist.

"Brett, I'm not punishing you. I'm just done with you."

This makes his eyes darken the way they always used to whenever I talked about opening my own bookstore one day. It's like I wasn't allowed to dream. He wanted me to act like all of my dreams had already come true because I was with him.

That should have pissed me off way more than it had while we were together.

"We're over." My voice is steady, but my heart is pounding hard. With Brett still my boss, I have to be careful. I can't risk losing this job before I sell my house, no matter how badly I want to get away from him.

His hand tightens around my arm. "I know I fucked up, but we're endgame, baby. Blake and Brett. I'm not going to lose you."

I try to pull away from him, but he tugs me closer, his grip on the edge of being painful.

"I'll do whatever it takes to get you back."

"Let go of me, please."

His jaw firms, his expression flashing with displeasure. I've managed to annoy him. He's used to me being an easier mark.

When he doesn't remove his hand, I wring my arm away and head straight to the back.

CHAPTER 7

BLAKE

My stomach is in knots. Holding my ground around Brett is something I'm still getting used to, so after our conversation, I need a minute to compose myself.

I go over to say hello to the dishwasher, Frank.

Frank's been working at Frostbite since the eighties, when this place was still run by Brett's dad, before Brett's dad became the mayor. Frank's usually listening to music, but today, the radio clipped to his belt is tuned to the local news station.

I prop my hip against the counter. "My mom used to put that station on every morning."

He glances at me over his shoulder, his smile hidden beneath his thick white mustache. "They're sayin' there's a storm comin'."

"Really? The sky was clear when I got in ten minutes ago. Second week of November is too early for snow."

He turns the water off and wipes his hands on a towel. "The weather's been all over the place these past few winters." He turns up the volume on the radio so that I can hear the hosts talking about what's supposedly the biggest winter storm in years heading our way.

I frown. "It wouldn't be the first time they were wrong." They better be. A big storm isn't something my old Honda can handle. I haven't even put on the tire chains I bought last week. I thought I still had plenty of time before the snow hit.

Frank shrugs. "Hope you're right. I've gotta help Howie fix his roof this weekend, and that ain't gonna happen if we get ten inches of snow like they're talkin' about." He scans me up and down. "We miss ya around here. You been hidin' from us."

A fist appears around my heart. With the exception of Brett and Melissa, the people working at Frostbite Tavern are good people. I used to stick around after we wrapped up with the day shift and have a meal with everyone, but since the incident, I just go straight home.

I'm embarrassed.

In Darkwater Hollow, everyone knows everyone's business, so what happened between Brett and me is public knowledge. Some people look at me with pity. Others with a smugness that implies they knew Brett and I would never work.

Most times, it just feels like the word IDIOT is a flashing neon sign right above my head, and everyone can see it.

"I've been busy," I say. It's not exactly a lie. I've spent the last few months doing all kinds of projects around the house so it'll be easier to sell it.

Frank gives me a sad smile. "Got any plans for Thanksgiving? That friend of yours going to come 'round?"

"Del? Not this year."

"What about your brother?"

I snort. "As always, Maxton's busy in LA." So busy, he didn't even come back for Mom's funeral. Del's company in San Francisco had a retreat that same week, but Del got permission to skip it so that she could be here for me. All I got from Maxton was an apology text.

"Ain't good to be alone for the holidays, sweetheart."

"Who knows, maybe I'll go to California to see them."

We both know I can't afford the flight, but Frank doesn't call me out on my lie. He just pats me on the shoulder and says, "If Kate and me were hosting, I'd have ya over at ours, but we're goin' to Leslie's this year."

The pastor's wife. The same woman who once tried to get me and Maxton kicked out of our middle school because she didn't like having "those grimy Wolfe kids" in the same classroom as her sons.

I force a smile because I don't want Frank feeling guilty when he has no reason to. "Sounds like it'll be a fun evening."

I go back to setting up for the lunch hour, and by noon, most of the dining room is filled. The radio hosts were right. The temperature's dropped below freezing, and flurries are coming down outside. Everyone wants to warm up with some coffee and tea.

I'm occupied with the new espresso machine Brett bought a few weeks ago, churning out lattes, while Brit and Carly, the two servers working today, do their best to carry them to the tables fast enough.

By two, just when I think we're past the worst of it, another wave of patrons floods the dining room.

"Where is everyone coming from?" I ask Brit when she comes by to grab some orders.

"The electricity's cut out on the north side of town. The snow's way worse over there, so a lot of people drove up."

Shit.

I glance out the window. Even here, it's coming down thick, which means when my shift ends at four, I might be stuck here. I can't leave early when we're this busy, so I just gotta hope my car will be able to make it out. It's only a fifteen-minute drive back to my house.

I'm in the middle of making four lattes when Brett appears by my side.

"Listen, Mel's going to come in a bit early."

My stomach sinks, and I nearly drop the steamed milk I'm pouring. "You promised me I wouldn't have to work with her."

"I know, but it's getting nuts in here. You need help." He reaches up and flicks one of the paper orders clipped in front of me. "You're way behind."

I'd rather walk home in this weather than work with Melissa. I place the lattes on the counter for Brit and turn to face Brett. "Can't you get behind the bar for a bit?"

He scratches the back of his neck. "I've got a lot of paperwork to catch up on. And I've got to make the rounds. Make people feel welcome."

Anger bubbles through my chest. "I thought I made my boundaries clear."

"You were the one who said you didn't want me to fire her."

I grit my teeth. No matter how angry I was—still am—with Melissa, I don't need her losing her job on my conscience. I know what it's like to worry about being able to pay your next water bill.

I wipe down the steamer wand with a rag. "You made me a promise. I guess I should have known that means nothing."

Anger flashes in his eyes. "Don't be difficult, B. There's a freak storm coming, and a lot of people are here to warm up. Have some perspective, yeah? This is more important than your personal issues."

My cheeks heat. My personal issues?

A sliver of doubt snakes through my chest. Is he right? Am I being selfish? After all, the world doesn't revolve around me and my problems.

I suck in a breath. I'm a big girl. I can deal with Melissa for a few hours.

There's no time to mull it over, because a moment later, Melissa appears behind Brett. I let out a disbelieving huff. She must have come in while Brett and I were talking, which means he really waited until the last moment to give me a heads-up.

Her dark hair is pulled back into a high ponytail, and she looks at me like she just killed my puppy. All guilt and nervousness.

"I'll leave you girls to it." Brett squeezes past her, his work here done.

But my work is far from over. I force my anger down and start on the next order.

Just stay focused.

Melissa clears her throat. "How can I help?"

"You can start another pot of coffee and check on the people at the bar," I say in a monotone voice. This is the first time we've interacted since I walked in on them. I've done my absolute best to avoid her for the last four months.

She grabs a pack of coffee grounds from the shelf above and pours it into a white paper filter.

"Blake, I was hoping we could talk."

"I'm busy."

"You never answered my texts."

"I blocked you."

"Why would you do that?" She sounds genuinely puzzled.

Gee, I don't know.

"I'm sorry, okay?" She puts the filter into the filter basket and slides it into the machine.

This day is quickly going from bad to hellish.

"Please, hear me out. I hate that our friendship is so fucked up now."

Maybe she should have thought of that before she slept with my long-term boyfriend.

"Everyone makes mistakes, right?"

I can't help it. I snap. "Can we not do this right now?"

She shakes her head. "I feel so bad about breaking you two up. I wasn't thinking. It just happened, I swear. Brett really wants to get back together with you."

Did he put her up to this? My pulse is racing. I can't handle this.

Before I lose my shit in front of everyone, I finish the orders I'm working on and transfer them to the counter. I walk all the way to the other end of the bar, away from Melissa and her bullshit. It's only about ten feet, but it's enough to allow me to breathe easier.

I clutch the counter and count backward from ten.

I'm at six when the door to the bar opens, and Rowan Miller strides in.

CHAPTER 8

BLAKE

Flurries blow into the dining room, making the scene at the front of the restaurant look like the inside of a snow globe.

The door slams shut behind Rowan.

He brushes the snow off his leather jacket, stomps his boots twice on the welcome mat, and adjusts the black cap he's got on his head.

I swallow and flatten my palms against the bar top. The man knows how to make an entrance.

He kept his word the evening he moved in. When I woke up the next morning to check the state of his front lawn, the trash was gone.

And he somehow managed to convince Elijah to keep the music down. I've gone over there half a dozen times to no avail, but one visit from Rowan, and it's all sorted.

I mean, I'm not complaining, but I really don't get how that man manages to wrap everyone around his little finger.

It's been a few days since he moved in, and so far, he hasn't done anything more to piss me off, but he also hasn't crossed anything off the list.

Exactly like I expected. I doubt that fence is ever going to get fixed.

Rowan walks up to the empty hostess stand, and a few heads turn to look at the new visitor.

A table of women giggles. Rowan shoots them a grin and glances around the dining room, searching for a place to sit.

I roll my eyes. The way they fawn over him is pathetic.

Can I admit he's a fine male specimen? Sure. He's fit, tall, and attractive. He's got the kind of smile that promises a good time—even if you'll likely regret it in the morning—and his eyes light up and get all squinty when he laughs.

But looks aren't everything.

Doesn't it bother anyone that he goes through women faster than a kid through Halloween candy? Or that he's slept with someone's wife?

Clearly not, because they're *still* giggling.

Carly hurries over to welcome him with a menu tucked under her arm and points at a small table by the window, the one I've seen him and his business partner sit at before. Rowan looks at it for a beat.

And then he looks at me.

My cheeks heat.

Carly asks him something, and he nods. She steps aside, and he walks past her and heads straight toward the bar.

Straight toward *me*.

I jump into action, meaning to look busy and not like I was staring.

Pick up the rag. Wipe down the service area. Organize the knives.

A stool scrapes against the floor. "Hey, Sunshine."

His voice sends electricity zapping down my spine. It's the most unnerving feeling.

I lift my gaze to him. "No."

A brow arches. "No?"

"That is the first and last time you're going to call me that."

His lips twitch. "But it fits so well."

"Don't tell me you drove all the way here just to annoy me. Or did our street lose power too?"

"No, we're fine."

"You probably should have stayed home, then."

He drags his palm over the scruff on his jaw. "Sorry to inconvenience you with my presence, but I've got nothing to eat at home. Haven't had time to go grocery shopping."

I ignore his snarky remark. "Busy with the house?"

"Very. But don't worry, I haven't forgotten your list."

I hum in response and slide him a menu, certain he's got my list somewhere at the bottom of his trash can. "You can order from me."

He picks it up and gives it a quick scan. "I'll have a bowl of soup, and the burger with fries."

"You got it."

"And a coffee."

Melissa appears next to me. "We just made a fresh pot."

The enormous smile on her face and the sugary tone fills me with irritation. Guess she's moved on from Brett. Then again, she's always been like this. Brett's gotten angry with her on more than one occasion for flirting with certain customers while ignoring the other tables.

I go to the terminal at the end of the bar to put Rowan's order in.

"Huh." I breathe out as a realization hits.

Of course. Brett wasn't just mad she wasn't doing her job. He was mad because he was already sleeping with her. And stupid me went as far as to comfort Melissa when she got upset about his scolding.

Anger and humiliation thicken my throat for a long second before I force the feeling away. No need to relive it. But I do need to get the hell out of here before she tries to talk to me again.

I spend the next thirty minutes pouring beers and making drinks, trying to stay focused on the task at hand, but my gaze keeps drifting to Rowan. Carly brings Rowan his soup, then his burger. He eats fast, clearly hungry.

There's something strangely attractive about seeing him devour his food.

I bite down on my lip and force my gaze away.

I blame Del for all of this. When I talked to her last night, she insisted on sharing more gossip from Aunt Lottie about Rowan's exploits.

The words "fucks like a beast" may have come up.

When I told Del there's no way dear old Lottie used that terminology, she laughed and said I should just find out if it's true on my own.

That girl needs to get her head checked. There's no universe in which I'd sleep with Rowan Miller.

But she may have made me just *a teeny bit* curious. After all, Brett's the only guy I've ever slept with, and our sex life was always focused on his pleasure. Whether I came or not didn't seem important to him.

Would Rowan be rough or gentle? Serious or fun? Kinky or vanilla?

He removes his jacket, revealing a weathered, gray T-shirt that stretches across his ridiculously broad shoulders. There are tattoos all over his corded forearms.

Hmm. Definitely kinky.

"It's finally slowing down."

I jolt at Melissa's voice. Jesus. I didn't even hear her come up beside me.

"Everyone's got their orders," she says. "They're just going to linger here until the electricity comes back on."

That's my cue to leave. I undo my apron. "Hopefully, it won't be long."

Melissa lowers her voice. "Since we're both stuck here for a while, I think this is a good time to talk."

Oh. My. God. Why can't she take a hint?

I ball the apron in my hands. "There's nothing—"

"Look, I want us to be friends again. It's totally over between Brett and I. Honestly, I don't know why I even slept with him. He's *so* not my type. I was just lonely, I guess, and I wasn't thinking. And he said you two were having problems and—"

"Melissa, *stop*." Not only do I not want to talk to her, but Rowan is sitting *right there*. I don't want him listening in on my business.

Melissa's bottom lip juts out. "You used to be nicer."

Yeah, and all the good it did me.

"I've got to go," I mutter and hurry to the back before she can try to stop me.

I need to tell Brett I'm done, and then I'm out of here. When I walk into his office, he's watching some action flick on his laptop. I resist the urge to roll my eyes. I thought he had work to do.

"Everything's calmed down. I'm leaving."

He startles. "All done?" His gaze moves to the window. "It's pretty crazy outside, B."

"I'll manage. Good night."

I walk out of his office and reach for my phone to check the weather, but it's not in my pocket.

Shit, I think I left it somewhere behind the bar.

Brett follows me back into the dining area. "If you stay until we close, I'll drop you off."

Five more hours around Melissa? I'd rather shove an ice pick through my eye. "I'm good."

I step behind the bar and glance around. Rowan's still eating, and our gazes snag for a split second before I remember what I'm here for.

Where the hell did I leave my phone?

Ah, there it is, right by the sink.

I grab it and turn around to leave, but Brett blocks my way. "You don't have snow tires on."

Annoyance pulses at my temples. He's right, I don't. Which is extremely stupid when you live in Missouri, but I thought I had at least another week before the first snow, and my tire chains are sitting uselessly in my shed.

Still, I've got to get home. The weather forecast, which is playing on the TV right above me, keeps saying it's only going to get worse as the night goes on.

"It'll be fine. It's only a fifteen-minute drive."

"It'll be close to an hour in this weather," Brett insists. "That is if you even make it in that tiny Honda of yours."

"I'll take my chances."

Brett's brows pinch together. "B, this is crazy, you can't—"

"I can drive you."

My head snaps toward Rowan. His expression is unreadable, but when he looks at Brett, there's something in his eyes that makes the tiny hairs on the back of my neck stand straight.

Rowan presses a paper napkin to his lips, crushes it in his fist, and slides off his stool. "C'mon, Blake."

Heat skates over my skin. I can't accept a favor from him. "No, that's okay."

"We're going to the same place."

He's...got a point. We live next door to each other.

It's just a drive. Don't overthink it.

Pushing away my apprehension, I give him a nod. "Okay. Thank you. I just need to clock out and grab my purse."

"Take your time." Rowan grabs his jacket from a hook under the bar and starts putting it on.

In the back, Brett accosts me again. "That guy is not taking you home."

I put in my locker combination. "Yes, he is."

"Did you hear what he did with Abigail? The guy's an asshole."

I scoff. "You really think you have any moral high ground here?"

Shock flashes across Brett's face.

What? He didn't think I'd call him out like that? It's probably not the smartest thing to do given he's the one signing my paychecks, but I'm too angry to hold my tongue.

He narrows his eyes. "What's gotten into you? Your behavior is getting out of hand."

My behavior. *My* behavior?

I take a breath. "I've just had to work side by side with the woman you cheated on me with. You promised me I wouldn't have to see her, and you lied. Again."

67

"I. Had. To," he seethes. "Look, I'll just take you home right now, okay?"

"No, Brett. Rowan is taking me home." I grab my purse out of the locker and walk over to the timesheet taped on the wall.

Brett hovers behind me as I scribble in the time. I hate how close he's standing. "You don't even know that guy."

"He's my new neighbor."

"*What?* Blake—"

I push past him and through the door to the dining room and—

"Oof!"

I fly straight into a wall. A very firm, very muscular wall. Big palms wrap around my biceps.

"You all right?"

I tip my head back to look at Rowan. He's so freaking tall that I swear my neck ends up arching up ninety degrees.

God, he smells *incredible*. Leather. Oak. A hint of smoke, but not the kind that comes from a cigarette. Has he been by a bonfire? A fireplace, maybe? I get the most ridiculous urge to bury my nose into his T-shirt.

He'd definitely reconsider his offer to drive me home if I did that.

"Yes." My voice comes out like a squeak, and I take a step back. "Sorry."

His dark hazel eyes spark. "Ready to go?"

"Uh-huh."

"Where's your coat?"

I gesture at the rack by the entrance. "Over there."

"Hold on a second. Blake, we were in the middle of a conversation."

I step aside and turn to look at Brett. His voice is on the edge of a shout, loud enough to get the attention of a few patrons sitting at nearby tables.

My face starts to burn. Why won't he drop it?

Rowan steps closer, his shoulder brushing against my own. "Is there a problem here?"

Whoa. I've never heard him use *that* tone before. It's the kind of tone that warns there better *not* be a problem, or else.

Impotent anger flashes in Brett's eyes. I see how he sizes Rowan up, and my neighbor's definitely got the size advantage.

"No," Brett snaps.

Rowan smiles. I didn't think a smile could be threatening, but his certainly is. "Good. Then we'll be on our way."

CHAPTER 9

NERO

Outside, the snow's coming down thick, and there's about an inch already on the ground. Blake and I leave footprints behind us as we walk toward my truck. Mine are twice the size of hers.

She keeps shooting me looks, like she's unsure of what to make of me.

Good, because I've got no idea what to make of her either.

Since I moved in next door, she's been popping randomly into my head multiple times a day.

I've got no idea why.

I mean, yeah, I'm a bit intrigued by her and I think she's beautiful, but so what? Some men like a challenge. I'm not one of them. I've always embraced the philosophy of working smarter, not harder.

Why expend my energy chasing after women who don't seem interested in me when I can easily find one who is?

Especially in Darkwater Hollow. Sometimes, all I have to do is breathe in their direction, and they start panting.

But not Blake.

Why the hell not? What is it that she doesn't like?

My looks can't be the problem, so it must be my personality, but how can it be my personality if she doesn't even know me?

No, it must be my reputation that's got her panties in a knot. She alluded to it last time. Why does she care about how and who I spend my time with? It just doesn't make sense.

There's some stubborn part of me that wants to figure that shit out and see if I can change her mind.

You promised Sandro to take it easy, remember?

Right.

When we get inside the truck, Blake clears her throat. "Thanks. You really came to my rescue back there."

"No problem. It's not like it's out of my way."

Did I think she'd be at Frostbite when I decided to come here in the middle of a fucking snowstorm? I may have suspected it given her car wasn't in her driveway.

But I didn't come here *for* her. That would be ridiculous. And I hadn't intended on offering her a ride home until I saw her boss.

I didn't like his face, or his voice, or anything about him. I sure as fuck didn't like the way he looked at her like he owned her. And when he kept insisting on driving her when she clearly wanted nothing to do with him, I had no choice but to intervene.

I turn on the ignition. "I like to do the occasional good deed to make up for my many sins. Something tells me you're keeping a list of them."

"Why would you say that?"

"You seem determined not to like me. The problem is I'm a pretty likable guy." A smirk tugs on my lips. "You making a list of all of my perceived wrongs would help keep you on track."

She lets out an annoyed sigh. "You're right. This interaction alone is giving me ideas for a few bullet points."

I chuckle and glance over at her. She hasn't buckled up. "Are you ready to go or..."

She arches a brow, oblivious to the fact. "Yes. Why?"

I sigh, undo my belt, and reach across her. "I know women tend to get flustered around me, but please try to keep your head on straight. We're about to drive in dangerous conditions." I grasp the belt buckle suspended by her head and draw it toward me, my knuckles accidentally brushing over the tip of her breast in the process.

She sucks in a breath.

I ignore the electric jolt to my groin and slide her buckle in with a sharp click. "There."

Her eyes lock on mine, and some color spreads over her cheeks.

So she's not totally immune to me.

Oh, I could do it. I could have this prickly bartender under me in less than a week if I wanted to.

I smirk and pull away to clip my own belt back in.

She clears her throat. "If you were looking for an excuse to cop a feel, you could have gone for something a bit more subtle."

My smirk melts right off. Heat prickles across the back of my neck.

"That's not what—"

"And for your information, I'm perfectly capable of putting on my own seat belt."

This snarky little...

"Then you should have done it instead of just sitting there," I mutter.

She scoffs a laugh.

I roll my shoulders back, dust off my slightly bruised ego, and start to pull out of the lot.

The snow's nasty—soft and slippery—so I'm going to have to be careful.

"Your boss is an asshole, by the way," I say as I turn onto the road.

"I'm aware."

"He always been like that?"

She lets out a low breath. It makes me glance at her. She's biting down on the corner of her full bottom lip.

Why am I looking at her lips instead of the road?

Jesus. Fuck. I need to get it together.

"You probably know he's my ex? Things between us are tense at the moment."

That guy is her ex? "I didn't know that."

"Really? And here I was thinking it was hot gossip."

I tap against my earlobe. "In one ear, out another. I don't give a fuck about other people's lives."

"Then you're an anomaly in this town. Most people here can't help but stick their noses into other people's business. Anyway, he cheated on me with the other bartender who was working tonight."

Oh. *Oh.*

Okay. I'm starting to get it. She probably thinks I'm like her ex—a cheater—hence the immediate dislike. She's wrong though. I don't cheat. I make it very clear I'm not interested in anything serious, that I'm not looking for commitment.

But it feels like right now is not the time to clarify that.

She sounds too casual, like she's making an effort not to let on how much that fucker really hurt her.

"When did this happen?"

"Four, nearly five months ago." She brushes a speck of dust off the dashboard. "He says he wants to get back together, but I don't think he knows what he wants."

The thought of Blake being with that asshole does something unpleasant to my insides.

I turn the windshield wipers on. They struggle to keep up with the rapidly building snow. "Why wouldn't he fire her if he wants to fix things between you two?"

"He offered. I told him not to."

"Why the hell not?"

74

"Not a lot of other jobs in Darkwater Hollow."

"So you're worried about the job prospects of a woman who fucked your boyfriend?"

She crosses her arms over her chest. "I don't like sending bad juju out into the world, okay? I treat people how I want to be treated. I know that might be a foreign concept to you."

"Ouch."

A beat passes. "Sorry, that was rude."

"I'm seriously regretting driving you."

"I can get out at the next light." She reaches for her seat belt, like she's really going to do it.

"Relax, I was kidding. It would take a lot more than that to make me regret bringing a woman home."

She clicks her tongue. "Do you have to say it like that?"

"Like what?"

"Like you're— Ugh, forget it."

I laugh. "Get your head out of the gutter, Sunshine."

Her fists clench in her lap. "Don't call me that."

I ignore her protest because the nickname is growing on me, and she'd better just get used to it.

"Okay, so the ex cheated on you, you don't want the other waitress gone, and you're still there because of the same lack of job prospects?"

She blows out an irritated breath. "I thought you said you didn't care about other people's lives?"

I shrug. "I don't. But we've got a long drive ahead of us, so we might as well pass the time. This is more melodramatic than those telenovelas my nonna loved to watch."

"Nonna? Is that Italian?"

"Born and raised in Sicily."

"I never had a grandma," she muses. "What was she like?"

"Strict. She swore a lot. And she made the best fucking chicken cacciatore you can imagine."

"Oh yeah?"

A grin pulls on my lips at the memory. "When I was a kid, about nine or ten, she'd have me, my mom, and my stepdad over for dinner every Saturday. There were usually just four of us, but she'd make enough food to feed an army. There was nothing that woman was more afraid of than running out of food for her guests."

The memory is bittersweet because they're all gone now. Nonna died in her sleep ten years ago at the ripe old age of eighty-five, and my mom and stepdad went the way most do in my old world.

A territory war. Drive-by shooting. They were having lunch at their favorite restaurant in Jersey.

"So it's just you?" Blake asks as we get on a ramp to the high-way. "No siblings?"

"I'm an only child."

"I could have guessed. You have that kind of energy."

"I'm going to pretend that's a compliment. What about you?"

"I've got a brother. He doesn't live here anymore."

"Where did he go?"

"California. LA. He's a chef at some fancy restaurant. I haven't seen him since he left home at eighteen."

"Is he older or younger?"

"Two years older."

"And you never had the urge to leave this place?"

"Would if I could." She sniffs and doesn't elaborate.

I almost ask, but then I remember I'm not supposed to get involved. Just by looking at this girl, I know she's got a sob story, and I don't need to hear it.

The world outside the car is a blur of white and gray, the snowflakes swirling in a frenzied dance. The road markings are impossible to see. I adjust my grip on the steering wheel, and in my periphery, I can see her looking at the tattoos on the backs of my hands.

"What's up with all the tattoos?"

"I like body art. Most women like them too, but let me guess, not you."

"Why would you say that?"

"You seem to be determined not to like anything about me."

"Does that bother you?"

"Not one bit."

"I'm pretty sure you're lying. What does that one mean?" She points at my right hand.

"*La mia rotta è fissata per un mare inesplorato.* My course is set for an uncharted sea. It's a quote from Dante."

She gasps. "You're literate?"

"I know. Shocking."

She laughs, and warmth spreads through my chest at the sound. Ahead of us, a few cars crawl at a snail's pace, their taillights peeking through the falling snow.

"I don't think Darkwater Hollow qualifies as unchartered sea. Where were you before this?"

"New York. I—"

Fuck.

I wasn't supposed to say that. Our story is that we came here from Vegas.

I slipped.

That's never happened until now.

Blake turns to me. "New York? Why did you leave?"

There's nothing left to do but backtrack and hope she forgets I ever brought it up. "I wasn't there for long. Before that, I was in Vegas. Sam, my business partner, and I worked at a construction company, but we both got tired of that place. So we decided to move somewhere quieter and start our own thing."

We turn off the highway, and that's when the car starts to slide.

CHAPTER 10

BLAKE

There's a subtle shift in the car's steady hum, a gentle lurch that morphs into a sharp slide. My stomach drops as the car begins to skid, the tires losing their grip on the surface beneath us.

I clutch at the armrest, my knuckles whitening, eyes widening in alarm.

The scenery outside the window spins as the car pirouettes across the road. I yelp and hear Rowan swear. He fights for control, wrestling the wheel back and forth. The sound of the tires skidding on the snow is punctuated by the staccato beat of my own racing heart.

The flashback crashes into me like a brutal wave.

"Hold on, kid."

"I'm scared, Daddy!"

A sudden warmth spreads through my body, subtle at first but rapidly intensifying. There's a furnace inside me, and it's just been ignited. The heat comes from deep within my core, radiating outward like ripples on water.

"I don't want to do this!"

"Shut your mouth, girl."

My skin prickles. Sweat beads across my forehead. I'm right back there, on the back of my father's bike in the Ring of Fire, my hands slippery against the leather of his vest, and my eyes squeezed shut. The roar of the crowd is in my ears, so loud it's deafening. He rides at high speed in an impossibly tight circle. All I can do is hold on and pray we won't crash.

I brace for impact, but then as quickly as it started, the sliding stops.

For a moment, the only sound is the engine idling.

Then Rowan's voice fills the air. "Hey. You okay?"

My heart is inside my throat, my nervous system in overdrive. I press my palms to my chest and try to inhale.

I can't.

There's a strange, almost suffocating quality to the air now. It feels thick, harder to breathe. My clothes cling uncomfortably to my skin, damp with sweat, and I'm aware of every layer.

There's no damn air.

"Shit."

I hear a car door open, then close, then open again. Cold air rushes inside and bites against my burning skin. A warm hand appears on my thigh. "Blake, look at me."

My eyes crack open. It takes me a moment to orient myself because the car is skewed and facing the wrong direction. Rowan is standing outside, between the open door and my seat, his concerned gaze on me. Snowflakes pepper his hair.

The hand on my thigh squeezes gently. Another comes up to brush against my cheek. "You're burning up."

"Panic attack," I manage to pant out.

"Let's get your coat off." He helps me pull the zipper all the way down and pushes the coat off my shoulders. "Take a deep breath."

I do. It's easier now that the vicious heat inside me is ebbing away. My breath is a puff of steam that quickly dissipates into the frigid air.

Rowan's eyes stay glued to my face as his hands gently press down on my thighs. There are thin gold shards slicing through his hazel irises. I hadn't noticed them until now.

He turns one palm up. "Take my hand."

I do it, sliding mine into his much bigger one. Even in my current state, I can't help but marvel at how nicely it fits.

"Breathe with me," he says softly, curling his fingers around me. "In and out. We're safe, Sunshine."

I swallow and do as he says. "We're safe."

"That's right," he rumbles.

My next inhale brings his scent into my lungs, and it makes the panic from moments earlier melt away.

"Have you been in a car accident before?" He runs his thumb over the inside of my palm. That tiny movement shouldn't make the hairs on the back of my arms stand straight, but it does.

"Once," I whisper. "I was with my dad, and I got really hurt."

"Hmm." The hand on my thigh gives me a gentle squeeze, and all of my awareness zooms in on the sensation. "No wonder you got so shaken up."

"I'm sorry."

"You don't need to apologize. Do you think you'll be okay if I keep driving?"

"Yes. I'm okay."

He nods, and his gaze drops to my lips for just a second before he lets go of my hand. "Good."

While he walks around the car to get back into his seat, I fold my coat across my lap. The place on my thigh where he had his palm simmers with residual heat.

I swallow. Great. Add a panic attack to the list of awkward moments with my new neighbor.

"We're almost home," he says as we start driving again. "I'll go even slower. Is there someone at home who can keep an eye on you? I haven't seen anyone else coming or going."

"No, there's no one else." I bite down on the corner of my mouth. "It used to be my mom and I, but she died earlier this year. If she were still around, I know exactly how the rest of my evening would go."

"Oh yeah?"

"She'd give me a big hug when I told her what happened and then insist we sit down for a cup of tea. It was our ritual. A cup of tea, every morning and every evening." I still haven't broken the habit of always making her a mug. God, I miss her so much.

He adjusts his grip on the wheel. "I'm sorry. What about your dad?"

"He died years ago. He was rarely around anyway." And he had a habit of showing up at the worst times with empty promises, stolen money, and little else. "You don't need to worry about me. I'll be all right."

His jaw firms, but he keeps his eyes on the road and gives me a small nod.

The car grows quiet, the noise outside muffled by the falling snow. All I can hear is my thundering heartbeat, and I'm worried Rowan can hear it too.

Snark and banter I can handle, but him comforting me? It's throwing me for a loop.

What did you think he was going to do? Toss you out of the car?

No, of course not. He did what any decent person would do.

So now he's decent?

I fold my lips over my teeth. This is confusing. I thought I had a solid read on Rowan, but now I'm questioning myself.

Is there more to him than meets the eye?

I shoot him a discreet glance. He's focused on the road and seems oblivious to the fact that my heart is still pounding.

And not just because of the near accident.

I wasn't totally repulsed by Rowan's touch. I should have been. But I felt...a lot of things, and disgust wasn't one of them. I'm not sure how to process that fact.

I put my coat back on and zip it all the way up. He glances at me but doesn't say anything.

As promised, we move slowly through the blizzard. After what feels like an eternity, Rowan finally pulls into my driveway.

I clear my throat and try to pretend like my perception of him didn't just tilt on its axis. "Thanks for everything."

"You sure you'll be okay on your own? I can stick around for a bit."

"I'm sure." I need to get out of this car and collect myself. "I owe you for the drive and for getting me home safe. Would have sucked to die on my birthday."

His brows arch. "It's your birthday today?"

"Twenty-three."

A genuine smile appears on his lips, and it makes something flutter low inside my belly.

"Happy birthday, Sunshine." He reaches over me and opens the door. "Watch your step."

Snowflakes land on my burning cheeks as I walk toward my front door. Right before I go inside, I glance over my shoulder and see Rowan watching me.

I give him a jerky wave, step over the threshold, and lock the door behind me. Then I stand there with my back pressed against it and take ten very deep breaths. Just when I think I've managed to calm down, I remember the weight of his hand on my thigh and how it felt.

Warm, sure, and safe.

I groan. Enough. I need to get a grip.

Shaking the snow off my Vans, I kick them aside and make my way to the deck at the back of the house. Cold air wraps around me as I pry the door open and stick my head out. That's better. I need to cool down.

Hold on a sec.

I squint my eyes at the fence between the Jacksons' backyard and mine. When I left this morning, it was broken.

Ignoring the fact that I'm only wearing socks, I step out onto the snow-covered deck and walk over to the railing at its edge so that I can see better.

It's not broken anymore.

I huff out, and my breath swirls in front of me in a plume of white.

He fixed it.

He actually fixed it.

A grin comes over my face. *Happy birthday to me.*

CHAPTER 11

BLAKE

"We got an offer?!"

"I told you we would." Nicole, the Kansas City realtor, is now officially my favorite person. "They want to close quickly."

I press my fingertips to my lips. "I can't believe it." We had three more showings in the week and a half since the storm, but I've been careful about getting my hopes too high.

"I only brought over buyers who I knew would be genuinely interested. I don't like to waste anyone's time, Blake," she says, matter-of-factly. I'm a little jealous of how much of a boss this woman is. "You should feel proud of the work you did on the house. I have to say, I was impressed with how well you fixed everything up."

I spin around the living room. It does look great after the fresh coat of paint and getting rid of most of the clutter. I even reorganized my books to have all the spines grouped by color so the living room bookshelf looks like a rainbow.

A grin spreads over my face. "Thank you. Thank you so much."

"You're welcome. I suggest you start packing. Since this is an all-cash offer, everything will move quickly. They'll transfer the money after the weekend, and you might be out of there in another week."

There isn't much I plan on keeping, but packing up the books will take time. It took me years to amass my carefully curated collection. For years, whenever I had any spare money left at the end of the month, that's where it went. I'm going to store them in a storage unit nearby until I figure out where to settle down.

"That's perfect. Can I ask who the buyer is?"

"A retired couple from New Jersey. They're looking to move somewhere quiet but close to their family in the city. Their daughter is pregnant, and they want to be moved in before the baby arrives."

"That's amazing. Thank you again."

"You're welcome. Happy Thanksgiving. We'll talk soon."

I hang up and jump around the house, squealing like a lunatic. It's finally happening. A few weeks, and I'll be out of here.

My hands are shaking as I dial Del's number.

As soon as she picks up, I burst out, "I got an offer!"

"I think you just blew my ear drum."

"Sorry, I'm just so excited."

"Um, yes, you should be. Holy shit, congrats!"

I sink down on the couch. "It's a retired couple with an all-cash offer. Nicole thinks we'll close in no time."

"Fuck yes. It's about time you caught a break."

"My whole body feels lighter. I think I've been carrying a lot of stress." I roll my shoulders and sigh.

"Working for your ex will do that to you. Not to mention dealing with your new neighbor."

"Are you fishing for info?"

She laughs. "Of course I am. You haven't called me in a few days. I want to know what happened after he fixed your fence last week."

"Nothing."

"Nothing?"

"Well, he cleared my driveway the day after the blizzard," I admit.

Del gasps. "Really?"

I couldn't believe my eyes when I looked out the window the next day and saw it perfectly clean. I almost burst into tears. I've been on driveway clearing duty ever since Maxton left, and it felt so nice to have someone do it for me. Frank came to drive me to work the day after since my car was still at Frostbite, and he even commented on what a good job I'd done. For some reason, I didn't tell him it was actually all Rowan.

"Is it terrible that I haven't thanked him? I haven't seen him coming or going since then, so it's not like I've been avoiding him, but still. Should I just go over there when his truck is in the driveway? What do I even say? I came out guns blazing the moment he moved in, and I've said some pretty rude things to him, so I feel like a bit of a jerk, but it's not like he's an angel. He's full of himself, and he's arrogant, and he did sleep with Abigail, we can't forget that, can we, but he's got this side to him—"

"Blake, sweetie, take a deep breath."

I grip my face. "Can we just not talk about him right now? I want to enjoy this moment."

"You got it. Okay, so what now? Have you decided where you're going to move to? Please, please, please just come here. We'd have so much fun."

"I wish. There's no way I'd be able to afford San Francisco."

"I know you could find a good job here."

"Have you forgotten I don't have a college degree? That makes my job prospects limited."

Del makes a thoughtful *hmm*.

I sigh. "I'd love to be closer to you, but I don't think I'd be able to handle the pressure of trying to survive in such an expensive place. Not right now."

"I hear you. What are you thinking then?"

"I don't know. Maybe somewhere in Texas? Now that the house is sorted, I'll finally have some more time to do the research."

"Dream big, baby girl. I think you should move to LA and become a model."

"Have you forgotten I'm five-three?"

"You could be a hand model."

I look down at the hand that's not currently holding my phone. "I don't think so. I haven't had a manicure in years, and my fingers are kind of stubby."

Del snorts a laugh. "Okay, I'm just trying to get some ideas going."

"And I'm grateful, because I really don't have a clue what I'm going to do." A flicker of nerves appears in my belly.

"What about that bookstore you've always wanted to open?"

"I'd need to save up more money for that." I scratch the side of my nose. "It feels like a big risk. I think I just want to find a steady job and get settled first wherever it is I end up in."

"That makes sense. Don't worry, you'll figure everything out. Today, you've got to celebrate. What are your Thanksgiving plans?"

"I was going to buy a frozen Thanksgiving dinner for one from Hy-Vee and watch a rerun of *Planes, Trains, and Automobiles*."

"Gah. Stop. You're making me depressed. I think you need company. Oh, I know! Go invite Rowan for dinner."

"Are you crazy?" I glance out the window that faces his front yard. Hold on. "Actually... That's not a bad idea."

"I know."

"He's probably spending the day alone too. He's got no family here, and it will give me a chance to repay him for everything he's done for me before I leave." It's been a while since I cooked for more than just me. If I go to the store right now, I should be able to pull something together.

"I'm full of great ideas. Go get 'em, tiger."

"Love you, bye."

I'm in such a great mood that I don't think about it twice. I slip on my Vans, jog over to Rowan's, and knock on his door.

It's cold out, so I hop from foot to foot while I wait for him to answer. I should have put my coat on.

Finally, the door opens, and Rowan appears on the other side.

My heart stutters inside my chest. His hair's wet from a shower, his beard is freshly trimmed, and his eyelashes seem thicker in the afternoon light.

Given that I'm leaving soon, it feels okay to let myself appreciate just how stupidly handsome he is.

He eyes my thin T-shirt for a moment before lifting his gaze to my face.

"Hey. I wanted to—"

He steps aside. "Come in."

"No, it's okay, I just stopped by to see if you have plans for Thanksgiving." My palms slide up and down my arms.

His gaze flashes with irritation. "Where is your coat? Do you want to freeze to death?"

"I'm fine. It's not that bad."

He rolls his eyes. "Your lips are turning blue."

"Oh my God, I just came over to ask..." I get distracted when he starts unzipping his big black hoodie.

"Um, what are you—"

He takes it off, steps closer, and wraps it around my shoulders. "Here."

Heat spreads through my chest. His hoodie is still warm from him. Still smells like him. My heart ping-pongs inside my chest like it's itching to burst out. I curl my fingers around the fabric and tug it closer.

"Thanks. Do you want to come over for Thanksgiving dinner?" I say in one breath before I chicken out.

A sexy—I mean, annoying—smirk stretches across his face. "You're inviting me over?"

"I just thought since we're both alone, it might be nice to have some company. I owe you for the drive home. And for clearing my driveway," I add, feeling my cheeks heat.

Standing in only a T-shirt, he braces his palm against the doorjamb. His biceps bulge, the tattoos on his arms shifting with the movement.

I can't tear my eyes away from them.

"I was going to have dinner with a friend."

My excitement dims.

Another *friend*? Jesus, he really doesn't waste any time, does he? After his unexpected acts of kindness, I'd almost forgotten about that side of him.

The pang of disappointment inside my chest is more than a little absurd. I clear my throat. "I shouldn't have assumed you'd be alone."

He drags a hand over his beard.

"Never mind." I take a step back, tugging his hoodie closer around me. "I'll ju—"

"Can I bring my friend with me?"

I blink. Is he serious? Are we talking about some kind of third-wheel scenario? That sounds awful. Everything inside me screams no, but...I owe him. And I don't like owing people.

So if that's what he wants, I guess I'll just have to go along with it. "Of course." I force a smile. "Does she have any dietary restrictions?"

A beat passes. Something entirely too amused flashes in his eyes. "My friend's a *he*. My business partner—Sam. And he eats everything."

Ohmigod. What is wrong with me?

I have to pray the relief I feel soul deep isn't blatantly obvious on my face. "Okay. Come at seven."

Rowan looks like he's holding back a laugh. "We'll be there."

It's only when I jog back home and close the door behind me that I realize I still have his hoodie wrapped around me.

CHAPTER 12

NERO

Sandro sighs.

"What?"

"I thought we agreed you'd take it easy with the women. Just today, I had two appointment cancellations. And one of them told me point-blank it's because of what happened with Abigail and you." Sandro paces the length of my living room. "Now you're dragging me to some new girl's house, where I'm supposed to do what? Be your wingman? It's like you don't listen to a word I say."

I grab my keys and head toward the door. "You don't need to do anything. I didn't want to ditch you, so I told her you're coming along. I thought you'd appreciate the gesture. Instead, you're giving me an earful."

"Hey, don't try to turn the tables on me. Are you trying to hook up with this girl tonight? Yes or no?"

Great question. Truth is, I'm a bit confused. I thought Blake and I left things on decent enough terms the night of the blizzard, but I sure as hell wasn't expecting her to invite me over.

She showed up at my doorstep without her coat on. I'd never seen her so excited. And when she thought I'd already made plans with another woman, her excitement dimmed.

So, yeah. I'm no mind reader, but I'm fairly certain she wants me. And I'm planning on testing that theory tonight. "We'll see."

Sandro pinches the bridge of his nose.

"Look, if it happens, she's not going to want anyone to know. If I won't tell, and she won't tell, what's the harm?" There's an unexpected prickle of unease. Something about Blake wanting to keep me a secret if anything does happen between us doesn't sit all that well with me.

Hmm.

"Uh-huh. They *always* tell. You're like a Pokémon every single woman in town wants to collect and brag about."

We step outside. "I'm telling you, she's different. It's that waitress from Frostbite."

"Which one?" His voice drops to a whisper as we cross my front lawn in the direction of Blake's house. "Don't tell me it's that blond who's never given you the time of day."

"That's her."

Sandro's jaw drops.

I grin and knock on her door. The lock turns, and Blake appears clad in a baby-blue off-the-shoulder dress that matches the color of her eyes.

I take in every detail. She has her hair curled into soft waves, a bit of makeup on her face, and a shiny gloss on her lips. There's a light-brown freckle on her cheek in the shape of a heart that I didn't notice before. Her blond hair, pure glistening silk, is pulled back into a high ponytail that would look great coiled around my fist.

When I drop my gaze to her bare legs, I have to bite back a groan. She looks good enough to eat.

Her smile is wide and unguarded. "Hi. Happy Thanksgiving."

"Happy Thanksgiving. This is my business partner, Sam."

She greets Sandro and takes a step backward. "Come in."

We file into the narrow entryway. She takes Sandro's coat before glancing over at me. I'm not wearing one since it's only about twenty steps from my house to hers. Her gaze slides over the navy-blue flannel shirt I have on. Something in the way her eyes flare tells me she likes what she sees.

She smooths her hands over her dress. "Thanks for coming."

"You look great." She'll look even better with nothing on. Hopefully, I'll get to tell her that tonight.

She tucks a strand behind her ear. "Thank you."

"You've got a great place," Sandro calls out from somewhere inside. "I love your record player."

She walks in the direction of his voice. I'm right behind her, close enough to take in her scent.

That damn vanilla makes my cock twitch.

The living room is small but cheery, with vintage furniture, lots of plants, and a brick fireplace. To the right of the fireplace is a huge built-in bookshelf—the books meticulously sorted by color.

"You read a lot?"

She seems a bit shy as she shoots me a look. "Yeah. Tons."

The image of her curled up in the small window nook makes something warm spark inside my chest. She's fucking adorable.

Blake leads us into the adjacent dining room. There are appetizers already on the table—olives, cheese and crackers, and some cold cuts. Sandro zeroes in on them immediately. The kid eats like a horse.

"I brought some wine." I hand Blake the bottle.

She turns it in her hand and reads the label. "Chianti, 1995. Produced in Tuscany, Italy." She glances at me. "This is fancy."

"Nothing but the best for you."

She gives me a funny look. "Thanks. If you want to crack that open while I finish up in the kitchen, that would be great. The bottle opener is right here. You two must be hungry."

"I'll come help you." I give Sandro a discreet wink, to which he responds with an eye roll.

In the small kitchen, Blake turns toward me. "There's not much to help with."

"It's not polite to leave the chef alone to do all the work."

"Did your nonna teach you that?" She walks over to the stove and checks on one of the steaming pots. She takes a wooden spoon and stirs whatever is inside twice.

I stop right behind her. She's so fucking tiny compared to me, her head only reaching my mid-chest. "She wanted to make sure her grandson was well-mannered."

The second she realizes how close I'm standing to her, her back stiffens. She stirs the pot once more and then slips around me and moves to the fridge. "Doesn't seem like she succeeded."

I lean back against the counter and grin. "I can be very well-mannered when I feel like it."

"Ah." She shuts the fridge, holding a bowl of tomatoes in one hand. "Then one day, you may still surprise me." She blows an errant blond strand out of her face. "I need to finish cutting some veggies for the salad. How are you with a knife?"

"I'm good with my hands."

She wraps her lips around her teeth to hide her smile from me. "Of course you are. If I asked you to try the gravy, would you say something equally ridiculous, like you're good with your mouth?"

I laugh at the way she drops her voice to mimic mine. "How did you manage to read my mind? By the way, both of those statements are true."

She gives me a cutting board and a sharp knife, a smile tugging on her lips. "You take the cucumbers, and I'll do the tomatoes. Your mind is quite easy to read."

We stand side by side, her cutting board a few inches from mine. "Oh yeah? Am I really that simple?"

Her knife work isn't bad, but mine's slightly better. It comes with years of practice. Cutting off a finger or a tongue is not as easy as one might expect.

My elbow brushes against hers. She blows at the strand of hair again. "You're not as simple as you want people to think, but not as complicated as you think you are."

The observation is unexpected. I turn it over once, twice, decide it's nonsense, and huff a laugh. "So you think you've got me all figured out."

"Not entirely. But I'm making progress."

I put my knife down and wipe my hands on a towel. The strand keeps slipping, getting in front of her eye.

"All right. Tell me what I'm thinking about now."

She glances at me, taking a moment to answer. "That I'm a bad host for psychoanalyzing you?"

I lift my hand and tuck the strand away, the tips of my fingers brushing against the shell of her ear.

Her breath hitches. Her knife slows and then stops completely.

I press my index finger against her jaw and guide her to face me. "No, Sunshine. Right now, I'm thinking about doing this." My palm slides around the back of her neck, and I lower my head and press my lips to hers.

The moment we make contact, I know something's different.

Electricity surges just beneath my skin, like a power grid coming back online after a blackout. My skin tightens. My heart picks up speed.

I'm buzzing. Does she feel it too?

I can't tell.

She's stock-still, letting me nip on her lips, letting me curl my hands over her hips. A gasp comes out of her when my fingers dig into her flesh through the fabric of her dress.

It's the soft graze of my teeth over her bottom lip that does it. She opens up for me, allowing my tongue to swipe against hers.

Fuck, she tastes like a chilled glass of wine on a hot summer day.

A low groan vibrates inside my chest.

I can already tell she's the kind of woman who'll test my patience by wanting to take it slow. But I don't mind. After all, the chase can be as thrilling as the kill.

CLANK.

We break apart at the sound, and my gaze falls to the knife she dropped on the floor. She turns and anchors her palms against the counter, her chest rising and falling with rapid breaths.

My own breathing is just as uneven.

That was only a kiss. What will it feel like to sink inside of her?

I'm hard as fuck. Why did I bring Sandro with me again?

"Rowan," she whispers. "Why did you do that?"

I pick up the knife and place it on the counter.

"Because I wanted to." And I want to do it again.

Her eyes are wide and stunned. "You can't."

I reach for her cheek. "Why not?"

She jerks away from me, not letting me touch her.

A flicker of worry appears in me. What is she thinking? I can't read her.

There's a slight tremble in her hands as she busies herself with transferring the tomatoes into the salad bowl. "Take this to the dining table, please." She practically shoves the thing at my chest, but when our fingers brush, sparks explode over my skin.

She lets out a heavy breath, but she won't meet my gaze, like she's determined to ignore our insane chemistry.

Oh, Sunshine. This is happening. Maybe not tonight, but soon enough. This kind of attraction doesn't just go away on its own. It has to be expunged, preferably over the course of many long nights between the sheets.

I float back into the dining room where Sandro's sipping wine over a pillaged plate of cold cuts. He arches a brow. "That look on your face is making me seriously uncomfortable. Dare I ask?"

"Be quiet." I place the bowl on the table and take a seat so that Sandro won't notice the bulge in my jeans.

He snorts into his glass.

A minute later, Blake comes in carrying the giant turkey. I take the tray off her hands and put it in the center of the table.

She hands me the knife, still refusing to meet my eye. "Will you do the honors?"

"Sure." I cut the bird and serve her and Sandro before putting some on my own plate.

Blake lifts her wineglass and clears her throat. "Thanks for coming, guys. I don't have any family in town, so my original plan was to get a Thanksgiving dinner for one from the grocery store. My friend who lives in San Francisco told me that's just sad."

Sandro laughs. "We're honored you thought we were a better alternative."

"Yes, well, I have something to celebrate today beyond just the holiday."

Oh? Wonder what that could be. It's not her birthday. Maybe she found another job?

Sandro grins. "What are you celebrating?"

Blake tips her chin up, her nostrils flaring on an inhale. "Today, I got an offer on my house. I'm leaving Darkwater Hollow."

A record that's been playing "Make It Wit Chu" in my head ever since the kiss grinds to a sharp halt.

Wait, *what*?

What the fuck?

"You're...*leaving*?" My shock is loud and clear, but I don't give a fuck.

Her eyes snap to mine. "Yes. I'm leaving."

"When?"

"The realtor said it should move quickly. Two weeks at most."

Two weeks? Two fucking weeks?

Okay, I can still have her in two weeks. I mean, she's halfway there already. She invited me over, which mea—

Hold on.

She didn't invite me because she suddenly realized she wants to sleep with me. By the sounds of it, she invited me because she didn't have anyone else to invite.

I was...her last resort.

Can't say that's a position I'm used to being in.

So when she said I shouldn't have kissed her, she meant it? She *actually* meant it?

My heart pounds out a disappointed rhythm against my rib cage. I take a long—very long—pull of my wine. It tastes sour. It's not supposed to taste fucking sour, but it does compared to her.

"How come you're moving?" Sandro asks, oblivious. "It's a nice place."

Blake sinks her fork into a piece of tomato. "It's not the house." She's silent for a moment, like she's carefully choosing her next words. "I had a bad breakup earlier this year, and I still work for my ex and there aren't a lot of job opportunities in Darkwater Hollow. I just want to get out of this town and start over somewhere else."

I fold my arms over my chest. "Have you even tried looking for something else here?"

"No. There's really no point," she says sullenly.

"Moving away over a breakup seems extreme."

Her gaze hardens. "I didn't ask for your opinion."

Sandro coughs. "I'm sure you're making the right choi—"

"Where are you moving to?" I demand.

"I haven't decided yet."

Now, I'm incredulous. "You're leaving in two weeks, and you don't know where you're going?"

Her fingers tighten around her knife. "Not yet. I'll figure it out. I'm sure wherever I pick will be an upgrade."

"Wow. You must really hate Darkwater Hollow," I grind out.

The light above the table flickers like it's picking up on the tension crackling through the air.

"I don't hate Darkwater Hollow. There was a time when I saw myself staying here forever."

"Oh yeah?"

"Yeah. I've always had this dream of opening my own little bookstore somewhere in town, but over the last few months I've realized it's better to start over somewhere new."

I huff a sardonic laugh. "Starting over isn't all it's cracked up to be, trust me on that one."

She arches a brow. "Do *you* hate Darkwater Hollow?"

"I like the nature. But the people are another matter. Some of them get on my nerves, you know?"

Her eyes narrow. "I know *exactly* what you mean. There are a lot of rude folk around these parts."

"Let's compare notes. I think it's pretty rude to send mixed sig—"

"The turkey is delicious!"

Our heads snap toward Sandro.

He's giving us a *what-the-ever-loving-fuck* kind of look. "Would it be rude to ask for seconds?"

"Not at all," Blake clips out. "I'm glad you're enjoying it. Have as much as you'd like."

My chair skids against the floor. "I need to use the bathroom." I feel like I might punch a wall. I don't even understand why I'm so angry.

She shoots daggers at me. "It's through the living room and down the hall. First door on the right."

In the bathroom, I lock the door behind me and get halfway to slamming my fists against the damned thing before I stop myself.

A growl escapes past my clenched teeth.

What. The. Fuck.

Okay, maybe she didn't invite me tonight because she wanted to hook up with me, but she *kissed me back*. She might be in denial about our attraction, but her body doesn't lie. There's something here. Something powerful.

If she wasn't fleeing this town because of her ex—fuck, I hate that guy—I would have broken her down eventually.

I don't *want* her to leave. I haven't given a shit about anything for the last four months, but I give a shit about this.

That kiss made me feel just a little bit alive after I've spent months feeling like a dead man walking.

And let's just rewind to the part where she has *no plan*. Is she crazy? A girl like her, alone and somewhere unfamiliar? She's asking to get robbed, raped, or worse.

Inside me, something dark begins to stir.

My reflection glowers at me, and I don't recognize him. I'm wearing fucking flannel, for God's sake. If the guys back home saw me, they'd laugh me out of the room.

Nero wouldn't be caught dead wearing this shit.

And Nero wouldn't let that girl go. Because Nero was willing to do whatever it took to get what he wanted.

I rake my fingers through my hair. I feel fucking impotent. Powerless.

And I hate it. So damn much.

Make her stay, Nero commands.

Let her go. She's just a girl, Rowan pleads.

I slip my hand inside my pocket and reach for the cufflinks.

Yeah, she's just a girl. But she's also something more. Something I desire the way I haven't desired anything since I got to this shithole.

That's when it hits me.

I can't let her leave.

And if I have to do a bad thing to keep her here, so be it.

Nero laughs, eager to come out and play.

I walk out of the bathroom. It takes one look at her fireplace for the idea to come to me—so elegant and simple.

As I move back inside the dining room, I make a show of rubbing my arms. "It's a bit cold in here. Mind if I start a fire?"

CHAPTER 13

BLAKE

Sam and Rowan leave around eleven p.m., and I'm so exhausted that I don't have enough energy to even begin to process that kiss. As soon as I finish clearing the table, I collapse on top of the bed. My head hits the pillow, and the next moment, I'm out.

In my dream, I'm sitting in a lush, green meadow, book in hand. Beside me is a basket of ripe cherries. They look so wonderfully sweet that I can't help but pop one after another in my mouth until I finish them all.

My back hits the soft grass. Above me, the sky is a clear blue peppered with white doves that soar high above. I smile. It's the perfect summer day.

"That dress looks good on you, Sunshine."

It's Rowan. He's here, lying beside me. I turn on my side to face him and meet his hazel gaze.

"Everything looks good on you," I tell him. "It's not fair."

He smiles. "What's not fair is that you pulled away from me earlier. Didn't you like how I kissed you?"

I bite down on my lip. A pleasant buzz spreads through my body. "I liked it. I more than liked it."

He props himself up on his elbow and tangles his fingers through my hair. "Then give me that mouth again."

My lips tingle with anticipation as he leans in, his handsome face coming closer and closer to mine. My eyes flutter closed.

Hold on. What's that smell? It doesn't belong here.

It's sharp and acrid... Is something burning?

My eyes spring open. Rowan isn't here anymore. Smoke pours into the meadow through the trees around me, so fast that it fills my nostrils before I can even get to my feet. My lungs seize. I cough and cough and cough, and then I'm awake and still coughing.

The meadow's gone, and I'm in my bed. I blink at my darkened surroundings, and even though I can't see the smoke, I can smell it.

Oh shit.

Adrenaline surges through my veins.

I spring out of bed, disoriented and head swimming.

Crap! I trip on my slipper and tumble to the ground, my knees banging against the carpeted floor.

What the hell is going on?

That's when I see it. Wispy white smoke oozes in from under the door to the hallway.

Fuck. Fuck. FUCK.

My heart in my throat, I force myself to get up.

I put out the fire in the fireplace before I went to sleep. I'm sure I did.

Or did I? I was so tired. I'd been cooking all day. It looked like it was out when walked by it, but I didn't check it thoroughly.

There's a clattering sound, and someone swears in a low, rough tone.

What the hell? Cold sweat breaks out over my back. Is someone here?

What do I do? Oh God, I can't think, and there's more and more smoke coming in from under the door.

Intruder or not, I've got to put it out. There's a fire extinguisher in the kitchen. That's what I have to get. And then I need to call 911.

Plan formed, I pull on a pair of sweats, slide my feet into my slippers, grab my phone, and rush out the door.

The sight that greets me in the living room is the stuff of nightmares. Flames stretch from the fireplace, clawing up the wall beside it and licking hungrily toward the big bookshelf. Even from this far away, I can feel the intense, oppressive heat. A loud crack echoes through the room as a burning chair to the right of the fireplace collapses, sending a shower of sparks into the air.

"Blake!"

I whip my head around in the direction of the familiar voice. "Rowan?"

Somehow, he's here, standing between the sofa and the front door. I don't know how I didn't see him as soon as I ran out of my bedroom. I pinch myself just to make sure this isn't another dream.

Nope, it's not.

He darts toward me and grabs my arm. There's a hint of panic in his eyes, and it makes my own fear balloon inside me. "I saw the fire from my house. We need to get out of here."

"Get out? No way. I'm not leaving until I put it out."

Books, my beautiful books, are already catching fire, their spines curling and blackening.

"It's spreading too fast. We—"

"I know it's spreading fast, which is why I need to put it out!" I try to move toward the kitchen, but he doesn't release my arm from his iron hold.

Frustration spikes through me. "Let me go, Rowan."

"You can't put it out. What do you have, a single fire extinguisher?"

"I don't have time to chitchat! I have to get it from the kitchen. Let go of me!"

Another loud crack.

"We're leaving," he declares like it's his decision to make.

I'm fighting him now, squirming in his grip. "Just let me deal with this." A cough overtakes me. Through watery eyes, I can see the flames reach toward my favorite special edition of *Pride and Prejudice*—the one I used to read out loud to my mom.

I have to save it.

Energy rushes through me, and I buck so hard that I take Rowan by surprise. His hold on me slips. I make it halfway to the kitchen before strong arms pull me back by my waist.

"You're going to get yourself killed," he growls into my ear, and then my feet are no longer touching the ground.

"What the hell!" I screech.

He throws me over his shoulder like I'm a sack of potatoes and carries me out the front door.

My blood rushes through my ears. He can't do this.

I pound against his back, furious. "Put me down! Rowan, I swear, I'll murder you. Put. Me. Down!"

He does—on the dead lawn outside of his house—and then he straddles me. His weight pushes down on my hips. He weighs a freaking ton, and I can't move an inch.

"What are you doing?!" I scream as I scratch at his chest.

He wraps one big palm around both of my wrists and presses them against my belly. "Keeping you alive while I call 9-1-1."

My heart gallops inside my chest. I don't think I've ever been this viciously angry with another person. "You have no *right*."

He shushes me. *Shushes* me.

"I'm calling to report a fire at house number three on Land-horne Lane," he says into his phone. "Please hurry, the fire's spreading fast."

I exhale harshly through my nose.

"No, we're not inside anymore. Yes, a safe distance away from the house." He turns the mic away from him. "No pets, right?"

"No pets," I spit out.

He repeats my answer into the phone. "Okay. We'll wait out here." He ends the call, tosses the phone on the ground, and looks back down at me.

"I hate you."

A muscle in his jaw ticks. "I know you're mad, but staying inside would be stupid."

I roll my head against the cold ground and look at my burning house. Dense smoke is seeping through the small opening I left in the living room window. I'm staring right at it when the glass on the window bursts.

I yelp. Rowan leans over me, shielding me with his body.

The anger leaks right out of me, replaced with despair. I'm not someone who cries often, but right now, all I want to do is wail. Tears start to prick inside my eyes. "Rowan, it's going to get so bad before they come." My voice has a tremble to it.

He sits up and presses a warm palm to my cheek. "I know, Sunshine. I'm sorry."

For a second, everything stills. I stare at him. He stares at me. My senses zoom in on all the places we're touching, on the strange intimacy of the moment, on the way he just carried me out of a burning building.

My lungs expand on a shaky breath. "Can you get off me? I can't feel my legs."

"Only if you promise you won't make a run for it."

"I promise."

He climbs off me and helps me sit up.

Through the broken window, I see what can only be described as an inferno inside my living room. My house's got wooden furniture. A wooden frame. And all my books.

How did this happen?

There's only one explanation. I fell asleep with the fire still burning.

Idiot.

You're such a fucking idiot.

The sound of a distant siren bleeds into the air.

"They're almost here," Rowan says. Something warm wraps around my shoulders. I glance down. It's another dark hoodie.

"The other hoodie you gave me is still inside," I mumble, like it matters.

"Don't worry about it." He sits down beside me.

"What if the fire spreads to your house?"

"I'm keeping an eye on it, but our houses are far enough that it's unlikely to happen."

That's good, I suppose. Just about the only good thing about this situation.

Pulling up my legs, I press my forehead to my knees. "Tell me this is a nightmare. Tell me this is not real."

A hand lands on my back and moves in circles. I don't mind it. I need comfort the way I need air, even if I'm not the type to ever ask for it.

Somehow, Rowan just knows.

My hands curl into his hoodie. "This can't be happening. The house… I just got an offer."

"I know. I'm sorry."

I bite down on my lips to quiet the sob that wants to escape me. I won't cry. I'm afraid what will happen if I start. What if I can't stop, like I couldn't last time? After I caught Brett cheating. The tears flowed and flowed like a river that had broken through a dam. You're supposed to feel better after you cry, but I didn't. I just felt drained.

The firefighters arrive in a cacophony of sirens.

I lift my forehead from my knees and look back at my house. The fire is raging through the living room. Sheer horror rushes through my veins. Will there be anything left after it's out?

One of the firefighters jumps out of the vehicle, sizes up the scene, and barks a few orders to the other men. When he sees Rowan and me, he jogs over. "Is anyone inside the house?"

"No," Rowan answers. "I got her out as soon as I smelled smoke."

He points at Rowan's house. "You're her neighbor?"

"Yeah."

"It shouldn't spread, but I'd prefer if you stayed out here until we get it completely under control. Do you know what caused the fire?"

I swallow. "I must have left the fire still smoldering when I went to bed."

Rowan looks at me, but I can't meet his eyes. I feel so damn stupid.

The firefighters move with a sense of urgency. They unroll their hoses, creating snaking white paths across my lawn. Soon enough, water blasts from the nozzles, colliding with the flames and making steam hiss into the air.

"How did you smell it so quickly?" I ask.

"My window was open. I was still up, and I just had a gut feeling something was wrong."

"Couldn't sleep?"

"No."

"How lucky," I mumble. Although it's hard to feel like luck is on my side as I watch my ticket out of Darkwater Hollow burn.

It takes the firefighters about a half hour to get it under control. The house is still standing when they're done, so I guess that's good, but the living room is ruined.

The paramedics arrive. They check Rowan and me for injuries and smoke inhalation and then tell us we can go inside his house. The sun is just starting to rise.

"I'll make you some tea," Rowan says as we pass through his front door.

"Okay. I just need a moment alone."

He gives me a long, pitying look before he nods and walks down the hall.

The window by his front door faces the yard, and when I stop right in front of it, I get a view of my house.

I managed to hold onto hope even after my mom died. Even after Brett and I broke up. But now, as I stand and look at my smoldering house, I feel that hope waver.

What if I'm not meant to leave this town?

No, I can't think that way.

I suck in a deep breath.

They say bad things come in threes, don't they? My house burning down is number three.

I have to trust it can only get better from here.

CHAPTER 14

NERO

The boiling water in the pot on the stove gurgles. I can hear the soft sound of Blake's sniffles over it, coming from where she's sitting in the living room.

My hands curl around the edge of the counter.

Don't panic.

Do not fucking panic.

Okay, I won't deny things may have gone a bit off the rails.

I didn't mean for the fire to get *that* bad. I meant for it to singe the walls, maybe damage the flooring. Nothing major —just enough to delay the closing by a few weeks.

But fuck. It got *bad*. That bookcase went up like a bale of hay. It reminded me of that time I started a fire at the docks in Brooklyn, and I had no idea they were keeping old firewood hidden beneath the tarps. The thing made the morning news.

This will probably make the *Darkwater Hollow Weekly* too.

I drag my palms down my face. This is why Nero's not allowed to come out and play. He doesn't belong in this town, around these people. He causes chaos and suffering, and that's all fine and good when his victims are deserving, but Blake isn't.

Guilt pulses at my temples. She looked fucking *devastated*. Seeing her so upset and knowing I'm the cause of it felt worse than getting waterboarded. My moral compass might be broken, but even I know that I crossed a line with this— in retrospect—impulsive plan.

I was so worked up when she announced she was leaving. I wasn't thinking clearly. I got what I wanted though. She definitely won't be able to leave now.

Neither Darkwater Hollow nor my house, because hers is too damaged to stay in.

She'll stay here, with me. I fucked up, and she's my responsibility now. She can live with me for as long as it takes to get her house repaired.

But when I go back out there with the tea and present the offer to her, her response is, "Thanks, but absolutely not."

I blink at her over the mug steaming in my hands. "What do you mean? Why not?"

She cocks a brow, like I should know I'm asking a stupid question. "Because I don't know you."

"We spent Thanksgiving together," I protest.

"Yeah, and you weren't exactly a well-behaved guest."

Fucking hell. You'd think she'd lose some of that bite after she just narrowly escaped a house fire, but there's a part of me that's thrilled I haven't broken her.

"Look, I'm sorry about the kiss. That was out of line."

"It was actually perfectly in line. It's what you do. Who you are."

I set my mug down beside hers. "Okay, is that fair? I saved you from near—"

She sputters. "Saved me? You dragged me out of there instead of allowing me to try to save my precious babies!"

"I'm sorry, your *what*?"

"My books! That was my life's collection. Some of those were special editions!"

Books. She's upset about her books. "I thought preventing permanent lung damage was more critical, but my mistake," I mutter.

"Some of those had sprayed edges—"

"I felt the fire hot at my back and thought we should probably skedaddle. How silly of me."

"And sewn-in bookmarks! It was my one guilty pleasure. Just the one."

"Bookmarks?"

"Books!"

I raise my palms. "You're right. I should have prioritized the books."

She huffs out a few angry breaths, her eyes narrow and accusing. Then, slowly, her expression shifts into something I don't like.

Heartbreak.

Yeah, I don't like that at all. There's a very caveman-like urge to pull her against me and tell her I'll replace all of her precious book babies if that will make her smile again, but if I touch her right now, she'll probably throw her tea in my face.

She wraps her hands over her knees and rocks back and forth a few times. "Look, I'm sorry. I know you had good intentions when you came over to check on me. I'm just.... You know. Kind of messed up right now."

The guilt spreads from my temples and down into my chest. I need to make this right. "Where are you going to stay if not with me?"

"I don't know. I'll figure it out. Right now, I've got other things to take care of. I need to call Nicole, my realtor, and let her know what happened. Then I've got to see what I can salvage from the living room." She sighs. "Doubt it's very much."

"You should probably call your insurance company before you go inside. They might not want you to touch some things."

She gives me a funny look. "What insurance? I don't have any."

I am aghast. "What? How is that possible?"

"The house is too old. My mom couldn't get a policy."

This is getting worse and worse by the minute. I rub my palm over my lips, doing my absolute best to hide my rising panic. "That doesn't seem right."

She shrugs. "Well, you know, capitalism."

She picks up her phone from the coffee table and unlocks the screen, oblivious to my internal meltdown.

So I just fucked her. Majorly. And not the way I wanted to.

Moving my head side to side, I crack my neck. I can fix this. I can fix all of this. Starting with her house.

I could buy the damn thing outright with the money I've got stashed away from my old life. But that would raise a lot of questions.

What if I just fix it for her? After all, I own a home renovation firm, don't I?

Sandro's going to crucify me once he hears what happened. Whatever respect the kid's still got for me is bound to go right out the window. But we're taking this project on, and it's officially our top priority. I don't care if we have to move some things around to make it happen.

I'll make her place even better than it was before. And I'll replace every single one of her books.

Blake groans and presses her palm over her eyes. "What am I going to say to Nicole? *Thanks for all your hard work, but I'm a stupid idiot who left a fire burning and burned down her house*?"

"You're not an idiot. It could have happened to anyone."

She peeks at me through her fingers before dropping her hand back down and picking up her mug. "I swear I put it out. I'm never lighting a fire indoors again." She takes a sip. "There's no point in delaying it, I guess. She's always up at the crack of dawn. She needs to tell the buyer's agent about what happened. The buyers wanted to move in quickly, which isn't going to happen anymore." A sigh. "They'll need to look for a new place."

My phone buzzes in my pocket. It's Sandro, another early riser. "I'll be right back," I say to Blake.

She nods.

I prowl down the hallway and turn into the formal dining room I haven't used even once so that Blake won't overhear. "Hello?"

"Happy Thanksgiving, you cranky bastard. How was the rest of your night?"

"You know, under normal circumstances I'd be cussing you out right now for waking me up at this unholy hour."

"These aren't normal circumstances?"

In the background, I hear Blake start talking on the phone to her realtor.

"Is someone in your house?"

Apparently, Sandro hears her too.

"Yeah, Blake's here."

He groans. "Seriously?"

"It's not what you're thinking." I peer down the hall. Blake's still sitting on the sofa in the living room, all hunched over, saying something in a strained voice. "There was a fire in her house, so I brought her over here."

"A fire? How did that happen?"

"How do you think?"

"Don't tell me you started it so you could convince her to come over," he says with a laugh.

I move deeper into the dining room, paranoid Blake will hear even though I know it's impossible.

Sandro's laugh trails off until all that remains is a loaded silence. "Hey, I was joking."

I grunt.

"Are you *serious*? Jesus fucking Christ. I can't believe it. You started a damn fire?"

"Keep your fucking voice down. Do you want to wake up your neighbors?" I snap. Has he forgotten how thin those walls are?

"You went back there after we left?"

"Hmm."

He's laughing again, so hard he's wheezing. "You're a crazy bastard. Absolutely deranged. *Jesus* Christ. I could tell you didn't like it when she said she was leaving."

"She has no real plan," I growl, keeping my voice low. "She'd be asking for trouble if she just up and left."

"Oh, so you did this for her benefit? Right. Got it."

"Fuck you."

He cackles again. "No, please enlighten me as to your rationale here."

"I just didn't want her to leave, all right? Not yet."

A beat passes. "Interesting."

His tone makes me purse my lips. "What's that supposed to mean?"

"Nothing. So how bad was the fire?"

"The living room's looking rough. The rest seems okay. She's not hurt."

"I gathered as much. And for how long is she staying?"

"A while." She just doesn't know it yet. "The firemen are still here."

"Based on how the two of you interacted last night, I'm surprised she agreed to stay with you."

I sniff. "She hasn't yet. But she will."

"Oh Christ. You should warn her you might burn down the rest of the houses in this town if she says no."

"You're a smart ass, you know that? I'm hanging up."

I walk back into the living room. Blake's just saying goodbye on the phone.

"How did it go?" I ask when she hangs up.

She winces. "Nicole was understanding. Told me to call her once I know what the repairs will look like. I need to board up the windows as soon as everyone leaves."

"I can do that for you. As soon as we're clear to go inside."

She opens her mouth as if to argue, but then stops herself. "I would appreciate that." She scratches her temple. "I've never been very good at accepting help."

Yeah, she definitely isn't. "I still think you should stay with me."

She shakes her head. "I can't."

"I promise I'll behave."

"It's not just that. It would be a huge favor, and I'd have no way to repay you. That doesn't feel right to me."

I sit up straighter.

Hold on.

That's it.

There *is* a way she can repay me.

"What if there's something you can do for me in exchange?"

She blinks at me. "Like what?"

"Pretend to date me."

Her left brow slowly arches up. "Huh?"

"I have a reputation problem. You must be aware."

She reaches up to fix her ponytail, looking adorably confused. "I'm aware of the reputation. I didn't realize it was a problem for you. Seems like a badge of honor if anything."

I pinch the bridge of my nose. "It's a problem. And according to Sam, it's a big one. We're losing business over it."

"You don't say," she deadpans, dropping her hands back into her lap. "Who would have thought sleeping your way through a small town might not be the smartest thing—"

Oh my God, this woman. I press my hand over her mouth to silence that non-stop stream of sass. "Date me. Tell everyone

I'm reformed. Other women are dead to me. You're the only one I want."

Her eyes have grown very wide. I lower my hand and watch her tongue dart out against her bottom lip.

"Um. No, Rowan. That's insane."

"In exchange, you can stay here for free. You'll be right next door while your house is getting repaired. And I'll—" I bite my tongue. No, I can't tell her about the renovations yet. It would be too much, and she'd get uncomfortable again.

"And you'll..."

"And I'll cook for you." My lips quirk up. "I'm a great cook. Italian roots and all."

She's looking at me like I'm an alley cat that might have contagious diseases.

"What do you think?"

She swallows. "Rowan, I don't know what to say. Do you really need to clean up your reputation this badly?"

"I do. You know Abigail MacDonald?"

She pales. "Yes."

I shrug. "Well...I didn't know she was married."

The flicker of repulsion in her eyes cuts me deeper than it should. "How is that possible? Everyone knows she's married to Wayne MacDonald!"

"Not me!" I insist. "I told you, I don't pay as much attention to other people and their business as the rest of this town does. I swear, I didn't know. But the court of public opinion is turning against me and I need to change that. It's affecting the business. I can't have that."

She stares at me intently for a while, like she's trying to decide if she believes me or not. Finally, she huffs. "So you want a pretend girlfriend to make people think you've settled down and won't steal their wives. And in exchange, I get to live here."

"Exactly." If Blake agrees, I'll kill three birds with one stone. She'll be taken care of while her house gets fixed. I'll be able to smooth things out with Sandro and work. And she'll have to spend time with me.

Lots of it.

She rubs her cheek and sighs. "Am I to believe you're going to keep your hands off other women while we're playing this charade?"

I don't miss the small flash of vulnerability in her gaze.

Her ex cheated on her, and the whole town knows about it. She doesn't want a repeat of that, even if our relationship is pretend. "Of course. The whole point is that I'm a reformed man, remember?"

Her teeth sink into her bottom lip. "I don't know…"

My heart pounds as I wait for her to make her decision. *C'mon, Sunshine, give it a chance.*

"Blake!"

She jumps to her feet at the sound of someone calling her from outside.

"Who is that?" I ask.

She swallows. "Brett."

CHAPTER 15

BLAKE

It's official. Rowan Miller is insane. How else would you describe a man who wants me to pretend to be his girlfriend so that he can fix his reputation as a womanizer?

A huff escapes my lips as I walk onto his porch.

The first thing I see is Brett's red BMW. Then I see Brett. He's talking to one of the firefighters, but when he spots me, he jogs over.

"Blake, oh my God!"

Before I know what's happening, he pulls me into a tight hug. A hug that's as unwelcome as it's uncomfortable. I squirm in his arms until he releases me, and then I take a big step back.

Talking to him is just about the last thing I want to be doing right now.

"Jesus Christ, B. How did this happen?"

"The fireplace, most likely."

"Did you go to bed without putting it out?"

The obvious judgment in his voice makes me bristle. "I thought I did, but I guess I didn't."

His jaw hardens. "This is why you shouldn't be living alone. You can't take care of yourself."

I blink at him, unsure I heard him right.

He stares back, as if he said something completely reasonable.

"What is that supposed to mean?" I demand, not caring the least bit that my voice is raised and some of the firefighters might overhear. "I took care of myself and my mom just fine for years, Brett."

He raises his palms. "I didn't mean to upset you. I'm just saying that staying alone in that house was always a bad idea. Maybe this is for the best."

Anger coils around my lungs. "Are you saying it's a good thing my house caught on fire?"

"I'm saying it could be a sign." He points at the sky. "Maybe someone up there doesn't want us apart."

Did he really just say God wants us back together? How delusional can he be?

And how the hell did I date this guy for three years? I must have had a brain-altering parasite.

"You think God burned down my house so that I would come running back to you?"

He nods. "Something like that. Let me help you."

"I don't need your help."

"Look, I don't know why you're isolating yourself and pushing me away. Everyone knows we're going through a rough patch, but we'll get back together."

My throat thickens with fury. "Brett, this is not a rough patch."

He frowns. "You're acting like a child, B. Enough already. Come stay with me."

There's no chance in hell I'm doing that.

Quickly, I run through my options. There's that old manor that got turned into an upscale hotel—a hundred dollars might get me a broom closet for the night.

There's also the Birchwood Motel, popular among the biker crowd and known for its seedy reputation. I could probably afford to stay there for a few weeks, but word of my whereabouts would likely get to Uncle Lyle. Last thing I need is my dad's old buddy coming around to offer his "help."

There are other hotels, but they're farther from here, and I want to stay close to keep an eye on the house.

There's nothing closer than Rowan's place. I should at least consider his offer. A few weeks of pretending to be his girlfriend in exchange for staying next door to my house? How bad could it be?

I grimace. Bad. Very bad.

It's hard to reconcile the guy who volunteered to drive me home in a blizzard and carried me out of a burning building with the guy who kissed me with no warning and slept with another man's *wife*.

Do I believe he didn't know Abigail was married? I want to. I really do.

But I'm hesitant to trust anyone, let alone someone as... confusing as him.

Agreeing to Rowan's offer would mean trusting him to a very large extent. I'd be living with him, for God's sake. I've never lived with a man before. Would I feel safe sharing a space with him? I don't know him all that well, so the answer should be no, but strangely enough, I have this weird certainty in my gut that he wouldn't harm me.

Maybe it's because of how he calmed me down after our near accident, or maybe it's just some animal instinct, but I've never felt unsafe around him.

That's more than I can say for most men.

So yeah, I think I could live with him, but what about the second part of the agreement?

If I agree to pretend we're dating, we'd have to put on a convincing act whenever we're out and about. At a minimum, we'd have to hold hands. Hug. Kiss.

Something hot and nervous twists inside my belly at the memory of doing just that in my kitchen.

The moment he leaned down, I knew what was coming, so why didn't I stop it? I could have kicked him. I could have screamed.

Instead, I kissed him back.

I'm a logical, rational person, but deep down, I'm also a romantic. Spending extended time in close quarters with that man is bound to be a test for any woman with a pair of eyes and a beating heart.

What if I forget myself again, the way I did with Brett? I don't want to put myself in a position where I'll only get hurt again.

Brett grabs my hand. "It'll be easier to fix things between us if we live together. Trust me."

The door behind me opens, and Brett's attention moves to a spot over my shoulder. His eyes narrow.

I don't need to look behind me to know it's Rowan. He must have heard us arguing and has come out to check on me.

I pull my hand out of his grasp. "I would rather be homeless than ever get back together with you."

"Don't be ridiculous." His voice is harsher and lower. It's the voice he uses at Frostbite when he wants to remind me that he's my boss. "C'mon. You've got no close friends. No family. Where else are you going to stay?"

Rowan stops close enough for his shoulder to brush against my own. A second later, I feel the warm pressure of his palm against the small of my back.

Brett pointedly ignores Rowan. "C'mon, B. Let's go."

My heart hammers inside my chest. Isn't it time I do something drastic to make Brett understand we're never getting back together?

"We both know you don't have any other options," he grinds out.

That's when I decide—screw it. I am so done with this.

"Actually, I do have options. I'm going to stay with Rowan."

Brett's eyes go very wide. "That's absurd."

"I've got things to do, Brett. You should probably go home."

"Blake, that's *absurd*. You are not staying with him. You don't even know him. He just appeared out of nowhere—"

"He came here from New York, and he was just over at my place for Thanksgiving. I know him well enough."

Brett shakes his head and takes a step forward. "Blake—"

Suddenly, Rowan's in front of me, blocking him from coming any closer. "She said you can go home." Rowan's voice is low and deadly. "This conversation is over."

Brett sputters. "Who the fuck do you think you are?"

"The guy whose property you're currently standing on."

"I happen to know the Jacksons. They're good friends of my dad. One call, and you're fucking out of here," Brett threatens.

Anxiety fans through me. I can't get Rowan evicted. Brett's family is powerful—maybe the most powerful family in town.

I'm about to butt in to try and defuse the situation, when Rowan says, "Go ahead. Call them. But I'm not sure what the Jacksons have to do with any of this, given I bought the house."

What? He *bought* it?

Brett's gaze stays on Rowan, but a hint of uncertainty passes through his eyes.

He didn't know either. He's not used to being challenged like this. Everyone in town treats him and his family like royalty.

But Rowan isn't like everyone. Maybe it's because he's new here, and he doesn't understand the power the Lewis family has.

Or maybe he just doesn't give a crap.

I kind of admire that about him.

Huh.

"Blake," Brett grinds out. "You can't be serious about this."

"I'm serious. I've really got to go. I'll see you at Frostbite."

When Brett doesn't move, Rowan crosses his arms over his chest. "You're still on my property."

He sneers at Rowan before spinning on his heel and stalking away toward his car.

I tug on my bottom lip with my teeth. I know Brett, and he's not the type to let a slight like this slip.

"Let's go inside," Rowan says, his voice a low rumble.

I nod, but as soon as we get inside and the front door closes behind us, I turn to Rowan. "You should be careful around him. His family is powerful."

His eyes darken until they appear nearly black. "I can handle him and his family."

I stand in his foyer, my breaths coming out short and quick. "So I guess we're doing this, huh?"

A small smirk creeps onto his lips. "I guess we are."

CHAPTER 16

BLAKE

The day doesn't seem to ever end. After Brett leaves, one of the firefighters accompanies me inside the house so that I can grab some clothes and essential items. I take the first things I can find in my bedroom and get out of there. I'm just not emotionally ready to face the damage head-on today.

I wait until the fire department finishes their investigation, confirming the fire most likely spread from an unattended fireplace, and provide my statement.

"I was sure the darned thing went out," I say to the fire marshal.

"Did you stir the ashes? Sprinkle some water on them?"

"Well, no," I admit sheepishly. I was too damn tired to do all that.

"Sometimes the fire might look like it's out, but the embers are still burning, and it can reignite."

"That must have been what happened."

While Rowan goes to board up the broken windows, I go back to his place and call Del to fill her in on what happened. The only thing I leave out is my fake dating agreement with Rowan, because I don't want him walking in while I'm freaking out about it with Del.

A fake relationship.

This is going to be interesting.

I set my phone on the coffee table in the living room and glance around—actually taking in my surroundings for the first time.

This place isn't as bad as I thought it would be. It's been what...two weeks since Rowan moved in? He's done a damn good job sprucing this place up.

If this is where I'll be living for the next little while, I might as well look around.

The living room and kitchen have been repainted, the kitchen cabinets look brand new, and the hardwood floor has a gorgeous shine that can only be a result of a recent refinishing. I've seen some contractors coming and going, so it's not like he's done all of this himself, but still, the man gets shit done. I'll give him that.

He must've also worked on at least a few of the bedrooms if he's got a room for me. Down here, it seems like it's just the master bedroom—the one he sleeps in—but there's probably two or three more upstairs.

I'm torn between wanting to go up there and feeling like I might be overstepping.

Better wait for him to come back and show me around.

I sit down on the sofa and moan with relief. Now that the adrenaline has finally left my system, I'm exhausted.

God, this sofa is comfy. My body melts into the cushions, and my eyelids grow heavy. I'm exhausted. I could probably pass out right now...

Clank.

I startle from the sound and sit up. My throat is dry, and my head feels like it's filled with cotton. I must have fallen asleep.

My eyes land on Rowan and the bowl of pasta he just placed on the coffee table in front of me.

"Eat."

He's standing on the other side of the table, clad in jeans and a black T-shirt that molds to his muscular chest entirely too well.

"You changed," I mumble, my voice still hoarse with sleep.

He glances down at himself. "A while back. I was covered in ash after boarding up the windows."

Right. He was doing me another favor while I was on his couch napping. My cheeks heat. "What time is it?"

"Just past seven."

"I was out for hours," I moan. "I'm sorry."

"There's nothing to apologize for. You were exhausted."

"I still am."

"Then eat and go to bed."

I pick up the bowl. The pasta smells amazing. It looks like pasta carbonara, which isn't the kind of thing you can make out of a box. "Did you make this?"

He hands me a fork. "Try it."

I twirl the spaghetti around my fork and take a bite. My tastebuds explode. "Oh Lord, this is *good*."

Rowan's lips twitch. "I feel like I should be offended at how shocked you sound. I told you I'd get you room and board, didn't I?"

I shove more pasta into my mouth, feeling completely famished. Or maybe it's just that good.

"This is my nonna's recipe."

"I think I'm in love with her."

He sits down beside me, his own bowl in his hands. It looks tiny in comparison, like it's a bowl meant for a doll. His T-shirt is just the right amount of tight around his rounded biceps and muscled shoulders.

The masculinity of this man is overwhelming.

I'm also still processing how weirdly...thoughtful he's being. And decent. He boarded up the windows of my house, and now he's feeding me? Who is this guy?

My perception of him is shifting in a very dangerous direction.

"You're not working tomorrow, are you?" he asks.

"It's my day off, thank God. I'm going to spend all day getting quotes for the repairs. I'll have to do what I can to secure the house before we get more snow, but fixing up the interior will take a while longer." The thought of how much the repairs are going to cost fills my lungs with dread. I've got a bit saved up, but there's no chance it'll be enough. "I'd rather know what kind of financial hit I'm looking at sooner rather than later."

What if it takes me a year? A whole year of working at Frost-bite and dealing with Brett, tightening my belt when it's already been pretty damn tight.

I swallow down the ball in my throat. One stupid mistake, and all the work I did on the house was for nothing.

"Your financial hit is zero."

I glance at him. What's he talking about? "I don't have insurance. I thought I already told you that." I take another bite.

His arm brushes against my shoulder as he lifts the fork to his mouth. "I'll take care of it."

I nearly choke. "I hope you're joking."

"I was the one who suggested starting a fire last night, so I feel responsible. Plus, you're my woman now, remember? What kind of a shitty boyfriend would I be if I didn't repair your house for free? I do own a renovation firm, you know."

His woman? This time, I really do choke on my pasta. Rowan pats my back as I cough.

"What is wrong with you?" I force out when I manage to finally breathe again.

"Weird way to say thanks, Blake."

I put my bowl down and turn to face him. "You are not repairing my house for free. That's ludicrous."

"I'll get Sam over here in the next day or two to scope out the project."

My head spins. "Rowan, it's been a long day. If this is your idea of a joke—"

"Take a deep breath." His hand appears on my knee. "Like I said, I'll take care of it all."

I stand up, needing to put some space between us. I'm starting to believe he's serious, and I'm having a hard time processing the sudden onslaught of feelings I'm experiencing.

"It's going to cost a fortune."

He puts his bowl down beside mine and leans back against the couch, throwing his arm over the back. "I'm doing what any good boyfriend would do."

"We're not *actually* dating."

"Our agreement is important to me. We need to sell this if it's going to work. What better way to show how serious I am about you than to work on your house?"

I feel so dizzy that I have to sit back down. "This is nuts. I already told you I'm not good at accepting help, and this is — God, Rowan. I'm not used to someone doing things like this for me." A mixture of gratefulness and vulnerability swirls inside my lungs.

His gaze burrows into me, intent and unrelenting. "Then you better get used to it, because I take care of what's mine, Sunshine."

My pulse picks up speed. There's something about the sure way those words roll off his lips that makes the hairs on my nape stand up straight.

For a moment, I catch a glimpse of yet another version of Rowan. Intense, possessive, *dark*.

But then he smiles, and it's as if it never happened. "Don't forget you're helping me too."

"I guess..." I trail off. Given the bombshell he just dropped on me, I'm starting to feel like this agreement is going to benefit me way more than it benefits him. Unless... "Rowan. Do you want something more in exchange?"

He cocks his head. "Like what?"

"I don't know. Maybe you're expecting me to be your sex slave or something. It's not like I have anything else to give."

Amusement colors his features. "I just want to remind you that I've never had any problems getting women to sleep with me. Coercion's not really my thing, unless you're into that."

"I am not into that."

"Then maybe don't look a gift horse in the mouth."

I press my lips together. He's right, of course. If he really wants to do this to help sell our dating act, why should I stop him? It must be worth it for him. For all I know, he's losing a ton of customers.

Rowan bumps my knee with his. "You good?"

No. But I think it's time I admit that Rowan's not exactly who I thought he was.

I meet his gaze. "I owe you a thank-you."

He smirks. "Finally."

"This is extremely generous." So generous that I know I'm going to do whatever I can to sell our act. I just have to make sure I don't get myself in trouble in the process.

"Then it's settled." His gaze caresses my face before it drops to my empty bowl. "You should get some sleep."

As if on cue, my mouth parts on a yawn. My eyelids feel like they're made of concrete. That long nap did nothing for me. "I'm going to be out like a log tonight. Can you show me to my room?"

Rowan stands up and helps me to my feet. He doesn't let go of my hand as he leads me down the hall, and I don't let go of his.

Only because I'm tired.

Definitely not because there's a tiny part of me that likes it.

I expect him to take me upstairs, but he doesn't.

He stops in front of a door that can only be—

"You'll sleep in my bedroom."

The surge of adrenaline that follows his words wakes me right up. I tug my hand out of his. "Don't tell me this is part of selling our fake relationship. No one's going to be watching us inside your house."

"The other bedrooms aren't ready," he says matter-of-factly. "When they are, you can take one of them. Don't worry, I'll sleep on the couch."

Oh. My cheeks blister. I really need to stop jumping to conclusions while I'm around him. "You sure?"

"I'm sure." He pushes the door open and reveals his king-sized bed. It looks brand-new, comfy, and inviting. My muscles ache, and I finally just...crash.

"Okay, thanks."

"The bathroom is through here." He gestures at a door to the left of the built-in closet.

I glance around the space, feeling like I'm intruding on his sanctuary. There aren't many personal belongings—only his clothes peeking through the gap in the closet doors, a gym bag on the floor, and some knickknacks on the nightstand closest to me. The sheets are a dark gray and look freshly changed. Maybe he changed them while I was napping. The duffel bag of things I collected from my house is sitting in the corner.

"Thank you again. For everything."

His jaw firms, and for a long moment, he just looks at me. "Don't mention it."

He leaves, and I walk over to sit on the bed. The duvet is cool and soft under my palms, and when I press my nose into the pillow, I pick up a subtle hint of his smell.

A wave of pleasure crashes through me.

You're losing it.

Lifting my face off the pillow, I glance to my right. There's a book on the nightstand. I pick it up and read the title.

La Vita Nuova. Dante.

Inside the book, I see it's got English and Italian side-by-side. I wonder if Rowan speaks Italian.

In the bathroom, I wash my face, do my business on the toilet, and take a quick shower. But when I pull one of the T-shirts I sleep in out of my bag, all I smell is smoke.

I drop it, zip the bag, and shove it under the bed. I can't sleep in that. I don't want to dream of the fire.

Better to ask Rowan for a shirt. I'll wash my things tomorrow and give it back to him then.

I pull on the hoodie Rowan gave me earlier today, zip it all the way up, and venture outside the bedroom.

Rowan's on the sofa, typing something on his phone.

"Could I get something to sleep in?"

His eyes snap to mine and then drop to my bare legs. His hoodie is big enough to almost reach my knees, but I'm suddenly very aware of the fact that I'm wearing nothing underneath. My thighs clench together.

Rowan's eyes are darker as he gets to his feet. "Of course." When he brushes past me to enter the bedroom, a pulse of heat appears between my legs. He rummages in the closet and tucks some stuff under his arm, probably planning for tomorrow. Then he pulls out a neatly folded T-shirt. "Here."

I take it from him and allow it to unfold. As expected, it's huge. It'll be as good as a nightgown on me.

"Does that work?"

"Yep." I squeeze the T-shirt. "I'll give it back to you tomorrow."

When he doesn't answer right away, I glance at his face. He's looking at the shirt in my hands, his thumb dragging over his bottom lip. The silence stretches until his eyes lift to mine.

There's a small scar right above his left brow.

"Keep it."

CHAPTER 17

NERO

Beep. Beep. Beep.

I mutter a string of curses at the phone as I jam my thumb against the snooze icon.

I'm not a morning person. Never been one. For most of my life, my work happened at night.

Now Sandro and I have meetings starting from eight a.m., sometimes even on a fucking Saturday like today.

We're pitching a plan for what might be one of the biggest projects we've done, and while the architect's running the show, I'll be on deck when we start talking numbers. The clients are a pain in the ass who like to hold mind-numbingly long meetings on weekends. Normally, I wouldn't care but I feel a pang of disappointment about leaving Blake on her own today.

When we bought the firm, we kept most of the existing staff. Handy Heroes had good people, but the owner was running the business into the ground. He barely had enough to cover a month of payroll when we scooped it up.

I wasn't a total stranger to the business. Back in New York, we controlled a good chunk of the cement industry. If a firm wanted to bid on a project worth more than three million, they had to be approved by us. The owners paid us ten percent of their contracts—or at least the smart ones did.

The dumb ones ended up at the bottom of the Hudson.

But in Darkwater Hollow, Sandro and I operate by the book. No intimidation. No racketeering.

Nothing that might bring any unwanted attention onto us.

No wonder I've been so fucking bored.

Not anymore though.

I sit up on the couch with a yawn and run my fingers through my hair. The alarm starts blasting again before I shut it off for good.

At least it hasn't woken Blake up. As I pass by the bedroom on my way to the guest bathroom, I don't hear a sound on the other side of the door.

She looked dead on her feet before she went to bed last night. She barely even argued with me when I told her to take my bedroom. The thought of her lying in my bed, in my T-shirt, fills me with satisfaction.

How would she react if I climbed in beside her, dragged her thighs apart, and tasted her until she came apart on my tongue?

I drag a palm over my face. Yeah, we've got a long way to go before that happens.

If she thought I was one hundred percent Satan when I first moved in, I've probably managed to get that down to seventy-five percent when I convinced her to fake date me.

Maybe even fifty percent after telling her I'll fix her house.

I have a feeling I'll have to get it all the way into the tens for her to even consider sleeping with me.

But this whole fake dating idea is brilliant. Sometimes I surprise myself. Now, I have an excuse to take her out on dates and treat her better than that prick ever did. And she's on the hook for going along with it.

We'll pretend for a while, but in the meantime, I'll be wearing her down. Bit by bit, every day. She won't be able to deny me forever. There's no woman who'd be able to withstand my charms in this situation. Not a single one. I've already won, Blake just doesn't know it yet.

And when she finally gives in, the real fun will begin. I'll fuck her so well she'll want to write a damn book about it so that she can revisit the memories. We'll get each other out of our systems, I'll fix up her house, and she'll go on her merry way.

And then everything will go back to the way it was before.

The way it was before.

Which...sucked.

I frown. I don't need to think about what happens afterward. That's a problem for another day.

I run the water and start brushing my teeth. Sandro's not going to be happy when I ask him to start working on her house along with the other projects we've got on our plate. But he's the one who's been up my ass about my reputation. He should be pleased I'm doing something about it, right?

My appointment is in Cedar Springs, a neighborhood about a thirty-minute drive from the house. I turn on the radio and start running through the agenda in my head.

A siren cuts through my train of thought. My eyes narrow at the reflection in the rearview mirror.

A cop car.

"What the fuck?" I'm not over the speed limit.

I do what any respectable citizen—aka not a gangster in hiding—would do and pull over.

The cop pulls up behind me.

A guy about the same age as me gets out of the car. He has slicked-back hair and a pair of aviators hooked on his crooked nose. He motions for me to roll down the window, one hand on his gun for no apparent reason.

"License and registration."

I prop my elbow on the edge of the window. "What's the problem, Officer?"

"Routine check." He shows me his open palm. "License and registration."

My teeth grind together. There's a gun in my glove compartment, but I keep the registration in the center console.

I hand the ID and the document to the cop, and I stare ahead while he looks them over. The ID's fake, but it'll hold up. I've got Rafe to thank for that.

"You live at One Landhorne Lane, right?"

"Yeah."

"Beside the house that caught on fire?"

I cock my head. "Were you there yesterday?"

"No, but some friends of mine were."

Something about the way he says the word "friends" tips me off.

Is this fucker friends with Blake's ex?

I give the cop a vicious grin that's made lesser men shit their pants. His eyes widen, but to his credit, he doesn't bolt.

"It was a terrible accident," I say. "Let's hope there won't be any more of those."

He pushes his sunglasses up to his head and frowns. "Rowan Miller. Your ID is from Nevada. What are you doing in Darkwater Hollow?"

"I live here now. Moved recently."

"What for?"

"I felt like it. It's a free country, Officer. Sure seems like a lot of questions for a routine traffic stop."

He drags his tongue over his teeth. "You need to get a state license if you live here now. I'm going to have to write you a fine."

"Go right ahead," I drawl.

He goes back to his car to write me a fucking ticket while I text Sandro I'm running late.

When he comes back, he hands me the ticket. "We're a tight-knit community here, Mr. Miller, and we protect our own. You might do well to remember that."

I give him and his cryptic message a two-finger salute. "Thanks for that. You have a good day now."

The fucker watches me drive off, a scowl on his face.

So Blake's ex has some bite to go along with all that bark. Too bad for him that his cop buddies won't find anything if they run Rowan Miller through the system.

If they looked up Nero De Luca on the other hand... *Ex-consigliere of one of the most powerful families in the Cosa Nostra. Nicknamed Angel of Death.*

If Brett saw my rap sheet, he'd bolt out of this town with his tail tucked between his legs.

Sandro and the architect are waiting for me with the client when I arrive. We spend more than three hours going over our proposal, break for lunch, and then get back to it.

It's not until we wrap it up in the late afternoon that I finally get Sandro alone.

"Let's grab a beer. I've got something to talk to you about."

"All good?"

"Yeah." I stop by my truck and swipe my knuckle under my nose. "Had an interesting incident this morning. Tell you about it at The Junction?" It's a local bar that doesn't get busy until after dinner, so it'll be quiet enough for us to have a conversation without being overheard.

Sandro gives me a curious look as he unlocks his car. "Sounds good. Meet you there."

Fifteen minutes later, we're sitting in a booth, beers in hand. Sandro got a Blue Moon, and I've got my usual Guinness. The owner, Denny, is behind the bar watching a replay of the game from this weekend on a flatscreen hanging in the corner.

Sandro takes a sip. "Long day, but I think it went really well. They loved the plan we presented."

"Yeah? The husband kept looking at me weird."

"Like I told you, the men of this town are wary of you."

"You'll be happy to know I've found a way to put their worries to rest."

Sandro's brow arches up. "Oh yeah?"

"I'm off the market. Blake and I are dating."

He rears back. "Come again?"

"She needs a place to stay, and I need a girlfriend. We made a deal."

My crisp explanation seems to make Sandro even more confused. "Hold on, so she's your fake girlfriend? Or is it for real?"

"Fake."

He looks shocked. You'd think by now he'd expect things like this from me.

Sandro drags a palm over his cheek. "Dude, if she ever finds out you started that fire..."

"She's never going to find out." How could she? "I'll start taking her out next week, and it won't take long for the whole town to know we're together. It's brilliant, isn't it?"

"I mean, yeah, I guess it could work..."

"We're going to fix up her house, by the way. I told her you'll be over soon to take a look at everything."

He drags his palm down his face. "Sure. Great. As if I don't have other things on my plate. But I don't get it. If we fix her place, won't she just try to sell it again and leave?"

"I don't need to fake date her for long. Just a few months to smooth things over and have the people in this town move on to some other scandal." A few months will also be enough for me to get Blake into my bed so I can get my fill of her.

At least I hope it will be enough. A woman's never managed to keep my interest for more than that.

But what if she does?

"All right, I'll go there next week." Sandro sighs into his glass. "So what happened to you this morning?"

"I got stopped by a fucking cop."

Concern flickers over Sandro's expression. "Why?"

"Blake's ex set him on me."

"Blake's ex?"

"Yeah, you know the douchebag who owns the bar she works at? He's also the mayor's son."

The concern deepens. "Dude, you sure you picked the right woman to be your fake girlfriend?"

"I'm not worried about it. I just thought you should know."

"Well, I *am* worried. I mean, it seems like you're diving head-first into a whole lot of trouble. He's setting the cops on you? What if he starts sniffing around some more?"

"You really think this fucker who probably hasn't stepped foot outside of Missouri his whole life is going to figure out who I am?" I scoff. "Please. He's not a real threat."

"You need to be careful." Sandro shakes his head. "Letting her stay with you is not a good idea, man. I've got a bad feeling about this."

"She's staying with me. End of fucking discussion."

"Her ex might be nothing, but his dad—"

"His dad personally delivered an invite to his Christmas Charity Auction to me. He's not looking for a fight. He's happy I invested in his town. I'll go to the auction, meet him, break bread, and put any doubts his son might have planted to rest."

Sandro stares at me for a few long seconds. "You know no matter what happens between you two, you can never tell her who you are, right?"

"You think I'm an idiot? Of course I'm not going to tell her anything." I have to lie to Blake the way I have to lie to everyone.

It's never bothered me before, but now, as I say the words, a hollow feeling settles in my chest.

CHAPTER 18

BLAKE

"Morning!" Del's chipper voice pierces through my ear.

I groan into my phone, still half asleep. "You woke me up."

"Girl, are you serious? It's eleven a.m. here, which means it's like one p.m. your time."

What? I jerk up, my heart rate skyrocketing. "You're kidding." A glance at my phone screen tells me she's not. Shit! I should have set an alarm. "Oh my God, I've slept through half the day. I've got things to do."

"Take a deep breath. You sound like you're having a heart attack."

Yesterday rushes back to me. The fire. Brett coming over. Rowan's offer—I still haven't told Del about it.

"Give me one sec." I lower the phone from my ear and listen for any sounds outside. It's silent. Rowan must have left for work a long time ago.

"Okay, you still there?" I ask.

"Uh-huh. What's going on?"

I tug the duvet closer to my chest. *Rowan's* duvet. "I'm going to be staying with Rowan for a bit. In exchange, he wants me to pretend to be his girlfriend. You know, so that everyone here will stop thinking he's a man whore."

Del gasps. "Come again?"

"I know. It's insane. And what's even more insane is that as part of this deal, he's fixing up my house. For *free*."

Del squeals. "That is nuts. But like in the best way ever. Let that man take care of you, girl."

I groan. "It feels so weird. I mean, he's getting the short end of the stick here, isn't he?"

"You're not the short end of the stick. Clearly, he thinks whatever you're doing for him is worth it. Now tell me more about this fake girlfriend thing. What are your responsibilities exactly?"

I gnaw on my nail. "We haven't really discussed it in detail, but at the very least, we'll have to be out in public together. I'll have to pretend to be into him."

"Can you do that?"

If she'd asked me that question two weeks ago, I'd have probably said no. But now? I don't think I'll have a hard time. In fact, I'm worried about how easy it might be.

Rowan isn't nearly as shallow and flighty as I thought he'd be. He's got a caring and generous side to him that I wasn't expecting. And being on the receiving end of that side? It feels good.

Maybe too good.

Brett's generosity wasn't like that. It never felt good to receive. He'd help me make my car payment now and then, but every time he did it, he'd make a big deal out of it, like it was my fault my mom needed something I hadn't been anticipating that month. And afterwards, he wanted me to lavish him with gratitude.

Compare that to Rowan, who seemed almost uncomfortable when I kept thanking him last night.

"Then you better get used to it, because I take care of what's mine, Sunshine."

A shiver runs through me. I fall back down on the bed. "I think I'll manage."

"And is there an end date to this arrangement?"

"I'm still planning on selling the house once it's repaired. So I guess we can keep doing this until then, unless he wants to end it earlier."

"That could be months."

"Correct."

For a while, Del's silent.

"What?" I ask.

"That's a long time to be playing pretend with someone. Especially someone who looks like he could fuck you into oblivion if given the chance."

"Did I tell you he kissed me on Thanksgiving?"

"No! What?! Are you joking?"

"I'm one hundred percent serious. It just shows you how chaotic the last twenty-four hours have been, I honestly forgot about it for a second. We were in the kitchen and he just went for it."

"Oh my God. How was it?"

"Um…" I swallow. It felt like being struck by lightning. "Good. But it can't happen again." And it won't.

"Uh, are you sure about this whole staying with him thing? You can always come stay with me."

"I have to be in Darkwater Hollow while the repairs are being done. I'll be fine," I say weakly.

"Just…be careful, okay? I don't want to see you get hurt."

"I won't get hurt." Rowan might be growing on me, but I'm not an idiot. I know better than to let my guard down around him again.

My phone buzzes twice. An email? It's probably my schedule for the week.

"Okay, I've got to get out of bed. Talk to you later?"

"Yep. Love you, good luck."

In my inbox, there's an email from Brett. He sends it around the same time every week.

But when I open the PDF, my jaw drops. He took me off the schedule for the next two weeks.

"That fucker!"

I scroll back to the top of the email and realize I missed the personal note he left me. *Take some time off, B. It'll give you an opportunity to reflect on your choices.*

My blood boils. "That petty, childish, miserable asshole!"

He knows I need the money, and so he's trying to squeeze me dry. Maybe he thinks I'll get desperate enough to come running back to him.

Honestly, what is wrong with him?

I jump out of bed, furious. I need something to distract me from my anger, or I might just drive over to Frostbite and cause a big scene.

Deep breaths.

No. I won't give that jerk the satisfaction of seeing how he's rattled me.

Instead, I get started on my long to-do list.

I take my duffel to Rowan's laundry room and dump my stinky clothes into the washing machine. After I start the laundry, I march over to my house.

The thought of seeing the damage is daunting, but I've got to rip the Band-Aid off. Rowan's going to fix it all. I just have to remember that.

The front door whines on its hinges as I open it, a new sound that it's never made before.

I take a cautious step inside, and my heart leaps in my throat.

The living room is ruined. Everything is covered in black soot. A strip of sunlight pierces through a hole in the ceiling, slicing through the husk that used to be my couch.

And the bookshelf... The bookshelf is an ashy graveyard of all the stories I love so much. The stories that got me through the hard parts of growing up. The stories that let me escape into fictional worlds where I could pretend to live the life of the heroine. A life full of romance, adventure, and opportunity.

A life I doubt I'll ever have.

My vision blurs for a few moments. I sniff and wipe the wetness that's somehow appeared on my cheeks.

Oh, there's no point in feeling sorry for myself. Who's that going to help?

It takes me a half hour to pack two suitcases of stuff, mostly clothes, some books I kept in my bedroom, and other essentials.

When I drag the heavy suitcase up Rowan's front porch stairs, I pull something in my back. By the time I'm done, I'm sweaty from exertion, my back aches, and I'm no less pissed off than when I started.

I take a shower. I wash my hair. I put on my freshly laundered clothes.

By the time dusk comes around, I've been stewing in my anger at Brett for hours, and it's close to boiling over.

I'm so damn tempted to at least call him and give him a piece of my mind, but even in my current state, I know that would only make it seem like his plan is working. He wants to get a reaction out of me. I refuse to give him that.

I'm clicking through the TV channels, trying to find something to keep myself away from my phone, when the front door opens.

Rowan is home.

I turn off the TV and cup my palms over my mouth. I have to tell him what Brett's done. How else can I explain why I'll be sitting at home for the next two weeks?

When he comes into the room, my breath hitches.

Oh boy.

Honestly it's just not fair that he looks like *that*. Today, his outfit's as ordinary as it can be—a gray T-shirt and a pair of jeans. Nothing special, right?

Wrong.

Somehow, this man has the befuddling ability to look like he's stumbled off the pages of *GQ*, no matter what he wears. I suddenly understand why some people are willing to pay hundreds of dollars for a simple cotton shirt—on him, that T-shirt looks like it's worth a million bucks.

And don't even get me started on those arms. Those tatted, muscled forearms are a work of art.

Heat creeps up my neck. If those arms had been on display when he kissed me in my kitchen, I think I would have let him do whatever the hell he wanted to me.

Wait, what? No. No, I wouldn't.

"Why are you shaking your head?"

My eyes snap to Rowan's. *Focus. You need to tell him about Brett.* "It's been a long day."

He tilts his head. "You okay?"

"I need a drink." Or two. Or three. By now, I've learned the difference between a bad mood I can fix with self-talk versus one that requires a liquid cure, and this is definitely the latter.

Rowan tucks his keys in the back pocket of his jeans. "What happened?"

"It's Brett. He took me off the schedule for the next two weeks. And he wrote a note. *Take some time off, B. It'll give you an opportunity to reflect on your choices.* That prick. I mean, who does he think he is? Yes, he's my boss, but this is obviously him retaliating because I didn't want to go stay with him. Isn't that illegal? Of course, he knows that even if he is breaking some kind of employment law, there's not much I can do about it. I just want to— Ugh! If you knew the kind of violent fantasies playing out in my head right now, you'd be terrified of me."

Rowan's lips twitch. "I'm quite curious about these violent fantasies, actually."

"They involve male genitalia and a hot branding iron." I stand up. Pain shoots through my back, but I manage not to wince.

"Well then, I suppose I should be glad your anger is directed toward Brett and not me." His eyes drag over my black tank top.

Shit, I'm not wearing a bra. I rarely do when I'm at home, but now that I've got a roommate, I'm going to have to start. I don't need Rowan to know that one lingering look from him is enough to tighten my nipples into points.

He's managed to get under my skin with that kiss. I need to stop thinking of him that way. Now. Otherwise this fake dating thing has a high chance of going *very* off the rails.

The last thing I need right now is to have my little romantic heart get attached to him. It might take a little while longer now, but I still intend on leaving Darkwater Hollow.

"Yeah, well, lucky for you, you're not the one screwing me over." Reaching down, I grab a plate off the coffee table I left from a sandwich I ate earlier and take it to the kitchen.

Rowan follows behind me. He leans against the kitchen counter, watching me rinse the plate. "This might be a good thing."

"How?"

"If you're off work for the next two weeks, we'll be able to move quickly with the repairs. If we have questions, you'll be on hand to answer them, which speeds things along. Sam's going to swing by tomorrow or the day after, by the way."

I shoot him a timid glance while I scrub at the plate. I still can't believe he's doing this for me. While Brett insists on making life as difficult as possible, Rowan is going out of his way to help me.

"That sounds great. How was your day? Hopefully better than mine."

"Got stopped by a cop. One of Brett's friends."

I nearly drop the plate I'm holding. *"What?"*

Rowan shrugs. "He wanted to scare me a bit. It didn't work."

A fresh wave of anger rolls through me. I turn off the tap and grab a towel to dry the plate. "That's it. I'm going to call him and tell him he can't do shit like that."

"You don't need to do anything, Sunshine. I'll handle it."

He doesn't sound at all worried. Doesn't he understand the problems Brett can create for him and his business? The Lewises are the most powerful family in Darkwater Hollow.

If they wanted to, they could find a way to run Rowan out of town.

It's a big deal. If Brett's willing to go this far because I'm staying with Rowan, what is he going to do once he hears we're supposedly dating?

I blow out a breath. "I don't understand why he cares so much about what I do with my life. Yeah, we dated for a long time, but it's not like I'm a big catch."

Rowan shrugs. "I get it."

"Huh?"

Warmth bleeds into his gaze. "Don't sell yourself short."

Del said the same thing to me earlier, but hearing it from her didn't make my pulse suddenly race.

I move to the cupboard to put the plate away, pretending like his comment didn't hit me right in the chest. Ugh. The shelf is just...a...bit...too...high.

A shadow comes over me. "Here."

I bite down on my lip as Rowan's hard body presses against me. He plucks the plate out of my fingers and effortlessly slides it onto the shelf I was struggling to reach.

Ta-dum. Ta-dum. Ta-dum.

What were we talking about again? No idea. His heat blankets my back, and I wonder what he would do if I leaned—

CONTROL YOURSELF.

Keeping myself perfectly straight, I lower down from my tiptoes. But he's too close. My butt grazes his thighs on the way down, and a flutter appears low inside my belly.

164

Oh God, this isn't good. I'm supposed to keep my cool around him but instead, I'm burning up.

There's a light touch against the side of my neck. I don't dare breathe as he moves my hair from one side of my neck to the other and says from somewhere close to my ear, "Get dressed. You said you needed a drink, right? I'm getting you one."

CHAPTER 19

NERO

Not even an hour after I left The Junction with Sandro, I come back with Blake.

I wave hello to Denny and do a quick scan of the other patrons. A couple in a booth, a lone guy at a high-top table nursing a beer, and a few older women drinking dirty martinis at the bar. Quiet for a Saturday.

"I haven't been here in years," Blake says, glancing around. "I think the last time was for Del's twenty-first birthday."

"Who's Del?"

"My best friend. She moved to San Francisco two years ago," Blake says, pulling out her phone to snap a picture of the neon sign above the bar. "I need to send her evidence that I went out. She's always on my case for spending most of my evenings reading. According to her, my spirit animal is the hermit crab."

I chuckle. "I can see that."

She shoots me a dirty look. "You strike me as a—"

"Lion. King of the jungle."

"I was going to say... Well, never mind." She heads toward a booth in the far corner.

I follow after her. "Say it."

"I'm worried you'll think it's unkind."

"Say it."

"Bird of paradise."

I snort. "That *is* unkind. A bird? Really?"

Blake slides into the circular leather booth that wraps around the table. It's warm in here, and she unzips her light-blue hoodie all the way. "It's not just any bird."

I slide in across from her. "Okay, I'll bite. Why that one?"

"The males engage in elaborate courtship displays to attract their females. Sometimes more than one per breeding season."

"So they're avian man whores. Bird whores? Got it."

Her laugh sends a zing down my spine. "I'm sorry."

"You should be. Now, let's see if this classic courtship display will work on you." I get back to my feet. "Can I get you a drink?"

She bites down on her lips, like she's holding back a smile, her eyes shining with amusement. There's a smile on my face as well.

It's easy talking to her.

"A double G&T," she says, rubbing the small of her back. "Hendricks, if they've got it."

"A double? We can go straight for the tequila shots if you prefer."

"Don't be a bad influence."

"Guilty as charged." I wink at her and walk toward the bar.

I order her G&T and a beer for myself. I wasn't much of a beer drinker until I got to Darkwater Hollow, but if I went around ordering Macallan 15—my go-to in New York—it might raise some eyebrows. Most places in this area don't even carry it, but The Junction does. I stare at it longingly while I wait for Denny to make the cocktail.

When I bring our drinks back to the table, Blake reaches inside her purse. "How much do I owe you?"

I slide the G&T over to her. "Courtship ritual, remember? They're on me."

"Rowan, you can't just keep paying for everything."

Oh baby, you have no idea.

"I'm starting to feel insulted you think I'm a guy who doesn't pay on a date. Plus, didn't you just lose your job or something?"

She huffs. "Thanks for rubbing it in. I didn't lose it. I'm just underemployed, okay? And since when is this a date?"

I take the seat across from her. "Might as well be one. This can be us testing the waters."

Her eyes widen as she grasps my meaning. "I-I guess you're right," she says, stumbling over her words. She glances around the bar like she's suddenly self-conscious about our potential audience.

Funny how she can be so feisty, but as soon as she thinks it looks like we're on a date, she gets all shy.

"No one's paying attention to us," she says, sounding relieved.

"Maybe we should have gone to a busier place," I tease. "But first, I have to make sure you can sell it."

She sucks on her straw and rubs her back. "Sell what exactly?"

"That you're in love with me."

Blake starts coughing.

I slide along the bench, moving closer to her, and pat her on the back.

She sucks in a harsh breath, wincing. "Ouch."

"Shit, I'm sorry. Did I hurt you?" I didn't pat her that hard.

She wiggles her upper body like she's trying to stretch it out. "I think I pulled a muscle in my back earlier today when I was moving my things to your place."

"Why didn't you wait for me to help you?"

She stretches again, and her face contorts with pain. "I was just angry with Brett and wasn't careful while lifting my suitcase up the steps. It's fine."

It's not fine.

This woman's insistence on not asking for help is going to get her killed one day.

I wrap my palms around her narrow waist and carefully turn her so her back is angled toward me. "Let me see."

"Hey! What are you doing?" she protests.

"Shh." I slide her hoodie off her shoulders before she can stop me. Goosebumps erupt over her skin.

"Rowan, this is ri— Oooh."

My thumbs dig into her tight lats. "Where does it hurt?"

"Lower," she breathes.

I skim my fingertips over her shoulder blades and down to her lower back. Her spine arches slightly in response, reminding me of a cat.

"To the right."

I apply some light pressure. "Here?"

"Mhmm."

I press my thumbs into the spot, kneading it gently. The tension in her body starts to ease, her shoulders dropping.

She's warm, pliable, responsive. If only she knew how good I could make her feel. I have a feeling this woman will be magnificent when she comes.

On my face. On my fingers. On my cock.

Fuck, I'm hard.

She turns her head sideways, giving me a view of her profile. "Rowan, this is—" Her eyelashes flutter. "Oh, *shit*."

I work my knuckles into the tight knot in her lower back, careful not to overdo it. She feels so fragile. So breakable.

But I know it's an illusion. There's nothing breakable about her. "Good?"

She drags her teeth over her bottom lip and turns to face away from me again. "Yes. That's good." Her head tips slightly forward, her hair falling into her face. "You don't need to keep doing it."

I'd like to do this all night if she'd let me.

"Tell me something about yourself."

"What do you want to know?" she asks softly.

"I don't know. Tell me about your friends and family. Things I'd know about you if we were dating."

"There's not much to tell. Both of my parents are dead. Mom was sick with cancer for six years, and I took care of her. I think I already told you about my brother, the one who lives in LA."

"He didn't help you with your mom?"

"No, he didn't help. He didn't even come back to bury her."

Indignation swirls in the pit of my stomach. What kind of a man leaves his sister and sick mom to fend for themselves?

"That sounds really difficult."

She sighs. "It was hard, but I would've done anything for my mom. I'm glad I got to spend those last few years with her. It might seem like Maxton took the easy way out, but he missed out on a lot too. One day, he might regret it."

"But you won't have any regrets."

"Not as far as my mom's concerned."

She rolls her head back and forth, like she's got a kink in her neck. I leave her back and start working on her neck and shoulders. She makes a happy sigh. I want to bottle it up and keep it somewhere safe.

Fuck. A warning siren flashes in the back of my head. When was the last time I was this fascinated with a woman?

"Maxton doesn't even know about the house fire. Doubt he'd care. Mom rewrote the will to leave the house to me after it became clear he was never going to come help take care of her."

"You haven't called him?"

"We haven't talked since he skipped out on Mom's funeral. Anyway, what about your family?" she asks. "You said you're an only child."

My story's well-rehearsed by now. "Dad was an electrician. Mom was a nurse. They're both gone."

"Where were you born? In New York?"

Her questions remind me I've already slipped with her once when she asked me where I came from that time I drove her home.

I'd hoped she'd forget it.

Sandro and I have Nevada IDs, and our records say we're both from Philly, but I told Blake that before I came to Darkwater Hollow, I was in New York.

I've got to straighten out my backstory.

"I wasn't born there, no. I'm originally from Philly, and I spent a long time in Vegas."

"And then you said you went to New York. I've always wanted to visit. Did you like it there?"

I clench my jaw against the onslaught of memories. "Yeah, I did. It's the only place where I felt at home."

Her breath hitches as I drag my thumbs over the tight muscles in her neck. "Why's that?"

"I had a good community there. People who I cared about and who cared about me."

Something tightens in my chest. I miss that feeling of belonging. Of being surrounded by people who understand me. Who know the *real* me.

I look down at Blake. If she knew who I was, how would she react? Would she be afraid? Or would she accept the darkness in me?

There's no point in wondering, I suppose. I can never tell her the truth.

"That sounds nice," Blake says, a note of longing in her voice. "Why did you leave?"

My movements slow. "Had a falling out with someone important to me. A friend."

She turns to look at me over her shoulder, but I don't want to talk about this anymore, so I slide one hand up under her shirt to distract her and meet soft, velvet skin.

She sucks in a low breath.

God, she feels so damn good.

A flush spreads up her cheeks, and the pulse in her neck speeds up. She picks up her sweating glass—there's only ice left inside—and rolls it back and forth over her clavicle.

I flip my hand under her shirt, letting my knuckles brush over her spine. I'm not working her muscles anymore. I'm just touching her, and the fact that she's not stopping me gives me a heady rush.

She turns, giving me her profile. Her lips are so fucking kiss-able, and I want nothing more than to tug her against my chest and claim them for myself.

Suddenly, she tenses and moves away from me.

"Shit." She puts her hoodie back on in a rush.

"What's wrong?" I turn to see what she's looking at.

It's the man who was nursing a beer earlier. He's now paying at the bar.

"Who's that?" I ask.

"No one."

Her nervous reaction suggests he's more than just "no one."

He puts on a leather jacket, and there's a large patch on the back—a raptor with a chain hanging off its neck. A member of a motorcycle gang?

I haven't heard of any active gangs in Darkwater Hollow, but there are definitely some in Kansas City.

The bigger question is why Blake seems to be scared of him. "Do you know him?"

"No." She pulls up her hoodie and tucks her hair inside.

"Then why do you seem afraid of him recognizing you?"

She swallows nervously.

After settling his bill and chatting with Denny, the man turns to leave. Blake is on high alert and watches his every move. Just as he nears the front door, he looks directly toward us.

His steps halt.

Slowly, a smirk appears on his lips.

I look over at Blake, gauging her reaction. When I see the small tremble in her hands, I know for a fact that she's terrified of him.

I'm going to find out why.

And then I'm going to make him pay for whatever he did to her.

The man stares at Blake for a long moment and then walks out of the bar.

As soon as the door closes behind the biker, Blake lets out a shaky breath. "I want to go home."

"Tell me his name."

She stands up. "Just drop it, Rowan."

My irritation spikes as she stalks away from me. This whole not-asking-for-help business is getting on my nerves.

She's still quiet when we get into my truck. "Blake, who was that guy?"

Her hands fist in her lap. "Look, no offense, but it's really none of your business."

My jaw clenches as I pull out of the lot.

Like fucking hell it's not.

But one glance at the closed-off expression on her face, and I know she won't give me anything tonight.

Fine. If she won't answer me, I'll get the answer to my question on my own. After all, in Darkwater Hollow, everyone knows everyone's secrets.

And I won't stop until I uncover hers.

CHAPTER 20

BLAKE

Given it's Sunday, I'm surprised to find the couch in the living room empty when I wake up the next day around nine a.m.

There's a note on the fridge in the kitchen. *Picking up some things from Home Depot. Should be back in the afternoon.*

I make myself a cup of green tea—just one—and sit down at the small breakfast table.

I owe him an apology, along with an explanation.

Going to The Junction was supposed to take my mind off things. Instead, I just created another problem for myself.

Uncle Lyle saw me getting all cozy with Rowan. Which means he's going to come knocking soon enough, demanding to know what happened between Brett and me.

My godfather isn't a good man, and the last thing I want is to put Rowan on his radar, the same way I've already put Rowan on Brett's.

I still can't believe Brett sent that cop to harass Rowan. What was he thinking? It's starting to feel like him wanting me back has little to do with any feelings he might still have for me, and everything to do with his ego. He should know I'll never take him back after he cheated. Status, looks, attraction—none of it matters if a person isn't honest with me. I thought Brett knew that, but maybe he didn't think the rules applied to him.

It's ironic how the town's golden boy turned out to be a lying piece of crap, while Rowan—the town's player—is far more decent than I pegged him to be.

Cocky—sure. Smug—at times. Smart assed—definitely. But it's starting to seem more and more like armor Rowan wears to hide what's really inside.

I've only scratched the surface with him...and I want to go deeper. Even though the smart thing would be to keep my distance so that I can keep my head on straight when we take our fake relationship act on the road.

I take a sip of the tea.

How is he going to react when I tell him my godfather is a member of a biker gang?

I should have told him earlier. Right after he asked me to be his fake girlfriend, so that he knew what he was getting as part of the deal. Maybe if he knew where I come from, or how most of the town sees me, he'd rethink linking himself up with me.

The fact that that day was pure chaos is a convenient excuse for why I didn't say a word about it, but deep down I know it wasn't just that.

A part of me relishes the fact that Rowan doesn't know my history the way the rest of the town does. That he doesn't look at me and immediately think "that's Rhett's daughter." I've rarely gotten a blank slate like that with anyone in my life.

But now that has to end. I have to tell him everything. Otherwise, I'm not being fair to him.

I eat a light breakfast and then go over to my house with the intention of sorting through the things that were damaged in the fire.

There's got to be at least a few things in the living room that I might be able to salvage. The fire didn't quite reach the side of the room across from the bookshelf where the TV is, so I start there.

It's funny how I spent months telling myself I needed to toss out all the little knickknacks collecting dust on the shelving around the TV, but now they feel precious. I clean the soot off the small animal figurines I used to collect as a kid and carefully wrap them in newspaper before putting them away in a cardboard box.

The DVDs are warped from the heat, so I toss them in a garbage bag.

In the drawer below, I find an old metal cookie tin filled with artwork—mine and Maxton's—from kindergarten.

God, it would have really sucked if these were destroyed.

I spend a while going through them and get a bit sentimental. I can remember drawing some of these. Neither Maxton nor I had any art skills whatsoever, but Mom always made it seem like we were bringing home Picasso masterpieces.

There's a family portrait. Stick figures, of course. Mine is just me, Maxton, and Mom, but Maxton's version from two years earlier has our father in it too. He's outlined in a harsh black. Maxton even drew a vest on the stick figure.

Dad always wore that vest. He was proud of it. The large center patch on the back meant he was a full member of the Iron Raptors, and his enforcer patch meant he had a high-ranking position in the club.

Anger slithers through my belly. He cared more about that fucking vest than he cared about his own kids.

In the bottom drawer of the TV stand, I find a picture frame with a photo of him. It's the only one I kept after I threw out the photo album Mom kept by her bedside with photos of them together before Maxton was born.

I didn't like those pictures. I didn't like seeing her smiling beside him. It felt like watching her get conned. She must not have known his true nature when she got pregnant with Maxton. And afterward, even though my father never wanted a family—definitely not the obligations that come with it—he refused to let Mom go. He'd come to visit every few weeks, just enough to keep her hooked on the small bits of attention he showed her.

At least Brett wasn't my dad. Yeah, he's a cheat and a liar, but he's not a damn criminal.

I put the photo of my dad back in the box and get back to work. I'm just about to wrap things up when I hear the sound I've been anticipating all day.

The deep, throaty roar of a motorbike.

The engine's growl crescendos as it approaches and then settles into a steady rumble as the rider idles at the curb. I wipe my soot-stained hands on an old towel and do my best not to let my nerves show as I make my way outside.

I knew he'd show up. I'm prepared.

Uncle Lyle, clad in a black leather jacket, cuts the engine, and the sudden silence feels almost startling. With him is a man—Steely—another old friend of my dad's.

They dismount their bikes.

Uncle Lyle doesn't say a word as he walks over. There's an unreadable expression on his weathered face, and it sends prickles down my spine.

"Blakey girl."

The smile I give him is forced. "Is everything okay?"

His eyes darken on me before he glances over his shoulder at his friend. "You hear that? *Is everything okay?* Like I'm some fucking stranger."

Steely chuckles while my palms break out in sweat. I never know what will set him off.

"It's been a while since you came by. I thought maybe something happened."

"Don't play dumb. We both know you're not. And I don't need an excuse to come by and check on you, do I?"

"Of course not." My tone is conciliatory. I'll say whatever I need to if it'll get them to leave before Rowan comes home.

He runs his fingers through his silver-streaked hair and drags his gaze over my body. "Come here. Give your godfather a hug."

I feel sick as I force myself to step into his open arms. He holds me close and tight for a few long moments, his hands drifting over my back and settling too low. My nostrils fill with the putrid scent of cigarettes and gasoline. Behind him, Steely smirks.

"I shoulda come by sooner." His voice is low in my ear. "I haven't seen you since the funeral. Thought you'd keep yourself out of trouble, but looks like I was wrong."

Whatever trouble he thinks I'm in is nothing compared to the trouble his reappearance will no doubt cause. Nothing good comes from men like him and my father.

I hoped that if I left Darkwater Hollow quietly, he'd forget about me.

"What happened with the house?" he asks, finally letting go of me.

"There was a fire."

"Where are you staying then?"

"With my neighbor."

"Your neighbor? That guy I saw you with last night?"

"Yeah."

"Huh." He drags his palm over his chin. "Heard you and the boyfriend broke up. So what was that last night? You on a date?"

What do I say? Lying will only delay the inevitable. The whole town's supposed to believe Rowan and I are in a serious relationship, which means Uncle Lyle will find out soon enough.

"Yes. Rowan and I are seeing each other."

He smiles, but it doesn't reach his eyes. "I went to Frostbite the other night. You weren't there, but Brett was. When we talked, he seemed sure you two will work things out."

God damn it.

I wrap my arms around myself. "I don't know why he thinks that. It's over."

"You should give the mayor's boy another chance. Or is he not good enough for you?"

Did Brett ask Uncle Lyle to talk to me about this?

He wouldn't do that. He wouldn't. He knows I can't stand Uncle Lyle.

But the two of them have always been a touch too friendly for my taste.

A slick grin unfurls over Uncle Lyle's face. "It's good to stay close to people who've got power, Blakey girl. You don't want to get on their bad side."

My thoughts race. If Brett asked that cop to stop Rowan, why am I so sure he wouldn't enlist my godfather's help as well?

My stomach churns. This is a fucking nightmare.

"I'm thirsty," Steely says.

My eyes snap to him. He arches a brow, like he's expecting me to do something about it.

Dad was like that too, barking out his needs and expecting Mom to take care of them with a smile on her face.

"There's some lemonade in the fridge. Would you like some?"

He nods. As I walk inside Rowan's house, I hear him say, "The ass on that girl. That's the eighth world wonder, right there."

Disgusting. He probably thinks I can't hear him.

"Watch it," Uncle Lyle says. "The only person who can comment on her ass is me."

Bile rises in my throat as a memory flashes inside my mind.

A hushed conversation in the kitchen. The words I overheard.

"I'll take good care of her, Valerie. She can finish up with school first. That girl won't need to struggle with a man like me by her side."

I was fifteen. I sat on the stairs and listened.

I didn't think Mom would defend me as fiercely as she did. I loved her, but I also spent my teenage years and onward wishing she were different. Wishing that she would stand up for Maxton and me. Wishing that she would tell our deadbeat dad not to come around anymore. But when it came to Uncle Lyle, she snapped. The sound of her slapping his cheek rang clear in the air.

Then there was another sound. Hard and dull.

After he left, I went down to the kitchen. My mom was dabbing a paper towel against her bleeding lip.

I lock the memory away, pour two glasses of lemonade, and bring them outside.

The ugly scar just beneath Uncle Lyle's Adam's apple bobs as he drinks. He must be pushing fifty now, just like my father would have been if he were still alive.

Instead, he was murdered at thirty-six by a rival gang member. I was twelve. Maxton, fourteen. Mom never recovered from the loss. I still think the cancer started because of it.

They hand me their empty glasses.

We're done here. What else is left to be said?

Leave.

Just then, I hear the roar of an approaching engine. Rowan's truck turns onto the road.

Shit.

Uncle Lyle and Steely watch Rowan pull into the driveway, their expressions deceptively neutral.

Frustration wraps around my throat, cutting off the air. I should have tried harder to get them out of here. Rowan's not the kind of guy who's easily intimidated, and that's a bad thing. He should be scared of these guys.

The truck's engine turns off. Rowan gets out, his movements as smooth and sure as a panther, and slams the door shut.

He walks over, his gaze skating over me briefly before he pins his stare on Uncle Lyle and Steely.

When he stops by my side, I'm flooded with a weird combination of anxiety and relief.

I feel safer with him here.

But it's not his job to protect me from these men.

The two sides assess each other. Rowan's taller and more muscular, but his physical advantage is no match for the gun my godfather always carries tucked into his belt.

An ominous grin spreads over Uncle Lyle's face. "What's your name, fella?"

"Rowan Miller. And you are?" There's an undercurrent of steel in his tone.

"Lyle. This is Steely."

"Can I help you gentlemen with something?"

Uncle Lyle tilts his head, scrutinizing Rowan with a piercing gaze. "Blake and I were just catching up on old times. You treating my Blakey girl well?"

"He is, Uncle," I say.

"You better treat her with care and respect, because you know you're just borrowing her, right?"

Ice slithers down my veins.

Beside me, Rowan grows very still. "I intend on keeping her."

Uncle Lyle's smirk falters for a moment. Like Brett, he's not used to people holding their own around him.

I shoot a discreet glance at Rowan. He doesn't look like himself. His normally relaxed demeanor has shifted to something far more intense. The lighthearted twinkle in his eye is gone, replaced by a cold, hard stare. His broad shoulders, usually casual and at ease, are now rigid with barely contained tension.

A shiver coasts down my spine.

When I look back at Uncle Lyle, even his expression is a bit unsettled.

But he laughs it off. "You hear that, Steely?"

"Yeah," Steely drawls. "You're new here, aren't ya?"

Rowan's jaw firms. "I guess I am."

"Then we can't hold your ignorance about the way things work around here against ya." There's a dark glint in Uncle Lyle's eyes. "You'll learn."

A drop of sweat slides down my back. God, why didn't Rowan drive home just a bit slower? I could have gotten rid of them.

I need to do something to deescalate the situation.

I inch myself in front of Rowan, hoping Uncle Lyle will think twice about hurting him if he'll have to go through me. "Thank you for checking on me, Uncle. It was good to see you."

Rowan's hand appears on my shoulder. He tries to push me aside, but I plant my feet and refuse to move.

Leave. Please, just leave.

At last, Uncle Lyle takes a step toward his bike. "I'll see you around, darlin'. Soon."

I force a smile. "Stay safe."

As their bikes rumble to life and drive away in a cloud of dust, I let out a shaky breath. That could have ended badly if Rowan had said one more wrong word.

But he doesn't look relieved as he turns me around with a firm grip on my shoulders. If anything, he looks pissed.

"C'mon," he growls. "We're going to go inside, and unlike last night, you're going to give me an explanation."

CHAPTER 21

NERO

Iron Raptors.

That's what was written on the back of those vests. I've heard of them—a gang from the Midwest—but our paths haven't crossed before.

Would have been great to keep it that way.

Rafe's last instructions to me were clear—find a place with no organized crime. That's why Sandro and I had stayed out of big cities, but apparently, those leather-clad roaches had made it out to the middle of nowhere.

The good thing is that they don't know me, which means they didn't recognize me as someone who shouldn't be alive.

But it's not me I'm concerned about at the moment. It's Blake.

"What were those guys doing here?"

She brushes past me, heading back toward the house. "Let's talk inside."

I follow after her, on edge. What would have happened if I didn't come back when I did? She looked tense and afraid, just like last night. What do they want from her? Does she owe them money?

It doesn't make any sense. She's a bartender who works at a local tavern and spends her evenings with her nose buried in a book. I can't imagine what business they could possibly have in common.

I shut the front door behind me and grab her by the arm. "Blake, look at me."

Her face is pale and guilt-ridden in the late afternoon light streaming through the window, like she's done something wrong.

And yeah, she fucking did.

"What were you thinking putting yourself in front of me like that?"

She leans against one of the walls in the foyer. "I was afraid he'd pull a gun on you. He's erratic, and he's got a short temper."

"So you thought it would be better for him to pull a gun on you instead?" I demand. God, I want to shake her for being so reckless.

"Ye—"

I grab her chin. "No. The answer is no. Never and under no circumstances. I won't have you put yourself in danger to protect me."

She jerks her face out of my grip, angry tears glistening inside her eyes. "God, Rowan! Don't you see? It's me who brought danger to your doorstep! That man out there—Lyle —is my godfather."

My brows furrow. Whatever I was expecting she might say, it wasn't that.

She makes a frustrated noise and flees down the hallway to the living room.

I move after her. "Your godfather? How did that happen?"

She sinks onto the couch and grips the edge of it with her hands. "My dad was a rider too." Her words come out like a confession. They're loaded with regret and resignation.

It takes me a moment to process.

Blake, with her quiet demeanor and bookish habits, had grown up surrounded by a world of violence and crime. A world not so different from my own.

"Were you close?"

"God, no," she says with a sad huff. "He didn't live with us, but he came around every few weeks. And when he died, Uncle Lyle told my mom and I that my father asked him to keep an eye on us."

That checks out. You always want someone to take care of your family after you're gone, but you should choose wisely, or you could end up in a situation like this. "What happened to your dad?"

"He was shot by a rival gang member. They had some long-standing feud, and one night, the other man got what he wanted."

"I'm sorry."

She wipes the back of her hand against her nose and stares at the floor. "I'm the one who's sorry. Lyle saw us out last night, and he wanted to know if I was seeing someone new."

"Why is that any of his business?"

"When it comes to me, he thinks everything is his business. It's why I've been careful not to mention to anyone in town that I was trying to sell the house. If he found out, he'd try to stop me from leaving."

I sit down beside her and nudge her chin up to look at me. "You don't need to apologize. But I want to know why you're so scared of him. Has he done something to you?"

She stiffens. "No."

My eyes narrow. I know the signs. "You're lying."

"He hasn't done anything to me, Rowan. But he's a bad man, and he's hurt my mom. I want nothing more than to have him out of my life, but I learned a long time ago that it's better to play nice around him. Telling him that I don't want him coming around would only make him angry."

There's a lot wrong with that statement. I open my mouth to argue, but she keeps going.

"He stayed away from me while I was with Brett, but now—"

"Now, he'll stay away because you're with *me*," I growl.

"Rowan, you don't understand who you're dealing with here. He's dangerous. He's not like us. He doesn't follow rules, and he doesn't play nice."

Oh, but I understand perfectly. "I'm not scared of him." I could put that man six feet under and come home in time for dinner if I wanted to.

She shakes her head, upset. "Your arrogance is going to get you killed. You *should* be scared of him. If they hurt you because of me, I won't be able to live with myself. I mean, you're helping me, and being this nice guy—"

I reach over and wrap my palms around her arms, trying to calm her. She's trembling.

Her lips part on a strained inhale. "Rowan, please. Tell me you get it."

What if I tell her the truth?

What if I explain to her that while she's with me, she's got nothing to worry about?

I wouldn't even need the gun I keep in my car to take care of those guys. I could do it with my bare hands.

And I'd enjoy every second of it.

But something holds me back. Something about the way she's looking at me—earnest and unguarded. I have this gut feeling that if I tell her the truth, her walls would come right back up.

So I take her hands into mine and say, "I get it. They're dangerous, and I'll be careful."

Some of the tension in her shoulders disappears.

"But for the love of God, do me a favor and never refer to me as a nice guy again. The fact that you think I'm one is frankly more concerning than those riders."

The frown lines in her forehead disappear. "Only you would find that term offensive." Her mouth twitches. "You *are* a nice guy, Ro—"

"Please stop. I'm breaking out in hives. I didn't save your books, remember?"

She bites down on her lip, suppressing her laugh. "You're right. You're not nice at all."

I grin. I like it a lot better when she's smiling. "There we go. Now tell me, how often do those guys come around these parts?"

"Darkwater Hollow? Not often. They're based on the outskirts of Kansas City."

I nod. "Good." If that changes, I'm going to have to do something about it.

"I know what you're thinking."

I arch a brow. I'm thinking about all the creative ways I can end Lyle's existence, so I doubt it.

She squeezes my hand. "You're probably second-guessing letting me stay with you. I'm broke, with a crazy ex, and a godfather in a biker gang. I've got baggage."

"I can handle it." In fact, I'd fucking love to handle it so that she never has to worry about those fucks again.

She just sighs. "I wish my dad never got Uncle Lyle involved with us. I don't know why he thought having him around would help anyone. My dad was bad enough, but Uncle Lyle is worse."

"Bad how?"

Her jaw flexes. "For my dad, the gang was number one. Followed by partying, women, and gambling. Family was somewhere at the bottom of his list of priorities. And Mom always made up excuses for him. She loved him 'til the day she died." Her expression darkens. "Never understood how she could stay so devoted to a fucking *criminal*."

The sheer amount of fury she wraps around that last word sends ice sliding down my spine.

"My father smuggled drugs for Mexican cartels. He hijacked cars and sold them for parts. He stole, and cheated, and *killed*." She looks me right in the eye. "How could she love a man like him?"

A pit opens up inside my stomach. "I have no idea."

"Neither do I." She tugs her hands out of mine and gets to her feet, frustration rolling off her in waves. "I need to shower. I'm covered in dust. Before they came, I was sorting through my things back at the house."

"Okay. I'll get dinner started," I say numbly.

I watch her disappear into the bedroom. A few moments later, the shower starts.

Fuck.

Fuck. Fuck. Fuck.

If only she knew who she was speaking to. If only she knew the things I've done. My record is no better than her father's, that's for sure. And to think I considered—

I can't tell her. I can *never* tell her.

I rake my fingers through my hair and let out a low breath. This shouldn't matter. My past life is exactly that—in the past. And I promised Sandro I wouldn't say a word to anyone, so what the hell was I even thinking back there?

All right. There's no point in freaking out. The important thing is that I kept my mouth shut.

Moving down the hall, I stop by the window that faces the front yard.

I don't like the thought of leaving Blake here alone while those bikers are sniffing around. What if they come by again while I'm gone? What if they do something to her?

She said they don't come to Darkwater Hollow often, but that doesn't mean they won't start now.

It's better if I'm here to keep an eye on her. I sift through my calendar in my head. I can move some things around to minimize my time at the office, but not everything.

Which means I'm going to have to...

Fuck, Sandro's going to kill me.

CHAPTER 22

NERO

It's a frigid morning in Darkwater Hollow, but the temperature inside my truck feels even colder.

Blake glowers at me from the passenger seat as I pull into the lot outside my office.

"You're very pushy, do you know that?" she snaps.

"It's just for a few days."

"I can't believe you're dragging me to work with you. I'm not a little kid."

"Trust me, I'm aware," I grumble.

We argued for thirty minutes this morning until she finally relented and agreed to come with me to the office. Seeing her so fired up made me want to tie her up, gag her, and give her a good spanking. Blake's stubborn, but I've got over a decade of experience negotiating with stubborn Italians. Even she's no match for that.

"I told you I can handle my godfather."

"He's our godfather now."

She gives me a confused look. "What?"

"As in, he's now my problem as much as he is yours. I don't want to risk him showing up to see you at my place while I'm not there. It's a liability."

"Isn't me hovering around your place of work also a liability? What if I spill coffee on an important document? Or jam the printer? Or—"

"Babe, just don't do any of those things and we'll be fine."

"*Babe?*"

I park the car, turn off the ignition, and turn to her. She's looking at me with alarm.

"We're dating, remember? We're in love. Do people look at each other like that when they're in love? No, they don't. So stop it."

Her eyes narrow. "How am I looking at you?"

"Like you wish you'd thrown me into the fire and left me locked inside your house."

"Too soon. Not funny," she says, but her lips twitch slightly.

I poke her cheek. "You're smiling. Now come here and give me a kiss."

"What!?"

It seems my tactic for getting Lyle off her mind is working. She's so comically aghast that I can't help but laugh. You'd think I told her to climb onto my lap and grind against my dick. "We need to practice. You have to kiss me at the office."

She shakes her head. "No, I don't."

"That's what couples do with each other. They touch, they kiss, they—"

She makes a crossing motion with her arms. "I'm anti-PDA. It's *yuck*. Gross."

I arch a brow. "Seriously? How old are you again?"

"Look, making out at your work is not something I'm comfortable with," she says emphatically.

I sigh. "It's going to be hard to make the town believe we're dating if you're anti-PDA."

She purses her lips, clearly conflicted. Finally, she relents. "I can kiss your cheek. That's it. The rest... I need some time to build up to it."

I turn my face. "Fine. Do it then."

She makes a small *ahem* and gives me a peck with her ridiculously soft lips. And it's just so fucking...cute. Something swells inside my chest.

"Happy?" she asks shyly.

"Overjoyed. You really sold it. I could feel you want to tear my clothes off."

She reddens. "That's not— What— Um—"

I press my palm over her mouth, cutting off her flustered stammer. "I'm joking, Sunshine. C'mon. I've got a call in ten minutes I'd like to be on time for."

We get out of the car. The day started off foggy, but some sun is starting to peek out from behind the clouds.

As we approach the front door, I intertwine our fingers. "Ready?"

Blake stares up at me, and she looks so determined. It's like she's about to walk into a bar fight instead of a sleepy five-person office. "Let's do this."

I snicker. "C'mon, Rambo."

The Handy Heroes office smells like strong coffee and fresh bagels. When Sandro and I bought the business, we also took over the lease. The space itself is nothing special—just a rectangular open area with four desks and my office in the back—but I've gotten used to it. As have the employees who have been here for over a decade under the previous owner. In fact, all three of them told us they would only stay if we kept the office in the same location.

People hate change. I get it.

"Morning, everyone. This is my girlfriend, Blake. She's going to be helping me out here for a few days."

Our estimator, Judy, peers at us over her half-moon glasses. "Blake, did you say?"

"It's Blake Wolfe," Arnie barks from where he's standing by the printer. "You know, Valerie's kid."

Judy adjusts her glasses. "Oh, is that right? Come here, dear. My eyesight's not what it used to be. Let me look at you."

I let go of Blake's hand and nudge her forward. She throws me a nervous look before walking over to Judy.

The two of them chat while I go to pour myself a coffee at the small kitchenette. Arnie appears beside me, his curly gray hair sticking out in every possible direction. I'm convinced the man has never met a comb. "She's a nice girl. Hardworking. Honest. Not your type."

I grab a mug off the shelf. "She's definitely my type."

He tsks and lifts the jug of coffee, pouring it for me. "You know what happened with her and the mayor's son, right? My heart just broke for her."

"Don't be a gossip, Arnie."

"I'm just saying, she's been through enough as is this year. First her mom passed, then the breakup, and now that fire at her house. She seems tough—well, she's had to be, hasn't she?—but we all have our limits. I'm not sure how well she'd handle another heartbreak."

Something uneasy settles inside my gut. Blake has been through a lot.

And that fire was all me.

But I'm fixing it, aren't I? I'm going to make that house look brand-new. She's going to get a better offer on it after I'm done, and one day, she'll think that fire was actually a bit of good luck.

Do you even hear yourself?

I bury the unease away and move to change the topic. "Where's Pete?"

"At home. Stomach problems."

"Again? What do we need to do to stop that man from eating dairy?"

"I already switched to lactose-free everything over here. Next, we'll have to sneak into his house and swap the milk out of his fridge while he sleeps."

"Good plan. Put it on my calendar. Something must be done. He can't keep missing days. Our projects won't plan themselves."

Arnie takes a sip of his coffee. "You remember you have that tile lady coming today at noon? She called ten minutes ago to say she'll be bringing lunch. I thought you two were going to go to Frostbite for your meeting."

Damn it. "I told her I didn't have time to go out. I was hoping we could keep the meeting to a half hour." The rep from Wonder Tiles can be a pain in the ass.

Arnie shrugs. "Good luck."

I look over at Blake. She's still talking to Judy. Does she want coffee? Probably. I pour her a cup and take it to her.

Her eyes light up when I hand her the mug. "Oh, thank you."

"You're welcome."

Judy glances between the two of us. "What's Blake going to be helping you with today?"

"Well, Pete's out again."

"Ah, yes, the poor dear."

"I was thinking Blake can organize the materials for the meetings Sam and I have tomorrow. Can you walk her through it?"

"Sure," Judy says with a smile.

"I'll be in my office, Sunshine. Knock if you need anything." When I lean forward and press a kiss to Blake's forehead, Judy makes a small gasp.

"Okay." Blake looks flustered as I pull away. She gives me a shaky smile. "Good luck with your call, honey."

My heart skips a beat. Oh fuck, I like that. I like that *a lot.*

I force a grin to hide my slightly bewildered expression. "Yep. Thanks."

In my office, I take a seat behind my desk and press my palms against my face. Fuck, what's wrong with me? Sometimes she makes me feel like a teenage boy, and it's fucking unsettling.

I drop my hands and lean back in my chair, staring at the computer monitor as it boots up.

This is when it usually hits—the gnawing anxiety, the feeling of something being off. It's not that I hate this job, but every morning I come here, lock the door behind me, and hear my stepdad's voice echoing in my mind.

You don't belong here. You will never belong here. You're a made man, through and through. It's in your blood, in your soul, in your heart.

Those whispers hit me like a ton of bricks to the chest.

Not today though. Today it's quiet.

And I think it's because Blake is here. Being around her makes all this feel less suffocating.

She wouldn't be around me if I was still Nero. A criminal, just like her dad.

Is she the silver lining in all of this? Did I lose everything so that I could have someone like her?

I let out a deep sigh and run my fingers through my hair. I'm not sure what I want from her anymore. The plan was always to eventually let her go. But now, sleeping with her doesn't seem like it will be enough. Of course, I still want to —physically, my body craves her in a way it's never craved anyone else. But my feelings for her are starting to inch into a territory that's decidedly more complicated.

Arnie's right. I can't hurt her. I can't break her heart. So where does that leave me?

A better man might end things right now, before we both get in too deep.

But that's not who I am.

CHAPTER 23

BLAKE

The desk I'm sitting at belongs to Pete Wiley, Handy Heroes' project manager. His son, Jake, was in the same class as me in middle school. He had bright-red hair, crooked front teeth, and a bright-blue backpack that someone stole from him one day.

Guess who got blamed for it?

Yep, me.

Someone emptied his backpack, took his pens and notebooks, and stuffed the empty backpack into my locker. It fell out as soon as I opened the locker during recess. I can still see Jake's furious face as he charged at me and called me a dirty thief in front of what felt like the entire school.

No one believed me when I said it wasn't me. I'd never broken a single rule until then, but it felt like everyone was waiting for me to mess up, and that day, they finally got their wish.

I was sure Mom would pick me up when the principal called, but she got the call when my dad was around, and he came instead. I heard the roar of his bike from where I was waiting outside the principal's office. The receptionist gave me a dirty look and muttered something about the apple not falling far from the tree.

Her words were a sharp sting right in the chest.

There's an aged-up photo of Jake framed on Pete's desk. When Judy gets up to get herself another cup of coffee, I flip it face down.

"How's it coming along?" she asks when she comes back around, steaming mug in hand. "Do you have any questions?"

"All good. Just waiting for this file to open." I point at the screen. "It must be a big one since it's taking a while."

Judy looks at the monitor. "Oh yes. That happens sometimes. Just make sure not to exit out while it's doing its thing, or the computer might freeze."

"Got it."

She gives me a smile and flips through the pile of documents I've printed out and meticulously labeled over the last few hours. "You're a quick study. You ever think about what you might want to do after you get tired of working at Frostbite? You've been there for a while, haven't you?"

"Almost four years." Brett and I started dating when I was about a year into the job. It felt weird to date my boss at first, but I got used to it. In fact, I thought it was nice we got to see each other every day.

I should have spent more time thinking about the downsides of that arrangement if anything ever went wrong between us.

The power Brett still has over me is driving me crazy. It's ridiculous that he can decide to not let me earn any money, and there's nothing I can do about it.

In some ways, I'm glad Rowan dragged me to work with him this morning. Not that I'd ever admit to it. He was heavy-handed and bossy when he declared he wasn't leaving without me. But at least now that I'm here, I can be useful. It's better to have something to do rather than sit around his house and do nothing.

There's a fluttering sensation deep inside my belly every time I remember how he said, "I won't be able to focus on my work if I'm worried about you, Sunshine."

Worried about me? I thought there was a high chance he'd kick me to the curb when he found out about Uncle Lyle. Instead, the man's *worried* about me.

It's...sweet.

"Well, keep up the good work," Judy says with a smile before patting my shoulder and walking back to her own desk.

She's nice. So is Arnie, who spent a half hour showing me how to use the printer. I wasn't expecting that. It's not that everyone treats me like dirt all the time, but I can usually sense people's underlying disdain even if they try to hide it under a layer of politeness.

Judy and Arnie seem genuine. Still, I can't help but wonder if they're acting this way because Rowan introduced me as his girlfriend. He's their boss, after all.

Lunchtime comes around, and as if on cue, my stomach starts growling. I get up and stretch my limbs. I could definitely eat.

Rowan hasn't come out of his office all morning. I'm wondering if I should pop inside to see if he wants me to grab him lunch when a woman walks through the front door.

She's gorgeous. Shiny black hair, full lips, legs for days. She's wearing an expensive-looking coat with a faux fur collar, tight jeans, and high-heeled leather boots.

Arnie gives her a wave from his seat. "Hi there. Can I help you?"

The woman gives him a perfunctory smile. "I'm Vanessa. Your boss and I have a meeting."

"He's waiting for you in his office."

She floats past Judy and me, filling my nostrils with her floral perfume, before giving Rowan's door two quick knocks.

His voice filters through the door. "Come in."

"Hey, big guy!"

My brows shoot up as Vanessa steps into his office and shuts the door behind her.

Big guy?

"Who is she?" The question bursts out of me before I can stop it.

Arnie moves some papers around his desk. "A sales rep from one of our tile suppliers."

"Very pushy," Judy mutters. "I think she's eager to hit her quota for the quarter."

I think she might be eager for a lot more than that.

I sink back down in my chair. Suddenly, I'm not hungry anymore.

"Do you two want to grab some sandwiches from Millie's?" Arnie asks.

"That's a great idea," Judy says, stretching her arms above her head. "Would you like to join us, Blake?"

I shoot her a distracted smile. "I think I'll grab something later. I want to wrap this task up so that I don't get confused."

"We can bring you something back?" she offers.

"Sure, that would be great."

I'm not proud to admit it, but I'm almost happy when they leave. It makes eavesdropping on the meeting in Rowan's office much easier.

If only the walls were a bit thinner. I can't make out what they're saying, save for a few words.

But I hear the laughter. Mostly Vanessa's. Then Rowan's too.

A pit opens up in my stomach, and in it swirls a foreign feeling.

It takes me a moment to realize what it is.

I'm...jealous?

My cheeks heat. I have no right to feel jealous. We're not actually dating, so why is hearing him laugh with that woman making me so irrationally upset?

I know why. He promised he wouldn't get involved with anyone while we're pretending. Maybe I should have clarified exactly what that meant.

For me, that means no flirting. And that amount of laughter feels a lot like flirting.

You're being crazy, a voice in my head advises.

But the pit keeps growing, and when Vanessa's high-pitched laugh turns into a giggle, I can't take it anymore.

I make a quick detour through the kitchenette before I burst through his office door.

"Hey. I thought you might want some more coffee?"

Rowan's head snaps to look at me.

The first thing I notice is that there's a whole desk between the two of them. The image of Vanessa pressed up to Rowan's chest that my mind conjured up a second ago disappears in a poof.

The second thing I notice is that Vanessa's fancy coat is slung over the back of her chair, and beneath is a sexy silky blouse that shows off her ample cleavage.

The simmering jealousy heats to a boil.

Rowan glances at the clock on the wall. "I don't usually drink coffee after noon."

Starting today, he does.

I walk over to him, a tense smile on my lips. "Is it already that late?"

Whatever he detects in my expression makes his eyes flash. "I guess it's only ten minutes after."

"And who's this?" Vanessa asks.

My hip brushes against Rowan's arm as I place the cup of coffee on the desk in front of him.

Jesus. You can literally see her lacy black bra peeking through the gap in her blouse.

What can only be described as some primal, animal instinct takes over my mind and body. I know I'm not thinking straight, but I can't help it as everything in me demands I stake a claim.

Rowan taps his fingers against the desk. "This is Blake Wolfe. She's helping us out today."

"A new employee?"

"No, she's..." His words drift off into a stunned silence as I sink lower and perch myself on one of the arm rests of his chair.

"His girlfriend." My smile feels like it's carved into my face.

Vanessa's eyes flare with shock.

I glance at Rowan to find him already staring at me.

His lips quirk.

"I see." Vanessa looks like she's swallowed something foul. "Have you...been dating for long?"

"A few weeks." It's amazing how easily the lie comes to me. Is Rowan going to correct me? Technically, it's only been a few days.

Shit, I'm sliding off the arm rest. Why don't my jeans have any grip? Oh God, I'm going to—

Rowan wraps his big hands securely around my waist and tugs me down onto his lap.

His. *Lap*.

"We live together," he says calmly, as if our current position is completely normal.

Vanessa looks devastated. "Oh, wow. Sounds like a whirlwind."

"When you know, you know," Rowan says.

My thighs clench. Oh God. He's playing along a bit too well. But I started it, so I have to keep it going.

I wrap an arm around his shoulders—or at least I try. I can't quite reach the other side of his stupidly broad frame. My gaze lands on Vanessa's half-open shirt, and I just can't hold it back. "Cute bra, by the way."

Her cheeks redden. She clears her throat and quickly does up a few more buttons.

I lean into Rowan and smile at her again.

Rowan slips his fingers under my T-shirt and caresses the sensitive skin just above the waistband of my jeans. A pleasant shiver coasts up my spine. "I know we're almost out of time, Vanessa. So back to that discount."

Wait, he's just going back to business like I'm not here hanging off him like a koala?

Vanessa brushes her hair back from her face and sits up straighter, her face a blank mask. "I'm sorry, but I don't think I'll be able to convince my boss to go that low."

I've got to give it to her, she seems to have gathered her wits about her quickly enough.

Rowan dips his fingers behind the waistband of my jeans and pulls me a few inches closer.

Oh. The seam of my jeans digs right against my clit, and the unexpected sparks of pleasure make me bite down a gasp.

"I thought you said that kind of thing is up to your discretion," Rowan rumbles behind me.

"Did I?" Vanessa purses her lips. "I misspoke. If you can get your orders up by about fifty percent next month, we might consider it."

He clicks his tongue. "I doubt we'll have that much demand in a holiday month."

Uh, crap. Did I just cost him this negotiation?

Sweat breaks out over my back. Is he going to be mad at me?

"That's too bad," Vanessa says flatly.

"I understand," Rowan says, a hint of regret in his tone. "Then I think that's all for today, right?"

"I believe so." She gets up to her feet.

I try to get off Rowan's thigh, thinking he will want to see her out, but his grip on my waistband only tightens. I have to bite down on my lip not to moan from the pressure on my clit.

"Thanks for coming by. And for bringing lunch."

"It's my pleasure."

"Do you mind closing the door on your way out?"

Vanessa's cheeks turn red. "Of course."

The moment the door shuts, I become acutely aware that I'm sweating like...everywhere.

Rowan turns my face toward him with a finger on my chin. "Hello."

"Hi."

His gaze flickers with amusement. Or maybe irritation?

God, I can't tell.

"You're on my lap."

"Correct."

"What happened to no PDA?"

I fold my lips over my teeth. How do I explain my momentary insanity? "Well, you see, it's important to keep our ultimate goals in mind."

"Which are?"

"To paint a portrait of you as a reformed playboy. A man slayed by a woman." I clear my throat. "By me."

He moves some strands of hair off my forehead, tucking them behind my ear. "Right." His gaze drops to my lips.

"And Vanessa was unaware of this when she walked in. And I saw how she was looking at you, and I stepped in before she could do something to damage the portrait."

"Like what?"

A drop of sweat rolls down the valley between my breasts. "Like...seduce you."

"Did you think she was seducing me before or after she refused to give me the fifteen-percent discount I wanted?"

His fingers twitch, and then he flattens his palm against the small of my back.

"Before. After. Both." The words come out as weak pants.

"Very interesting," he murmurs.

"Indeed."

"You know what else is interesting?" He looks at my mouth again.

"Hmm?" We're very close. So close that all I would have to do is tip a bit forward for my lips to meet his.

"She's gone," he says in a low voice, his breath coasting over my skin. "And you're still on my lap."

Am I? Oh, hell, what am I doing?

I scramble off. "Sorry. I forgot." My heart is beating right in my throat. "You're surprisingly comfortable as a chair."

Rowan quickly moves closer to the desk, hiding his legs underneath.

He probably wants to make sure I don't climb up on him again.

This is mortifying.

He clears his throat and runs his fingers through his hair. "I've achieved my higher purpose in life."

"Congratulations," I choke out. "We should celebrate."

I've lost it. I've officially lost it. God help me. What just happened?

When Rowan looks back at me, there's a bemused smirk playing on his face.

We both know I just embarrassed myself, and that's on top of costing him whatever negotiation he was trying to have before I barged in. Anguish blooms inside my lungs. I never do psychotic things like this—what the hell has gotten into me?

"I cost you that discount, didn't I?" I whisper, wringing my hands.

He leans back slightly and links his hands behind his head. "Generally, it's considered unprofessional to comment on people's undergarments in a business setting."

I grip my face. "Right. I can see that. Are you mad? I can't tell."

"Mad?" His eyes darken. "Sunshine, you climbing into my lap is more than worth the slight hit to my bottom line."

Heat crashes through me. I stare at him open-mouthed, unsure of how to respond to that.

The door pops open. "Hey, the client— Oh, Blake."

I whirl around. "Sam!"

He blinks at me and Rowan. "I didn't realize you'd be here. Actually, this is great. I was just at your house with an architect. Do you have time to chat? I can tell you what we're thinking in terms of next steps."

I've never felt more overjoyed about an interruption. "I've got plenty of time."

"Great. Let me just talk to Rowan real quick, and I'll be right out."

I hurry out of the office, not daring to look at Rowan. He's probably still eyeing me with that knowing smirk that seems to say, *Got you.*

CHAPTER 24

BLAKE

When I walk into the kitchen to make coffee a half hour before we're due to leave for the Handy Heroes office the next morning, Rowan is there.

I come to a sharp halt.

My jaw drops.

He's whisking something in a bowl and wearing only a pair of jeans that are slung low on his hips. My eyes slide over his tattooed back with the eagerness of a kid going down a waterslide. I've never seen a body like his in real life. He's all muscle and ink, the dark lines flowing along his tanned skin.

"Want eggs before we head out?" he tosses over his shoulder.

"Sure." It comes out like a croak.

He turns to pour the egg mixture into a hot pan, and I get a glimpse of his abs. All eight of them.

Yep, okay. The image of Rowan's sculpted torso has been officially burned into my mind.

I try my best to avert my gaze, pretending to be nonchalant as I walk over to the coffee maker. "How was the rest of your day yesterday?"

I ended up driving back here with Sam. He wanted to review some things at the house with me. He stayed until Rowan came home, but I was so embarrassed about my deranged behavior at his office that I said I was tired and hid from him in the bedroom for the rest of the night.

I'm not proud of it.

"Busy. How did things go with Sam?"

When I sit down on the chair, my panties stick to me.

Fuck my life.

"He's a sweetheart. He's working on a detailed plan for everything, and the work is going to start next week."

I tried to ask Sam how much the renovation was going to cost, but it was like he was deathly allergic to discussing anything attached to a dollar sign.

Just how much is Rowan spending on me?

He moves the eggs around the pan. "Good. I asked him to move quickly."

Despite my best efforts, my gaze slides back down his body. What would it be like to feel that body move over me?

My mouth goes dry.

"I thought we could make our official public debut today."

"What?" I ask weakly.

He transfers the eggs onto two plates. "Our relationship."

"I thought our public debut was at the bar."

"No one saw us."

"Where do you want to go tonight?"

He turns, flashing me his abs again. "Frostbite is an awkward choice since you're still employed there, so I made us reservations at Emerald Grill for seven p.m."

I blink, trying to remember how to speak. Emerald Grill is the second most popular restaurant in town after Frostbite, and it will be packed, even on a Tuesday night.

Rowan puts the plates down, sits across from me at the breakfast table, and smiles. "You up for it? After yesterday's performance at the office, I can't imagine you're not."

My cheeks heat. "Of course."

After all, it's about time I start earning my keep.

As EXPECTED, the Emerald Grill parking lot is packed when we arrive that evening. Rowan's long fingers are intertwined with mine as we walk up to the hostess stand, and while he seems completely at ease, my gut is a churning mess of nerves.

I'm not doing anything wrong. Brett and I broke up months ago, and he was the one who cheated on me. There's nothing strange about me moving on, but the fact that my supposed new boyfriend is Rowan makes it more complicated.

People will talk. And the thought of being subjected to all that gossip fills me with unease.

We follow the hostess through the dining room, and Rowan slides his arm around my waist, palming my right hip with his large hand.

His warmth seeps through the fabric of my dress, branding my skin. His touch feels practiced, like he's held me like this a hundred times before, but he hasn't. This must be how he's touched all of the women that came before me.

Disappointment flickers through me at the thought.

As we walk, it feels like everyone's eyes are on Rowan and me. I can guess what all of these people—most of whom I recognize—are thinking. *He picked* her? *He usually goes for prettier girls. Doesn't he know who she is?*

The dress I'm wearing is one of the nicer ones I've got—it's got cute ruffled sleeves and a flared skirt that ends midthigh. I've got a pair of tights on because it's too damn cold for bare legs, and they've got a bit of a sheen to them that I like. Completing the outfit is a pair of high-heeled boots I got from the sales rack at TJ Maxx.

If anything, I'm a bit overdressed. Rowan's only wearing a light-blue button-up shirt and a pair of jeans, but he looks like a damn male model, and I've never felt more self-conscious than I do now.

I'm praying for a table that'll give us a bit of privacy, but the universe isn't listening. The hostess puts us on the right side of the main dining area, where everyone can see us.

I slide into my chair, pick up the menu she leaves on the table, and clutch it in front of my face.

While Rowan's getting settled in, I try to get my anxiety under control.

Of course, everyone is staring at us. They stared when I first started dating Brett too.

With Brett, there was an explanation. We worked together for a year before he asked me out. People probably thought I spent that entire year seducing him or something crazy like that.

But how will they explain Rowan and me?

I can imagine their whispers. *Those two don't make any sense together.*

They're right. We don't. That's why this isn't real. Why it's just pretend.

But even pretending with him feels like I've accidentally gotten onto a rollercoaster to heartbreak, and I have no idea how to get off.

Rowan's gaze lifts to me. "What are you thinking?"

I close the menu without even looking at the items on it and put it down between us. "I don't know. I'm feeling a bit overwhelmed," I admit quietly. "Everyone's staring."

His eyes are warm and attentive. "They're staring because you look fantastic, and people like to stare at beautiful things."

Shock reverberates through me. He thinks I'm beautiful? I've never thought of myself as special before—

Oh.

Bringing the ice water to my lips, I swallow down my disappointment. "You're good at this. I almost believed you."

His thick brows furrow. "You think I'm lying?"

"I think you're in character. Which is fine. I mean, that's why we're here, right?"

Our conversation is interrupted by a waitress coming by to take our drink orders. He orders a bottle of red wine, sends her on her way, and then leans forward, bringing our heads close together.

"I don't need to be in character to appreciate a beautiful woman and her company."

My eyes trace his lips. A man like Rowan shouldn't have such perfect lips, full and shapely. He's tempting enough as is.

Even if he's lying.

I know I'm no great beauty. My nose is too pointy, my mouth is too wide, and despite being blond-haired and blue-eyed, there's something about how my features all come together that puts me far from the mainstream ideal.

But what's the point of arguing with him? Do I really want him to admit to me that even on my best day, like right now, I'll never measure up to the worst day of some of the other women he's been with?

I'm not a masochist.

"Thank you for the compliment," I say stiffly and pick up the menu to look at it again.

After we place our orders, I get up to use the ladies' room, keeping my eyes down as I weave past the other tables.

When I return, there's a pretty dark-haired woman sitting in my seat.

I stop a few steps away.

That's Casey. Del told me Rowan slept with her a few months ago.

Jealousy sinks its claws into my insides. Again? Is this what dating Rowan will be all about? Seeing other women salivating over him and questioning if I'll ever hold up to them?

It's a good thing this is fake.

All. Just. Fake.

It takes Casey a moment to tear her gaze away from Rowan to the shadow standing by the table.

A beat passes as she takes me in, and her confused expression tips me off to the fact that she momentarily mistakes me for a waitress.

But then she catches on.

"I'm sorry, did I take your seat?" She doesn't look in any rush to vacate it.

"Hey, Sunshine." Before I realize what's happening, Rowan grabs my wrist and pulls me onto his lap. I'm caught off guard and lose my balance, sinking all my weight onto him, but he doesn't even huff in discomfort.

Sitting on him feels like sitting on an iron throne. His muscles barely budge as I shift and try to sit up straighter. He wraps one arm around my waist and places his other hand on my thigh, keeping me in place. "Casey just stopped by to say hi," he murmurs, his lips brushing against my ear.

My cheeks start burning. How is it that I keep ending up in his lap?

Casey's eyes widen. "So this is..."

"My girlfriend, Blake Wolfe. Have you two met?"

Shock blooms across her face and some spiteful part of me gets a kick out of it.

"Of course. Everyone's met everyone around here at some point." She regains her composure. "Are you still working at Frostbite?"

I nod. "Yes, but I'm taking a few weeks off to deal with the house."

Rowan's thumb brushes over my inner thigh, setting off a swarm of butterflies.

Casey tucks a strand behind her ear, flashing her glittery fake nails. "There was that fire, right? What a nightmare. Good thing you were able to get out in time."

Maybe the best way to protect myself is to stay focused on what I'm supposed to be doing for Rowan as part of our arrangement. Why stop at making people think Rowan's settled down? Why not also make him into a hero? That's a sure way to help his business. He's been overdelivering on his side of the bargain. Now it's my turn.

"It was awful, but Rowan saved me. You know, I might have died if it weren't for him."

Casey gasps. "Really?"

"He was the first person to realize there was a fire, and he ran into my house to carry me out. He's a hero."

I twist to look at him, and for the first time since I've met him, he looks flustered.

"That's... Wow." Casey reaches for my glass of water before she remembers herself and pulls her hand back. "I'm sorry, I just can't imagine how frightening that must have been. You were lucky Rowan was around."

I cup his bearded cheek. "*So* lucky."

He turns his face and presses a kiss to the inside of my palm. "Feels like I'm the lucky one now that I have you living with me."

Casey's brows inch up her forehead. "You're living together? While the repairs are happening?"

I open my mouth to answer, but Rowan beats me to it. "That's what she thinks, but I'm determined to convince her to make the move a permanent one." He squeezes my thigh, as if I'm not breathless enough from just the way he's ensnared me with his gaze.

"After all, she belongs with me." The words rumble inside his chest, and something hot twists low in my belly. My pulse travels from the tips of my ears, down to my throat, and keeps moving lower until I feel it between my legs.

Rowan is clearly capable of putting on a performance worthy of an Oscar. He's so good, I almost believe him.

"Now, Casey," he says, still holding our eye contact, "if you don't mind, you're in my girlfriend's seat. We'd like to get back to our date."

In my periphery, I see her get to her feet. She mumbles something apologetic before she hurries away.

Our waitress appears with our meals. I try to get off Rowan's lap, but he puts pressure on my thighs.

"Stay," he murmurs into my ear.

"Rowan, we have an audience," I say out of the corner of my mouth.

"Good." His lips trace the side of my neck. "I want everyone in this restaurant to know you're mine, Sunshine."

My eyes flutter, and I relent.

It's not because I enjoy the feel of him under me. It's definitely not because I'm agitated and yet so horribly turned on I want to scream.

People are looking at us, so we might as well act all loved up, right?

I watch him twirl the spaghetti on his fork and lift it to my lips, and I open my mouth like I'm in some kind of a trance.

Jesus. When did I become the kind of woman that lets some man feed her?

But Rowan isn't just *some* man. I'm starting to think mind control is one of his many talents, because how else do I explain him managing to get so deep under my skin?

"How's your back, by the way?" Rowan asks. He puts the fork down and drifts his fingers down my spine before stopping at the spot he massaged a few days ago.

"Better."

He rubs a circle with his thumb, and I feel an echo of his touch someplace else. My skin's been buzzing ever since he pulled me onto him, and everything's more sensitive than normal.

When he rubs another circle, pressing harder this time, I do the most embarrassing thing.

I whimper.

"Fuck," Rowan mutters in a hoarse voice close to my ear.

That one word kills me. Wetness gathers in my panties. I'm burning up, my entire body feeling like it was just plopped into an inferno.

That's it. I *need* to get off his lap.

And so I do. Or at least, I attempt to. As I shift forward to get to my feet, my ass grazes something hard and alarmingly large inside his jeans.

Is that his...

I freeze.

Rowan exhales a low, strained breath. He wraps his palms around my waist, lifts me off him, and helps me back into my chair.

He runs a flustered hand through his hair. When he sees how I'm looking at him, he tugs on his collar. "What?"

"Are you... Are you hard?"

His eyes turn very dark. He reaches for my hand under the table, pulls on it, and puts it right on his lap.

And I feel... All. Of. Him.

"This is how hard you make me." His voice is pure gravel. "Remember that the next time you're questioning if I really find you beautiful."

If someone put a gun to my head right now and demanded I speak, I'd take a bullet to the brain.

Words? What are words? We haven't met.

He stares at me for a long moment, as if he wants to make sure I heard him.

Oh, I heard him. But I'm mute. Utterly stupefied.

And then the man releases my hand and digs into his pasta like he didn't just tilt my entire world on its axis.

CHAPTER 25

NERO

Blake busies herself with her food, but whenever her gaze jumps to me, she looks a bit like a deer in headlights.

It's fucking adorable how flustered she is. My cock stays painfully hard through the rest of dinner, and I realize Blake's been discreetly dabbing her napkin against the sweat glistening on her neck.

It's not that hot here. She's just as worked up as me.

I was concerned when I saw Casey walking over to our table, but what bothered me most about the unfortunate encounter was Blake calling me a hero. I didn't like that, nor the sharp pang of guilt that followed.

I'm no fucking hero. I'm a villain who's working hard on rectifying the mistakes he's made with her.

The waitress comes around and asks if we want dessert, but Blake shakes her head, saying she's full.

"You sure?"

"Mm-hmm." She can't seem to hold my gaze for more than a second without her cheeks turning bright pink.

"Let's grab the check then."

I pay for the meal and help Blake with her coat. She's silent through it all, staring at her feet like she's thinking really hard about something.

Did I go too far with her? I've never been known for my patience, and with each passing day, I can feel it running out. I want to kiss those lips, to hold her in my arms, to burrow deep inside of her.

I think she wants it too.

But she won't admit it, even to herself.

If I push her too much, she'll retreat.

Much like she's doing now.

As we're walking out, I hear someone calling my name. "Is that you, Rowan?"

It's Lottie Brown. The lady's about eighty years old, but she's got the energy of a teenager and the wardrobe of a go-go girl. I'm working on her kitchen.

She gets out of her seat, revealing the fuchsia sequin ensemble she's got on, and sashays over to us to the jiggling soundtrack of the stacks of bracelets on her arms.

I grin. She's a gossip, but she's got character.

I bend down to press a kiss to each of her cheeks. "You look lovely, Mrs. Brown."

"How many times do I have to tell you to call me Lottie?" She swats at my chest, the old flirt. "You're a sight for sore eyes, darling. I was expecting you yesterday, you know?"

"My apologies. I had to stay at the office. I'll be there next week."

"You better." Her gaze moves to Blake and then drops to our linked hands. "Blake Wolfe! Oh my goodness, are you two here on a date?"

I let go of Blake's hand to wrap my arm around her shoulders and pull her into me. "We are."

Her eyes widen with delight. "First date?"

"It's been a few weeks," Blake says. "I thought Del would have told you."

"I must have a chat with that girl. I tell her everything, and she holds out on me. Will I see you two at the mayor's Christmas party next week? I can't remember if I got your RSVP, Rowan. I told you I'm on the organizing committee this year, right?"

Ah, the mayor's party. That's been on my calendar for weeks. The whole town is supposed to show up, and Sandro told me he'll castrate me if I don't go. I'm supposed to work the room and get leads for our business.

But what I'm looking forward to most is showing Blake off.

"We'll be there," I say.

Blake shoots me a surprised look. "We will?"

I lean down and press a kiss against the crown of her head. "Did I forget to tell you?"

She gives me a tight smile that looks vaguely threatening. "You did."

She doesn't sound thrilled about it, and it doesn't take a genius to figure out why. Her ex will be there, along with his dad and the rest of his family.

But she doesn't need to worry. Brett won't bother her while I'm around.

In fact, I can't fucking wait to parade her on my arm in front of him.

"I'm so thrilled to hear that," Lottie croons. "Not to toot my own horn, but it's going to be the event of the year." She turns to Blake. "Oh, honey, can I ask you for a favor?"

Blake smiles. "Sure, Aunt Lottie. What is it?"

"You know the charity auction we always do as part of the event? Marissa, the woman who owns that Italian place near Kansas City, just dropped out. She had donated a cooking class, but she just lost her sister, so the poor thing had to pull out."

Blake looks gutted. "That's terrible."

Lottie pats her arm. "I know in the previous years you donated a mixology class. Can I convince you to do it again this year?"

Blake stiffens. "Uh. I'm not sure..."

"Well, why not? Surely you can spare a few hours for a good cause?"

"All right," Blake says, a hint of reluctance in her voice. "I'll do it."

"Wonderful! You two enjoy the rest of your night."

When we get outside, Blake turns on me. "I would have appreciated a heads-up. The party's next week."

I grin. She looks even more beautiful when she's mad. "It's for a good cause. What are you worried about?"

"For one, I have no idea what to wear."

"What you're wearing right now is fine. You'll look great in anything."

She shoots me a dark look before getting inside the truck.

At first, the silence feels comfortable, but as we keep driving, the mood shifts. Blake is turned away from me as she stares out the window, her hands resting in loose fists in her lap.

Is she that pissed about going to the party? Or is it the class Lottie convinced her to donate?

"You said you lived in Vegas. You a gambler?"

Her question catches me off guard. It takes me a moment to answer. "Not anymore." Saturday poker nights with the guys in New York used to be my favorite.

"You lost one vice," she mutters.

"Picked up a few others." Like obsessing over her.

"Hmm. Are the women a new thing?"

I bite down on my tongue. Why the hell is her head going there?

Probably because of Casey. I wish the woman hadn't come up to me, but it would have happened eventually. Somewhere, with someone.

Unease slithers down my spine. It would be unreasonable for me to expect Blake to suddenly get over the fact that I've slept around. She's made it very clear it bothers her.

"No, it's not a new thing," I admit, not wanting to lie. Haven't I lied enough?

"Usually, promiscuity is a sign you're running from something. Learned that after I spent hours googling why men cheat."

I stop at a light and look at her. "I don't cheat. I've always been upfront about my intentions."

She meets my gaze. "Which are?"

"With Casey and the rest of them?" I make a caveat so that she knows what's happening between us is different. "I made it clear to them that I wasn't looking for commitment or anything serious."

"I wish Brett was as honest with me. He was running from the fact that he was unhappy with me. I was never a good match for someone like him."

"Someone like him? You mean an asshole?"

Her laugh is soft. "His family is practically royalty in this town. And me? I already told you that I'm a nobody. The daughter of a criminal. White trash."

I don't like her talking about herself that way. "Don't ever call yourself that."

"It's what I am. My mom was born in a trailer park."

"We don't get to choose who our parents are. But we can sure as fuck choose our actions. Don't tell me you blame yourself for what Brett did."

"I don't blame myself, but I get it. I wasn't all that fun to be around those last few months before Mom died, so he found someone who was. I could feel him pulling away emotionally, but I was too wrapped up in my grief to do anything about it."

My hands tighten on the wheel. God, I'd love to smash that son of a bitch right in the face. "He wasn't right for you. If he was, he would have stuck by your side instead of straying from the commitment he made to you."

She whips her head around, piercing me with her glare. "Sure. But who are you to judge him, Rowan? You can't seem to commit to anyone for more than one night, or at least so I hear."

Anger sparks inside of me. I haven't fucking looked at another woman since she moved in, but of course, she hasn't noticed that.

"You've been in my bed for far more than one night," I growl.

"I'm the *only* person in your bed."

"Do you want to change that?" I challenge. "Judging by your performance at my office yesterday, it seems like maybe you do."

Her cheeks redden. "You're an asshole. You know we have a deal."

Frustration fans through me. "A deal. So all of this is you working overtime to meet the requirements of our deal?"

"Are you really asking that question? Or are you just trying to provoke me?"

I'm pushing it, but I'm too annoyed with her to keep myself in check. "Tell me, what went through your head when you felt how hard I was for you at dinner?"

She sputters. "W-what do you mea— What kind of a ques—
"

"It's a simple fucking question. What went through your head?"

Her fingers flex into tense claws on her knees. "Nothing. I drew a blank."

"Really? Because I bet if I'd slid my hand between your thighs just then, I'd have found you wet. And why do pussies get wet, Sunshine? I'm no genius, but I know a thing or two about women's anatomy. Women get wet when they're aroused. So what's arousing to women? That depends on the individual. But given what I know of you, let me venture a guess. I think the image that went through your head when you felt how fucking hard I was for you was me and you in a dark, empty corner of a library—you know, the kind with all those fancy books you love so much—and you're in a dress, one of those little fucking dresses that billow out from the waist. You've got your hands up on a bookshelf, your face eye level with a shelf of Italian poets, and you're holding onto it for dear life because I'm railing you. I'm railing you *so* hard and I've got my fingers over your clit, and your hair wrapped around my fist, and I'm biting your neck while you moan my name and beg me to fuck you even harder. That's what I bet went through your head."

There's silence and then a harsh intake of breath.

I tighten my hands around the wheel and look at her. "Did I get that right?"

She's staring at me with wide eyes and a parted mouth. Her cheeks burn a bright red.

I huff. "Would you look at that? I'm so fucking right I stunned you into silence."

She wraps her palm around the side of her neck, and I see it bob on a swallow before I turn back to face the road. We've reached our street.

"I have no desire to be another one of your conquests," she says, sounding out of breath. "I'm not like you. I don't sleep with others on a whim."

"The rest of the town already thinks you've slept with me." We pull into the driveway. "You might as well do it and have some fun for once."

"I don't need the kind of fun that leaves my heart broken. And I've long since learned I can't control what this town thinks, but I can control what *I* think. And what I think is that for you, sex is a crutch. Whatever pain you're nursing, sex helps you forget it. But the relief is short-lived, which is why you move on so quickly in search of your next distraction. I'm not a distraction, Rowan. I'm a person. And I deserve more than that."

She's out of the truck before I can utter another word.

It's for the best, because I've got nothing to say to that. She's right. I slept with those women because they were a distraction from the bored dissatisfaction permeating my new life.

I drag my palms over my face. No wonder she doesn't want to get involved with me if that's all I can give her.

She's pure, good, and selfless. If I want to have her, let alone keep her, I have to become someone better.

The question is...can I?

CHAPTER 26

BLAKE

"Ugh, I wish I was going to the party with you," Del grumbles.

I squeeze the phone between my shoulder and my ear as I slide the hot iron over my dress. "Don't you have your company's holiday party coming up this week?"

"Yeah, and I can guarantee you I'll be in bed alone by ten p.m., the same way I was last year. These nerdy software engineers have no idea how to have a good time."

"I think it's a good thing you're not going to be at the charity auction. We can't have you blowing money you don't have just because you feel bad for people who donated the items." Del has a track record of draining her savings bidding on things no one else seems to want, which will probably be my mixology class this year. One time, she spent three hundred dollars on a collection of empty perfume bottles.

"Hey, I have no regrets. If I was there, you know I'd bid the hell out of your class."

I groan. "I'm dreading it. It's going to be so embarrassing if no one wants it." And there's a good chance no one will, but I couldn't say no to Lottie. She's always been kind to me, and I loved her as a teacher.

Del tsks. "Don't be ridiculous. You're telling me you're not even a little excited?"

I set the iron aside and lift the satin dress I dug out of the back of my closet a few days ago. It's red with black polka dots, long sleeves, and a boat neck.

It should do.

"I wouldn't even go if Rowan weren't insisting on it. But he and I have a deal, so this is me earning my keep."

Nerves flutter in my stomach. Dinner at Emerald Grill was overwhelming, but tonight, the whole town will be present to witness Rowan and me acting like a couple.

We've barely talked since the night of our last date.

He's spent the last three days silently driving me to the office and then silently driving me back home. All week, he's looked like there's a lot on his mind. And Sam was around the whole weekend, walking me through the plans for the renovations and helping me clear the rest of my things out. When Rowan wasn't helping us, he made himself scarce.

Now it's Monday, the night of the party, and I'm desperate to break the ice that's set in between us.

Was I too harsh with him on the ride home? Probably.

I don't know why I went off on him like that.

Actually, that's a lie. I do know.

That date unmoored me. Rowan makes me feel all sorts of things, and the more time I spend with him, the less I remember all the reasons I should keep my guard up.

I felt like I needed to plant a stake in the ground and make it clear to both of us that it doesn't matter how my body reacts to him. Or how I've been dreaming of his hands on me again for days. Or how there's a tiny part of me that's excited about this party despite my nerves because I'll get a chance to be close to him again.

None of that matters, damn it.

If I give in and sleep with him, the confusing feelings inside me will grow wings, and I'm scared I won't be able to rein them back in.

Del snorts. "I'm sure he'd be happy to let you earn your keep in other ways."

"Stop it."

"Oh, c'mon. Don't tell me you still haven't fooled around."

"Not at all."

"You're really telling me you've been there for more than a week now, and nothing's happened between you two?"

I think back to the night after we went to The Junction. I think back to him standing shirtless in the kitchen, cooking eggs for me. I think back to how I cozied up on his lap, not once, but *twice*.

Oh, *something's* been happening.

But I can't tell Dell that. Not when I don't understand any of it myself yet. "I thought we were becoming friends," I say instead. "Now, I'm not so sure."

She laughs. "Based on what I've heard about him, that is not a man who has female friends."

"What would be the point of starting anything? I'm still planning on leaving this place once I've sorted everything with the house. Sam told me it should take four weeks to get everything done, but with the holidays coming up, he tacked on another week. So that brings us to mid-January."

"Why not just have some fun with Rowan in the meantime?"

That's exactly what Rowan said after our date. *You may as well have some fun.*

I rub my forehead. "You know I don't do casual sex. If I sleep with him, there's a good chance I'll get attached and get my heart broken when it's time to leave."

"It's not like you *have* to leave."

I flip the dress over to iron a wrinkle I spied on the other side. "What do you mean?

"I mean, you can fix up the house, sell it, and use the money to open that bookstore you always wanted in Darkwater Hollow. Then you wouldn't have to end things with Rowan if you didn't want to."

"Del, haven't you heard enough from me and Lottie about Rowan? He doesn't do relationships. He's not looking for anything serious. In fact, he'd rather let me live with him and pay a fortune for my repairs than give a genuine relationship a chance."

Del sighs. "I hear you. It just seems like such a waste. Especially since it sounds like you two are getting along."

More like I go from being enthralled by him to wanting to strangle him.

But tonight at the party, I have one task.

I have to convince everyone I'm in love with him.

I WALK OUT of the bedroom an hour later, determined to play it as cool as a cucumber tonight, only to nearly stumble over my feet when my eyes land on Rowan in the living room.

He's standing by the window looking out at the backyard. The crisp white dress shirt and the dark-wash jeans fit him sinfully well, as if whoever made them used a pattern with exactly his measurements in mind. He tugs on the sleeves and rolls his boulder-like shoulders back.

Just watching his absentminded movements sends lava dripping into my bloodstream.

He slides on the blazer he's holding, the action so fluid and practiced, it's like he's done this a thousand times before, even though I know he hasn't. I doubt he's had to dress up like this often working in constriction.

It's a shame.

When he turns to face me, there's a fire blazing low inside my belly.

Our eyes clash. Rowan holds my gaze for a moment and then allows it to slide lower, taking me in inch by inch.

I can barely breathe as I wait for him to speak. Being seen by him is a full-body experience—my skin sizzles, my heart pounds, and my nerve endings flutter.

When his eyes finally return to mine, there's a distinct hunger in them.

He looks like he wants to take a bite of me.

And right now, I think I'd let him.

Maybe he senses my weakness, because he stops in front of me and drags a knuckle over my clavicle. "You look good in red."

My nipples pebble. If I weren't wearing a bra, he'd see it and know that he was right that night after we left Emerald Grill.

He did make me wet that night. He made me so fucking wet. And then he somehow managed to do it all over again when he pulled a fantasy I didn't even know I had from somewhere deep inside my head and recited it to me in that low, sexy voice.

"Thank you," I breathe.

Snow floats through the sky as we drive to the historical manor where the party is taking place. The air inside the car is so charged that neither of us dares to speak.

I think back to my conversation with Del. Everything I said to her is true, but I'm not all logic. And a very illogical part of me wants to forget about my legitimate concerns about Rowan and see where tonight might lead.

We find a spot in the busy parking lot and get out of the car. Rowan's palm is pressed against my lower back as we join the other guests streaming inside the venue.

The manor is one of the few historical buildings scattered throughout Darkwater Hollow. It's beautiful, with intricately carved wooden ceilings, art depicting biblical scenes on the walls, and a grand ballroom where the dinner and auction will be taking place.

The ballroom is brimming with people by the time Rowan and I make it inside. It takes me only a moment to spot Brett's sister and mother on the other side of the room.

They shoot me a glare, like they can't believe I've dared to show my face here. They've never liked me. Neither has the rest of Brett's family. His dad has always been cordial, but he's the mayor. He has to put on a friendly front to his constituents. I've never deluded myself into thinking he was happy about his son dating me.

I ignore them and follow Rowan toward our designated table.

As soon as I see the people who'll be sitting with us, my stomach turns.

There are four couples. I know three of them only in passing, but the fourth pair—James and Sarah—were in my grade in high school. One time, Sarah took my clothes while I was taking a shower in the girls' changing room and hid them under a bench far from my locker. It only took me five minutes to find them, but I spent those minutes imagining I was going to have to go out into the hallway in only a towel, and the sheer panic I felt stayed with me for years.

She shoots me a cold look when Rowan and I take our seats.

Annoyance prickles over my nape. It's been years, but she still clearly has a problem with me.

I scan the three older couples at the table. Their vibe is also decidedly frosty as they send us a smattering of nods and thin-lipped smiles. Two of the women avert their gazes when I try to make eye contact.

Okay, what's going on? I've only ever served these people at Frostbite, and I don't recall any of them being particularly rude to me.

Is it what I'm wearing?

I glance down at my dress.

Rowan leans in and whispers, "The only way we could have gotten a worse table is if they'd sat us with Abigail and her husband."

I tip my head toward him. "What do you mean?"

"The two guys sitting across from us are friends with the husband. I've seen them hanging around together."

Crap.

"Bad luck," I mutter.

This is not a good start to our night. I know Rowan's goal is to get some new leads for his business to replace the clients he and Sam have recently lost, and the couples at our table would be the perfect place to start. But how can Rowan convince them to work with him if they don't even want to say hello to us?

I need to help him. He's new to this town, but I'm not, and I know that if he can win over the people sitting with us, it will start a chain reaction. If there's one good thing about the Darkwater Hollow rumor mill, it's that it goes both ways.

I take in a steadying breath. Well, here goes nothing.

Plastering on an earnest smile, I lock eyes with the woman sitting closest to me. "Hi. Emily, right?"

Hesitantly, she turns my way. "Hello."

"I think you know Lindsay Kennedy? She's my best friend's mom."

Her expression brightens. "Oh, yes, Lindsay and I lived next door growing up. Shame she left a few years back." She folds her hands in her lap. "How's Delilah?"

"She works at a tech company in San Francisco now. I was just on the phone with her before we came here, and she was very upset she's missing the party."

Emily smiles. "I think a lot of people have fond memories of these parties. The community doesn't quite come together like this at any other time during the year."

"You're completely right." I lean back and put my hand on Rowan's forearm. "By the way, have you met my boyfriend, Rowan?"

In my periphery, I see the table slightly perk up at the word.

So they're all eavesdropping, huh?

Good. The bigger the audience, the better.

"I don't believe so, but I've heard tons about you, Rowan." There's an amused glint in Emily's eyes. She gestures at the man beside her. "This is my husband, Jonah."

Rowan extends his hand with a charming smile. "Nice to meet you both."

Jonah nods in greeting and shakes Rowan's hand, relaxing slightly as the tension at the table eases.

Ice broken.

I'm not a particularly charming person—not like Rowan, at least—but after working at a bar for four years, I've learned how to talk to just about anyone. The best way to get someone to like you and leave a bigger tip is to ask them tons of questions. People love to talk about themselves.

So that's what I do with Emily and Jonah. I ask about their kids, their plans for the holidays, and their favorite hiking spots around town.

"The trail in Whispering Woods is our favorite," Emily says. "It's only a thirty-minute drive, and the view of the lake is unforgettable."

"We'd love to go." I shoot Rowan, who's been letting me drive the conversation, a smile. "Darkwater Hollow is a beautiful place. I'm proud to call it home."

Jonah nods. "That's good to hear. A lot of young people are leaving these days. I know there are more opportunities in bigger towns, but if everyone leaves, Darkwater Hollow will disappear in a few generations."

Rowan's hand is resting on the table, and I place my palm over it. "This is why I'm so proud of Rowan. His business, Handy Heroes, employs four people, and they're only getting started. I've been helping out this past week, and I think it's the kind of company that can make a big impact in the community."

When I look at Rowan, he's staring at me with some unreadable emotion in his eyes.

"I've heard about the work your company does," Jonah says.

"You did an amazing job on my mom's house," James says begrudgingly, jumping into the conversation. "She won't stop mentioning it whenever I call her."

Sarah shoots daggers at her husband, but Rowan grins. "What's your mom's name?"

"Felicia Sutton."

Rowan barks out a laugh. "She's a delight. Sharp as hell, too. Did she tell you how she wiped the floor with me during a poker night she threw for me and my guys?"

James chuckles. "No, but that doesn't surprise me one bit. You should see her when she goes to Vegas."

Rowan runs his palm over his beard. "That was a great project. The first one we finished after we bought the company, actually."

Emily glances at Jonah. "We've been talking about redoing our living room for ages. Maybe it's time we pull the trigger? Do you have any availability in the next six months, Rowan?"

Jonah clears his throat. "We've got to get a few quotes before we commit to a firm, honey."

"No commitment necessary for us to give a quote," Rowan says. "Our prices are competitive."

I inch my chair closer and wrap my hands around his arm. It's solid muscle. "Very competitive. You won't believe how sweet this man is. My house sustained some damage from a recent fire, and he insisted on fixing it for me. He won't let me pay him a penny."

"That was a girlfriend special," Rowan says. "Don't advertise it to everyone, Sunshine."

Emily is smitten. "That's so sweet. We'd love to talk more about this, Rowan. Do you have a card?"

I watch Rowan talk to them, noting how easily he can hold a conversation, and how subtle he is about pitching his company. It doesn't feel like he's selling, but by the time the bread rolls come out, he and Jonah are already discussing their budget.

Triumph blooms inside my chest. I think I managed to do it.

Me. The girl this town hates.

The conversation is interrupted by the servers bringing out large dishes of food—family style for the table to share. Rowan throws his arm over the back of my chair and leans in. "I'm in awe of you," he whispers, his lips close to my ear.

A pleasant shiver zings up my spine. Truth is, I never would have had the courage to put myself out there like that if I didn't have him sitting beside me.

I turn and open my mouth to respond, but when I see how he's looking at me, I forget what I wanted to say.

He stares at my mouth as he lifts his hand to my cheek and brushes away a strand of my hair. "Did I tell you how unbelievably beautiful you look tonight?"

I feel his words brush against my lips. We're so close, we're breathing the same air.

"You didn't."

He brushes his knuckles over my jaw, caressing me like I'm something precious. "Then I'm an idiot."

The entire table must be watching us, probably trying to hear what he's saying to me, but it's as if the room has faded away, leaving just Rowan and me in this charged space. No matter how I try, I can't convince myself he's doing this for our audience. There's no hint of falseness in his dark, hazel eyes.

My heart thumps against my rib cage, the sound growing louder and louder inside my ears, and for the first time since we started this, I begin to think...this doesn't feel like pretend.

CHAPTER 27

BLAKE

"Good evening, everyone! Thank you so much for joining us tonight!"

The shock of the voice blasting through the speakers sends my heart into my throat. I jolt away from Rowan and look toward the stage where Lottie is standing talking to the audience. The faces around the table come into focus, and with them, an uncomfortable sensation of being under a microscope.

I pin my gaze onto my plate and hide my face behind the curtain of my hair. I don't want anyone to see whatever drama is playing out across my face, especially not the man sitting next to me.

My cheeks burn. Lottie's announcement that the charity auction is about to start barely registers. I glance at the paddle by my plate—on it is the number thirteen.

An omen for how the rest of my night will go?

No matter how deeply I try to breathe, I can't seem to get enough air.

The look Rowan gave me just now—warm, tender, and so damn possessive—is branded into my memory. What if he's starting to feel something more than just meaningless lust for me? Keeping my heart guarded was already hard enough when I thought sex was all he wanted.

I shiver, trying to shake off the lingering sensation of his gaze.

The auction begins, Lottie announcing the first item—some kind of vase hand-painted by a local artisan. People call out their bids, but it all seems distant and muffled to me. My head spins.

The vase goes for two hundred dollars.

"The next item is a mixology class donated by Blake Wolfe!"

Oh no.

"For those of you that don't know, that means making all kinds of yummy cocktails. Yes, a boozy afternoon with the best bartender in Darkwater Hollow. Who wouldn't want to bid on that? We're starting the bidding at a hundred dollars," Lottie says into the microphone.

In my lap, my hands curl into fists. I was so thrown off my equilibrium by that near kiss that I forgot to worry about my own item coming up for bidding, but now my nerves flare to life. No one's going to bid, I just know it. I thought when I graduated high school that I was done with being humiliated in public, but it looks like I was wrong. And this time, I've got no one to blame but me. Why did I agree to Lottie's request? I'm supposed to be putting myself first, not doing stupid favors just because I want Lottie to like me.

"This is your chance, folks! Remember, it's for a good cause!"

My skin heats to the point of discomfort as I watch Sarah's lips curve into a mocking smirk directed at me. I don't know why I'm even looking at her, but I can't seem to rip my gaze away.

This evening is another reminder that I'm nothing to these people. Why would they want something donated by the daughter of a criminal? I come from a chain of broken homes and broken families, and everyone in this town thinks they're better than me.

"One hundred to number fourteen!"

Fourteen? That's right beside me...

My head snaps to my right. Rowan's got his paddle up, his arm stretched high over his head like he wants everyone to see it.

"What are you doing?" I say under my breath.

"Bidding." Rowan lowers his paddle.

"Do we have two hundred?" Lottie calls out.

I blink at him. "Why?"

"I've always wanted to learn how to make a mean cocktail."

"Two hundred to number twenty-three!" Lottie calls out.

What? Someone else bid?

I crane my neck, searching for the other bidder. When I see who it is, my eyes widen.

Brett.

My ex stares at me from where he's sitting a few tables over, his gaze sharp, and his lips pressed into a thin line.

Dread prickles over my skin. If he wins, I'll have to spend time with him one-on-one. Even a few hours would be torture. Why did I—

Rowan raises his paddle. "Three hundred!"

They go back and forth. Five hundred.

And back and forth. Seven hundred.

And back and forth. Nine hundred!

By this point, I'm sweating through my dress. Our entire table is staring at me, some with amusement, and some with disbelief.

This feels like a civilized version of a duel.

And the thing that makes even less sense is that they're dueling over *me*.

"One thousand to number fourteen!"

Holy shit. That's more than what I earn in a week at Frostbite.

Rowan seems completely calm, but Brett's face is turning red.

"One thousand one hundred to number twenty-three!"

Rowan raises his paddle and calls out. "Five thousand."

Hushed whispers travel through the room. I'm stunned. I have no idea what to even think.

I see Brett's father lay a hand on his arm, stopping him from continuing this madness. Brett scowls but doesn't bid again.

His expression darkens even more. "I gathered as much." He reaches into an interior pocket of his blazer and pulls out a folded piece of paper. "I want you to look at this."

"What is it?"

He unfolds the paper and hands it to me. "Rowan's background check."

I frown, confused. "Why do you have this?" My gaze drifts over the document.

"Look." Brett points at a line on the page. "Huge gaps in his history. Didn't you say he moved here from New York? He didn't, Blake. It says he was in Vegas."

Rowan told me he lived in Vegas, so that isn't news to me. And the fact that New York is missing... What is that supposed to mean? I have no idea what a background check entails. Is this even real?

I give the paper a shake. "Where did you get this?"

"I asked the police chief to run Rowan through their system."

My eyes narrow. I can't believe him. "Were you hoping he had a criminal record or something?"

Brett's cheeks redden. "There's something off about that guy, Blake. You're too wrapped up in him to see it, but I'm watching out for you."

Fury pulses through my veins. How dare he? "My God. You were hoping to dig up some dirt on him, and all you got is *this*? What do you think this proves?"

"It proves that he's a liar," Brett bites out.

"You think this is a good use of police resources? You've got everyone in this town in your pocket, huh?"

He clenches his fists. "I asked the chief to do me a favor because I'm worried about *you*."

"If you actually gave a shit about my well-being, you wouldn't have stripped me of my income for two weeks."

"I did that so that you would come live with me! I would have taken care of you!"

"I don't need you to do anything except stay the hell out of my business," I snarl.

Brett's jaw clenches. "What's this I hear about you dating him? Lottie was spreading that bullshit earlier today before I told her to stop talking about things she has no clue about."

"I don't owe you an explanation." I turn to leave.

"Goddamn it, Blake!" He seizes my arm and jerks me closer, his touch rough enough to make me wince in pain. "Do you really think you'll ever find anyone better than *me*? I'm getting fucking tired of you playing hard to get. I took a chance on you. You know what my friends said to me when they found out we were dating? They told me I should just fuck you and then find myself someone who wasn't born in a fucking trailer park. But I didn't listen to them. I gave you my love. I gave you everything. You don't get to just throw all of that back in my face."

My throat thickens. His words feel like needles piercing my skin.

"You're going to marry me. You're going to have my children. And you're going to be a good wife who knows her place, because the life I'm offering you is the best life you could ever get. Are you so stupid that you don't see that?"

A mix of fear and anger churns inside me at his poisoned words. The man I thought I knew, the man I thought cared about me at one point, is showing a twisted sense of entitlement that makes my skin crawl.

He never saw me as an equal. Never saw me as worthy. The whole time we were dating, he thought he was doing me a favor.

I was just a poor stupid girl he probably thought he'd saved.

"Remove your hand, or I will," an icy, commanding voice says.

I twist my head to look over my shoulder. Just seeing Rowan approaching sends relief rushing through me. At first glance, he looks relaxed and at ease, but his eyes tell a different story. Darkness swirls within them, along with a clear warning.

"Who the fuck do you think you are?" Brett snarls as he drops my wrist. "And what the hell do you think you're doing with her?"

"What's going on between Rowan and I is none of your business," I snap, moving to stand beside Rowan.

"It's all right, baby. No need to spare his feelings." Rowan slips his arm around my waist and pulls me flush against his body. "Here's what I'm doing with her, Brett. I'm treating her right. I'm earning a place by her side, not taking it for granted. And I'm taking care of her. You didn't know how, but I do. It's time you move on. Blake certainly has." He pulls me closer and crushes his lips against mine.

CHAPTER 28

NERO

The kiss is nothing like that time I kissed her in her kitchen. That kiss was probing. Gentle. I wanted to ease her into it.

Now? I'm kissing her like I'm claiming her. Like I'm a predator, and she's my prey. My lips crush against hers, devouring the breathless gasp she makes. Her fingers curl into my lapels.

Blake needs to understand that I'm done playing games as far as she's concerned. I've spent the last week thinking about what I want and what I'm willing to do to get it, and in the process, I've realized a number of things.

When I was in New York—even when I thought I was on top of the world—there was an achy loneliness buried deep inside my chest.

The women I dated always had certain expectations.

I was Nero De Luca. The Messero consigliere. Powerful, dangerous, cunning.

I had a role to fill. A name to live up to.

Sometimes it felt like I was reduced to just the name and the reputation.

My impenetrable armor.

I've never let a woman see the man beneath.

But in Darkwater Hollow, everything is different. The pull of my old life is waning with each passing day, because being here no longer feels like being sentenced to death by slow-acting poison.

It's starting to feel like the start of a new life.

My stepdad wouldn't have approved, and that thought still stings. I loved that stubborn old man.

For Renzo, the mob was everything. There was no life outside it.

When he married my mom, he could have chosen to ignore me, but instead, he took me under his wing. The two of them were unable to have kids, but I was always Renzo's boy.

He called me son. I called him dad.

He taught me how to be a protector and a provider—something my biological father never knew how to be. He taught me how to be a damn good mobster, the kind that rises through the ranks. He taught me the meaning of loyalty. He was the most loyal man I'd ever met.

To put all that aside, willingly, feels like a betrayal in some way, even if I'm here out of loyalty to Rafe. But if I want to adapt to my new environment, it's what I have to do.

Can I do it?

I don't know. Breaking some of my old habits has been difficult. But I'm going to keep trying, because I know one thing with absolute certainty.

I want Blake to be a part of this new life. Our relationship might be fake, but there's never been anything fake about the way I'm drawn to her.

I want to make this woman mine. Even if it means I need to lock Nero away and never allow him to come out again. My past is darker than a moonless night, but what Blake doesn't know can't hurt her.

My tongue presses in, seeking entrance. She opens up for me and lets me probe her deeply. Her taste floods my senses. God, she's so fucking sweet that I could live off kissing her alone.

Then I remember that son of a bitch is still watching us.

I pull away with a low snarl.

Blake blinks at me, looking dazed. Then she glances to the right. "He's gone," she whispers on an exhale.

She's right. Brett left.

Good fucking riddance.

I found her here just in time to hear Brett saying what his family thought about their relationship.

That was bad enough, but what came next was even worse.

Is that the kind of bullshit he fed her all those years they were dating? Did he make her feel inferior to him?

She's breathing hard, her chest rising and falling. Anxiety flashes in her eyes. "I'm not sure taunting Brett was a smart idea."

"I'm not fucking sorry. He was touching you. He doesn't get to fucking touch you, Sunshine." If I'm locking Nero away, that means I probably shouldn't kill the motherfucker. But I don't need to go that far to get him to leave her alone.

If I need to sit at Frostbite all day and keep an eye on her when she goes back to work, so fucking be it.

Blake swallows. "You didn't need to do that for the sake of the deal."

I cup her cheek. "This isn't about the deal."

"What is it about, then?" Her voice is no more than a hoarse whisper, and she looks terrified all of a sudden, like she knows the next words out of my mouth are likely to send us right over the edge of a cliff.

I get it. Some part of me is scared too. But I've never let fear stop me from getting what I want.

"Every word he said to you was a lie. You're so much better than him. You're beautiful and kind and clever, and you deserve the entire fucking world, Sunshine."

Her eyes start glistening. "Rowan…"

I brush her hair off her face. "I can be an asshole, and I can be a selfish prick, but even in my worst moments, I'd never tear you down like that." I kiss her again. "I know my place, baby. It's kneeling at your feet."

She steps into me and presses her forehead against my chest, her body rattling with silent sobs.

I drag my palm over her back, trying to calm her. The auction's started up again, and the hallway is abandoned, but it still doesn't feel private enough. I don't want anyone to watch us anymore. I just want to be alone with her.

A few moments pass before she glances up at me with eyes that glisten like cool lakes.

What does she see when she looks into my eyes? Dark, murky waters?

"Let's get out of here," she whispers.

I grab her hand and tug her to the coat check. Lottie's voice echoes against the walls of the lobby as she calls out the bids, but when we step out through the main doors, everything quiets.

Thick snow shimmers in the air as we cross the parking lot toward my truck. I help her get inside and then stand there, my hand on the open door.

She stares at me, her nose tinged with pink and her lips slightly parted. My hand reaches out for her, needing to touch her, needing to make sure she's not upset anymore. I drag my knuckles over her jaw before I brush the snowflakes from her hair.

She sucks in a shaky breath. "Would you have kissed me if Brett wasn't there?"

I trace the curve of her cheek. "I spent all night wanting to kiss you."

Her eyelashes flutter. "I don't know what's real with you and what's pretend."

I take her hand, slide it under my jacket, and lay it right over my pounding heart. "This is real."

There's awe in her eyes, but also fear. My thumb brushes over the racing pulse on the inside of her wrist.

I don't want her to be scared. I want her to feel safe. Desired. Worshiped. I want to make sure she forgets every single word uttered tonight by her ex.

"We've got a fifteen-minute drive home," I say in a low voice. "I'm going to spend those fifteen minutes thinking about all the ways I'm going to make you come tonight."

Pink blooms over her cheeks.

"And I want you to think about why you might not let me do that. Make one of your lists on your phone. Make it thorough."

"Why?"

"Because I'm going to work through each one of your objections. If we do this, I don't want you to have a single hesitation. I want you all in. Deal?"

A beat passes. "Deal."

We get on the road. The silence crackles with the tension that comes from both of us knowing I'm planning on tearing her clothes off as soon as we walk through the door. Blake's profile is thoughtful when I glance at her, her mouth pursed into a determined line. She takes out her phone and starts typing something in.

Good girl.

And I do exactly what I told her I would. I think about how I'm going to bury my face between her legs and devour that pussy until my chin is dripping with her wetness. I think about how she'll writhe beneath me as I fuck her nice and hard. I think about all the sounds she's going to make for me —the whines and the moans and the cries.

Maybe I'll have her sit on my face for a while. She'll be shy at first, but then she'll get into it. That'll be fun.

We pull into the driveway and tumble out of the truck.

Inside the house, I press her back against the front door. Our mouths find each other, hungry and desperate. Her taste floods me with euphoria, no less potent than a drug.

The kiss is hot and needy and takes me to the edge of feral. Fuck, I want to be inside of her so badly. Instead, I work on retaining a small semblance of control.

She squirms against me, kissing me back with enthusiasm, oblivious to the battle raging inside my body. She wraps her arms around my neck, sliding her fingers into my hair. My body's buzzing, and I'm just about to pick her up when she suddenly pulls away.

I let out a breath and press my forehead against hers.

Here we go.

"All right, give it to me. Objection number one."

She pants against my lips. "It'll complicate everything. I was just getting used to this. You're starting to feel like my friend."

I drag my tongue in a long line up her neck. "You do this with all your friends?"

She moans. "No."

"We're not going to be friends, Sunshine."

"Del warned me about that."

"What?" I ask, pressing kisses along her jaw.

"She said you're not the kind of man who has female friends." Her fingers tangle with my hair, and she tugs me away from her neck.

Our eyes meet. "What else did your friend say about me?"

"She said I should sleep with you."

I smirk. "I like her."

"I told her that was a bad idea."

"Why's that?"

"What if we do this, and I do something wrong—"

"That's impossible."

"And you decide you don't want me here anymore."

"Also impossible."

"I have nowhere else to go, Rowan." The words come out in a vulnerable burst.

My palm moves to cradle her cheek. "Good, because I have no intention of letting you go anywhere."

She leans into my touch. "Is it stupid that I want to believe you so badly?"

"It's not stupid, because I'm not lying. But I don't blame you for being concerned. I get it. My history has always bothered you. But I'm not like your ex, Sunshine. "

Her throat bobs on a hard swallow. "No, you're not."

"I don't stray, and I sure as fuck know a good thing when I find it."

She considers me for a long moment, and then she leans away, as if getting settled in against the door at her back. She wraps her hands around my lapels and pulls me into her. My thigh presses between her legs. Her cheeks are flushed, and her eyes are hooded.

"Kiss me," she whispers, and God, those are the sweetest words I've ever heard.

We kiss until we're both panting.

We kiss until she's grinding against my leg.

We kiss until I'm wrangling with her coat, desperate to get it off her.

I was afraid of stepping off the cliff, but now that I've done it, I realize I'm not falling.

I'm fucking flying.

Her coat puddles around her feet.

And I get down on my knees.

CHAPTER 29

BLAKE

There were a few more things on my list, but one look at Rowan kneeling before me, and it's over.

Whatever resistance I had rips to shreds.

I surrender to the need that's been building inside me all evening, and *God*, it feels good. Like the first bite of a rich chocolate cake. Or a sinful afternoon nap in the middle of a busy day.

People say willpower is a limited resource, and I've officially reached my limit for tonight. I know I might regret it later, but right now, I just don't care.

Rowan lifts the skirt of my dress with one hand, bunching the fabric in front of my belly, and swipes his knuckles over the cotton covering my pussy.

The touch is featherlight, but it still sends an electric jolt through me. My lips part on a harsh inhale. We didn't bother turning on the lights when we stumbled into the house, and the foyer is dark. When one sense is dulled, the others are heightened, which must be why every single one of my nerve endings feels like it's on high alert.

"Open your legs," Rowan murmurs, an irresistible command that I follow without question.

He drags his knuckles over me again and again, on one side of me, then the other, then right over my seam.

I'm mesmerized. Snared. When he finally slips two fingers inside my panties and probes my entrance, I make an undignified needy sound because I want nothing more than for him to shove those fingers deep inside of me.

"So wet for me," he murmurs. "God, I can't wait to taste you."

My arousal tangles with a thread of anxiousness as he shoves my panties aside and presses his lips to my sopping entrance.

He groans with satisfaction. The sound is so raw, so *tangible*, that for a moment, I forget that I've rarely been able to come this way. He tastes me with long, thorough licks, and my panties stretch tighter and tighter around his fist until I hear the fabric *rip*.

"Oh God," I moan as he chucks the scrap of cotton to the ground and slides two fingers inside me.

Finally.

My inner muscles contract around him. He sucks on my clit while he curls his fingers in a come-hither motion, rubbing something inside, something unknown, something that makes my pussy flood.

Heat consumes my body. I've been placed in an inferno. I want this dress off, I want my bra off, I want *everything* off, and I want to come, goddamn it.

I want it *so* bad.

My hips rock back and forth, searching for a release that's just out of reach.

Frustration rears its ugly head. With Brett, it so rarely worked that he stopped trying. I knew I needed him to go for longer, but I wasn't good at asking because of my unwillingness to ever be an inconvenience.

Shame prickles over my cheeks.

Rowan's mouth on me disappears. "Baby? Why'd you go so still?"

My gaze drops to his perfect face. Even in the dark, I can see how his beard glistens from me. "I don't think I'll be able to finish like this," I whisper.

He arches a quizzical brow, giving my nub a light pinch that threatens to buckle my knees. "I'm just getting started."

My heart ping-pongs against my ribs. "It...might take a while."

I can barely see his smile, but I can hear it when he says, "Perfect. I don't like to rush my meals."

Oh.

"Carry on then," I choke out when he tugs on my clit again.

He gets back to it with a low chuckle, pressing his face at the apex of my thighs and lapping at me with his tongue.

He's good at this. So good that I have to dig my nails into the door to stop myself from crumbling to the floor. When my legs tremble so badly the hard surface at my back isn't enough to support me, I drop my palms onto his solid shoulders and hold on for dear life.

I feel like I'm about to explode.

So, so, so close— *There*.

My orgasm sweeps through me like a hard wave. I surrender to it just like I've surrendered to him.

It's glorious. Magnificent. The best thing I've ever felt.

Moans flood from my mouth, loud and unrestrained because I'm too damn fucked up to care. I slide down the wall, still holding his shoulders with my remaining strength to soften my landing, but my ass never hits the floor.

The next thing I know, he has my trembling body in his arms, my inconvenient dress still wrapped around me, and he's carrying me deeper into the house.

My breath leaves my lungs as he drops me onto the bed. Suddenly, the feel of the fabric sticking to me is unbearable. Why did I wear this tight, long-sleeved monstrosity? What kind of a lunatic am I?

I go up onto my knees and wrestle with the long skirt. "Can you help me get this off?"

Rowan flicks on the small bedside lamp, flooding the room with dim light. Together, we pull the dress over my head. The bra—my other enemy—comes off next. I groan with relief at having cool air brush against my skin.

This is much better.

When I raise my gaze to Rowan, I find him still standing by the side of the bed. He's staring at me with a look that makes my pussy clench.

It's dark, ravenous, possessive.

It takes me a moment to realize this is the first time I've been naked in front of him. Shockingly, there are no self-conscious whispers in the back of my head.

How can there be when his gaze alone makes me feel like something precious?

He reaches out and caresses my face, dragging his thumb over my cheeks, my jaw, my bottom lip. "You're so fucking pretty, Sunshine. Pretty all over." He traces the sides of my breasts with his knuckles, teasing me, tormenting me. I want his mouth on me, his teeth on my nipples. Instead, he cups both of my cheeks with his hands and claims my lips in a hungry kiss.

When we break apart, I'm done playing. I want him inside of me.

"Clothes, off," I beg. How is he still fully dressed while I'm completely naked?

He shrugs off his blazer and makes quick work of the buttons of his dress shirt before taking that off too.

My pulse hammers in my ears at the sight of all that tanned skin. His body is pure, lethal power.

My gaze slides over the tattoos that cover his chest and arms. From over here, I can just barely make out the scars smattered all over his torso.

He's got a lot of them. What happened?

His hands drop to unbuckle his belt. He pulls it through the loops with a soft hiss and tosses it onto the ground.

The movement shouldn't be erotic. It shouldn't make my skin heat. It most definitely shouldn't make me even wetter than I already am, yet here we are.

I swallow, unable to take my eyes off his body. He pushes his jeans and his boxer briefs down his legs in one fell swoop.

Oh fuck.

My gaze latches onto his hard length, and for a moment, I'm genuinely unsure what I'm supposed to do with *that*, but my cunt seems to have its own agenda, because it floods eagerly, sending wetness trickling down my thighs.

Rowan prowls toward me in all his naked glory, and I fall backward on the bed, my heart in my throat. He climbs over me, bringing his face to hover above mine, and grins. "You look worried."

"Very." I press my palms against his bare chest. "Can I just get another look at that?"

With a deep chuckle, he rolls over, taking me with him. I end up straddling his thighs while he folds his arm under his head like a pillow and watches me watching him.

My gaze drops lower. And lower. And...*fuck.*

I look down at myself. "How the hell is that going to fit?"

"Baby, we'll make it fit."

Tentatively, I drag my fingertips from the base to the head of his cock.

He twitches and lets out a hiss.

I do it again, mystified, terrified, and oh so turned on. My pussy clenches, begging to be filled, but there's something else I want to try first.

I slide down his thighs and bend until my mouth is lined up with his cock.

Rowan stops breathing.

Slowly, I take him into my mouth. I get a few inches past the head, but I have to handle the rest with my hands. There's so much of him, and it takes me a few moments to find the right pace.

He groans. "*Fuck* me."

I swirl my tongue around his tip before taking him back into my mouth, trying to go deeper.

A hand appears in my hair, guiding me. "God, you're such a good girl," he murmurs. "Taking me so well with that mouth."

His praise makes my heart beat faster.

He coils my hair around his fist and pulls me off him. "Come up here. I want to drown in your pussy while you're sucking on my cock."

We maneuver my body until my cunt is hovering above his face, and then he tugs me right down, like he really does want to drown in me.

His next groan vibrates right against my clit, and it makes me whimper.

We go at each other, his tongue deep inside me, his cock sliding in and out of my throat.

The only time he takes a break is to tell me, "You taste so fucking good, I could live off this cunt, Sunshine," and that one sentence does things to me.

I take him deeper. My eyes water, saliva drools out of my mouth, my makeup is likely ruined. I'm not really breathing, just panting around him, and I'm so turned on, I feel crazed.

When my pussy starts clenching, he pulls me off him, making to sit upright on his face, and cups my breasts with both of his hands, squeezing them hard. I plant my hands on his hard abs and grind against his face, riding my orgasm. I've never done this before, never been devoured like this, never taken my pleasure like it's owed to me, and God, it's magnificent.

Rowan drinks from me until the spasms inside me weaken, and then he rolls me off him and gets off the bed.

I'm about to protest when I realize he's grabbing a condom from the nightstand drawer. His gaze spears mine as he rips open the plastic foil. "I can't fucking wait to be inside of you," he says in a hoarse voice. "You're so ready, baby. Look at the mess you're making on the bed."

I don't need to look down to know he's right. Even after coming twice, everything down there tingles with anticipation.

A shiver of pleasure rolls down my spine as he grabs me by my ankles and tugs me to the edge of the bed. He positions himself between my thighs, his hands gripping my hips.

I make a strangled noise as he sinks into me with one smooth thrust. When he pulls out and sinks back into me again, my eyes roll to the back of my head. I've never felt so stretched, so full, so *right*.

A warm hand cups my cheek. "I want you to look at me while I fuck you. I want you to see exactly how crazy you make me."

My eyes stayed glued to his as he fucks me slowly at first, then fast and hard, and that's dangerous, because I can see how much he's enjoying this, and it makes me feel all kinds of wild.

This isn't how it ever was with Brett. This isn't how I imagined it could ever be.

A burst of confidence rushes through me, and I find my voice. "You feel so good."

His eyes flash with satisfaction. "Oh yeah?" He reaches between us, his thumb finding my clit. "And your pussy feels like heaven wrapped around me."

He leans forward, anchoring his palms on each side of my head, and starts going faster. His mouth finds my breast, his teeth tugging on the hard bud of one nipple before moving on to the other.

I slide my nails down his back, pulling him closer. I don't know how he's doing this, but I'm about to come again, and he's been holding back this whole time. I whimper when he changes the angle of his thrusts to just the right spot.

"Please," I beg, not knowing what it is I'm begging for. "Please."

"Fuck," he groans, his movement growing frantic. His eyes squeeze shut, and just as everything inside me breaks, he moans with his release.

I clutch him, my legs wrapped around his waist, my fingers digging into his biceps. All my coherent thoughts scatter to the edges of the universe. There's nothing but the roar of my blood in my ears, and the hard buzz of my climax in every inch of my body.

He collapses on top of me, keeping his weight on his forearms. His forehead is pressed against mine as he makes a few more shallow thrusts. "God, Sunshine. You're going to get me addicted to this," he says in a raw voice.

My heart pounds, and at the back of my mind, something starts to flicker in warning, but I'm still too incoherent to make out exactly what it is.

He pulls out of me and goes to the bathroom to get rid of the condom.

I stare at the ceiling, slowly becoming aware of the mess between my legs. "I should go get cleaned up," I mumble weakly once Rowan comes back to bed.

My legs feel like jelly as I stand up. I take a moment to orient myself, noticing the clothes scattered all over the floor. In my current state, there's a high chance I'm going to trip on something, so I bend down and pick up my dress and Rowan's jeans.

Something clatters loudly against the ground.

"What's this?" I ask, picking up the two silver objects that must have fallen out of his pocket.

Rowan quickly sits up in bed. "Let me see."

It takes me a moment to realize they're cufflinks—silver with two black diagonal stripes.

"I've never seen you wear these." I turn the cufflinks over in my palm. There's something engraved on the inside part. "NDL," I read aloud. "What does that stand for?" The letters are slightly faded but still visible. Could be the brand that made them, but the letters don't look like they were stamped at a factory. It's almost like the letters were etched by hand.

I toss them in my hand. For such little things, they're heavy.

"I have no idea," Rowan says.

I look back up at him and catch a strange expression on his face, but then it's gone. He smiles at me and opens his hand. The second I give the cufflinks back to him, he tosses them into the nightstand drawer by the bed, slams it shut, and gives me a shrug. "I got them for cheap at a secondhand store. They belonged to someone else."

"They look expensive. That's a good find." My voice trails off as he climbs off the bed and prowls toward me, his cock already swelling once again.

He backs me against a wall and presses his lips to my neck. "Let's save the cleanup for when we're done here."

"We're not done?"

He grins. "Not even close."

CHAPTER 30

BLAKE

When I wake up, there's a heavy arm slung over my waist, and a muscular thigh wedged between my legs.

My eyes fly open.

Oh. *Oh.*

Last night comes back to me in a series of R-rated snapshots.

I bite down on my bottom lip and carefully turn my head to steal a glance at Rowan's face.

He's still asleep, thank God.

There's an ache between my legs, my jaw is sore, and my lips feel puffy and raw.

Well, I know who's responsible for all that.

After we did it the first time, we did it again. And then once more. It's like we both couldn't get enough. The desire that had been building day after day of being in his presence, the desire I'd worked so hard to repress, had become a living, breathing thing, and it wouldn't rest until it got its fill. My body giving out finally ended things. He was still pulsating inside me, milking the last tremors of my orgasm out of me when my eyelids drifted shut, and I passed out.

It's not that I had doubts he'd be good in bed. I just hadn't anticipated that he'd blow my brain to smithereens in the process.

Then again, with the amount of practice he's had...

A sour taste appears in the back of my throat. *So much for not becoming another notch.*

I ease myself from under his arm. The clock on the nightstand says it's almost eight thirty, which means we're late getting to the office.

Should I wake him up?

I take another look at Rowan's sleeping face and decide against it. He's the boss. Surely he can come in late now and then.

And no one's going to miss me much. Pete came back halfway through last week, so the extra tasks Judy had been giving me to do dwindled to practically nothing.

Carefully, I slip out of bed, grab some clothes, and take them with me to the living room to get dressed.

Not far from the house, there's a trail that runs through the woods along a narrow creek. When I was younger, Mom would bring me there often. *"Fresh air and a long walk is the best way to sort out your thoughts,"* she used to say.

I have a lot of thoughts that are in desperate need of sorting, so that's where I head.

The drive doesn't take more than fifteen minutes despite the fresh layer of snow on the road. When I get out of the car, cold air bites at my face. I tuck my scarf into my coat and zip it all the way up before slipping on a pair of gloves I found in one of the pockets. My car's the only one in the lot, and there's something comforting about the absolute solitude.

I walk toward the entrance to the trail and turn right at the fork.

Here, the world seems hushed and contemplative. Silence reigns, disturbed only by the occasional chirp of a bird or the creak of a branch. I inhale crisp air and focus on the crunching of my shoes on the snow.

A sigh escapes past my lips.

What now? I wish I could lose myself in the current that swept me off my feet last night and simply see where it takes me. But that's a recipe for getting hurt, and after what happened with Brett, I'm not ready to risk that again.

I can keep my heart safe if I manage to get my head back on straight and remember one important thing—I can't fall for Rowan.

It's just that I wasn't expecting the very real connection between him and me. A physical connection—yes, but it's not only that. He's funny. He makes me laugh. He makes me feel like I'm someone who matters. But do I really think I'm the one who's going to get him to abandon his old ways when it comes to women?

No, I don't.

It doesn't matter that admitting that makes my chest sting. I need to be practical. Rational.

There's a big difference between sleeping with someone once and wanting to be in a relationship with them. Even if Rowan likes me more than his typical one-night stand, him saying that he might be interested in something more serious isn't something I'm able to trust.

That man isn't looking for commitment. He wasn't looking for it with all those women he slept with before me, and he's not going to be looking for it with me.

But what am I looking for?

I've never thought of myself as someone who could keep things casual with a man I'm interested in. I fall too hard, care too much.

But what if I could figure out how to not do that this time around?

After all, I'm still planning on leaving Darkwater Hollow. Rowan and I have an expiration date, and he's as aware of it as I am.

It might take anywhere from a few weeks to a few months to sell my place once I put it back on the market, but Nicole got me one offer, and I'm confident she'll be able to do it again.

Which means my plans didn't get demolished, just delayed.

I stop by the bank of the creek and peer down at the glassy surface. The once-flowing waters are now still beneath the ice. There's an orange leaf frozen there, suspended in space and time, just like me. But when the weather warms, it'll keep moving.

I've had plenty of time to think about my next steps since the fire, but the truth is, I've barely thought about them at all. When I try to imagine my future, all I find are muddled images.

It's time to change that.

Yes, I have to push myself to figure out what I'm going to do after I leave Darkwater Hollow. The only way I can get through the next few months without getting too wrapped up in that man is if I can stay focused on my future and remember that whatever is happening with Rowan and me is temporary.

I won't make the same mistake I made with Brett. I won't buy into a fantasy of something serious with Rowan only to have it ripped away from me. I know better.

I have to be ready to leave when the time's right. I'll be the one walking away.

By the time I make it back to the house, I'm calmer, more centered. I feel like I can let myself have this time with Rowan as long as I have my exit plan in place.

Inside the house, I go in search of him. I find him in the bedroom, still in bed.

Propping my shoulder against the doorframe, I can't resist soaking all of him in.

My eyes trace over the rounded shapes of his biceps, the washboard abs, the V that disappears beneath the sheet that's bunched around his hips... He's a masterpiece. A masterpiece I get to enjoy until I leave.

Shouldn't that be enough? I won't ruin it by longing for something more.

"Why are you up so early?"

I glance at his face. He's awake, looking at me with hooded, sleepy eyes.

I smile, hoping the pang of sadness in my chest isn't reflected on my face. "Early? It's past ten. Aren't you late for work?"

A lazy grin tugs on his lips. "I told Sam I'm not coming in today. Come back to bed, baby."

And so I do exactly that.

CHAPTER 31

NERO

I can't get enough of this woman.

In meetings, I'm hopeless. Our clients' words might as well be meaningless babble. Sandro pulls me aside and tells me to wake the fuck up because my new reputation as a committed boyfriend won't be enough to save us if I'm mentally checked out.

When I'm not in meetings, I'm with her.

On Wednesday, I get as far as the front door of the office before I press her against the building and kiss her until we're both panting.

On Thursday, I call her into my office for lunch, roll up my sleeves, and make a meal of her on top of my desk.

On Friday, I tell her we're going to look at some paint samples, but we only make it as far as my truck before I pull her onto my lap and fuck her in the parking lot.

Saturday is blissful. There are no distractions and no interruptions. We stay in my bed for most of the day, insatiable to the point of absurdity. We order pizza and feed it to each other, and in the evening, we curl up on the couch and watch her favorite movies.

Her laugh makes my chest ache. I want to record it and play it back over and over again. The thoughts running through my head feel like they belong to a different man, or maybe this is just what it feels like to fall for someone. You lose old parts of yourself to make room for newer, better ones.

When Sunday morning rolls around, I find myself thinking of reasonable excuses I could give Sandro for not showing up tomorrow. I'm a terrible partner, a terrible boss. I used to be so fucking responsible when I was running shit in New York, and now look at me. I'm a fucking mess.

Blake's snuggled against me, her cheek pressed to my chest, one leg and one arm thrown over my body.

She wakes up with a loud yawn. Her eyes meet mine, and a happy smile tugs on her lips. She props her chin on top of my hand and whispers, "Hi."

"Hey. Sleep well?"

Keeping our eyes locked, she presses a kiss to my chest. "Like a baby. You?"

I haven't had a single bad dream since we started sharing this bed. "I always get great sleep after a good bout of cardio."

She snickers, and a blush colors her cheeks.

She seems content. I was worried she'd pull away after that first night and let some of her old doubts about me creep in, but that hasn't happened.

Thank fucking God. I don't know what I'd do if she pushed me away again.

"So about tomorrow…"

She groans. "I'm going back to Frostbite tomorrow."

Fuck. I forgot about that. Has it really been two weeks?

I swallow my disappointment at not having her all to myself. "How you feel about that?"

"Awful."

That opening is all I need. "Then don't go."

"I need the money."

"I've got lots," I murmur. "You can have it. Let me take care of you."

Her brow arches. "I thought your business was in trouble just a few weeks ago."

"Back on track now," I say. It's not a lie—things really are turning around—but it's not my income from Handy Heroes that I was referring to. I still have access to my offshore accounts, and there's more than enough there. For me, Handy Heroes was never about the money. It was about staying busy and productive. Something to keep me from going insane. But now that I have Blake, I'm tempted to just give the entire business to Sandro to run so that I can spend more time with her.

If I tell him that, he'll never let me hear the end of it.

Blake sits up, settling in beside me with her legs crossed under the sheet. "I can't take your money."

"Why not?"

She gestures between us. "This is new. Very new. And we're both hopped up on endorphins. You're not thinking straight."

"Me giving you money is not a big decision."

She swallows, her crystal-clear blue eyes focused on my face. "I know you're just being sweet, but I don't want your money, Rowan. It's important for me to be able to take care of myself."

She's being rational about this, while I'm feeling all kinds of irrational. I don't want to slow down. I don't want to be cautious.

I want her to be mine, in every possible way, and I want to provide for her. Yes, because it'll make her life easier, but also because it makes *me* feel good.

"Is it because of Brett?" My knuckle traces the contour of her cheek. "Because he was your boyfriend and the guy who signed your paychecks?"

"Partially," she admits.

"It wouldn't be like that." I don't want to use my money to control her. I want to help her.

"I know, but—"

"I could give you the money up front, however much you need, no questions asked. It doesn't make sense for you to keep working at a place you hate if you don't have to."

"I'm sorry, but no." There's a resolute look in her eyes that tells me she won't change her mind. "Whenever my mom took money from my dad, that money was never truly hers. It came with strings attached. I know you're not like him, but I still can't accept it."

I concede. For now. "Okay. If this is your last day of freedom, we should do something fun."

The smile I adore is back. "What do you have in mind?"

"You pick."

She shrugs. "You're the fun one."

"That's true. How about that lesson I won at the auction?"

Her nose wrinkles. "I've seen inside all your cupboards. You don't have any of the stuff we'd need."

I know a place that has it all. "Why don't we do the class at Frostbite?"

"It's closed today. And even if it were open, Brett would never let me use it for this. He's a sore loser."

"Don't you have a way to get inside?"

She looks taken aback. "Are you saying you want to break in?"

"It's not breaking in if you have the key."

"Rowan, that's crazy."

I smirk. It's adorable how appalled she is. "It's not like we'll use up much liquor with just the two of us. What's the harm?"

Her eyes are wide. "What if he catches us? He'll be furious. He might call the cops."

"Sunshine, he won't catch us. C'mon, tell me about the cameras, and I'll devise a rock-solid plan."

"Uh-huh. What are you, some criminal mastermind?"

My laugh is a tinge too loud. "I'm full of secret talents."

She brings her thumb to her mouth and gnaws on her nail, thinking. "I don't know…"

"If we get caught, I'll take the blame," I offer.

She keeps chewing on her nail.

"Isn't there a tiny part of you that wants to do something to get back at him for being such a dick?" I poke at her ribs.

That gets through to her. I can see a small spark in her eyes. "He is a dick. And I mean…we wouldn't be hurting anyone."

"Not at all. Just a bit of harmless mischief."

She drags her palms over her face and sighs. "Okay. There's a camera at the back entrance. There's also one at the front, but it's been broken for the last few months. Break-ins aren't really a thing around here, so Brett hasn't been in a rush to fix it."

I grin. "Then we're golden."

As EXPECTED, the parking lot outside of Frostbite is abandoned when we get there in the midafternoon. We use Blake's key to get in through the front door and walk through the empty dining room all the way to the wooden bar at the back.

Whatever jitters Blake had on the drive over are gone now. She takes off her jacket, slings it over the bar, and goes around to the service side while I take one of the stools across from her.

"What should we start with?" I ask.

"Something easy. An old-fashioned." She glances at the shelves stacked with liquor. "I need a bourbon."

A minute later, she's got all the ingredients set out in front of me—a bottle of Buffalo Trace, angostura bitters, sugar, and a bit of water.

"You've never made one before, right?"

I shake my head. "When I feel like bourbon, I usually drink it straight."

"This will be just a little sweeter and more flavorful." She takes out two tall glasses from behind the bar and slides one my way. "First, we're going to mix the sugar, bitters, and water together in here."

She walks me through the right amounts, correcting me when I do it wrong. A smirk tugs at my lips. I like seeing her in her element.

"Okay, now measure out two ounces of bourbon and pour it over the ice. Then you'll need to stir everything together until it's chilled."

"You're a stern teacher," I comment. "It's kind of turning me on."

She gives me an amused look. "This is a serious lesson. Pay attention."

I laugh. "Oh, I'm paying attention."

When she's satisfied with my mixing, she gives me a strainer and a smaller glass with a single ice cube inside and tells me to strain the drink into it. She comes around the bar and climbs up on the stool beside me.

"What do you think?" she asks me after we take our first sip.

"Delicious. Let me try yours." She slides her glass my way and takes mine.

I watch as her lips press to the rim of my glass. Her drink is perfectly balanced. Mine's too heavy on the bitters.

"Not bad for a first try," she says. "Let's see how you handle the next recipe."

"I'm feeling a bit overwhelmed with all this new information. I think it's time for a break."

She laughs. "Whatever you want, Rowan. You paid five thousand dollars for this experience, remember?"

I stand, lift her to sit on top of the bar, and step between her legs. Sitting up there, she's nearly at my eye level. I wrap my palms around her thighs.

"Whatever I want? Dangerous words, Sunshine." Slowly, I undo the buttons of her shirt. She's wearing a light-blue bra underneath with a front clasp that's all too convenient to pop open.

When her tits spill out, I let out a low groan. My cock swells. So fucking perfect. I bend down to capture a nipple with my mouth. She moans and arches her back, pressing into me like she's eager for me to do the same to her other breast, but I pull away and pick up my drink.

She hisses when the cool glass makes contact with her skin. With hooded eyes, she looks mesmerized as she watches me roll the glass back and forth over her nipples until they harden into points. I tip the cocktail and let a little bit of the amber liquid run down her chest. I lean in and catch the rivulet with my tongue.

She lets out a moan. "Oh God."

"Tastes even better this way," I murmur and drag my tongue over her hot, wet flesh.

She buries her fingers in my hair, tugging me closer. If there's one thing I love about fucking her, it's when she shows me how needy she is for me, how badly she wants more.

I suck on her tits until they're pink and scattered with hickeys, and then I push her shirt and bra down her arms. Sliding my hands under her ass, I move her from the bar to one of the barstools.

It's the perfect height.

Her jeans come off, along with her panties, and then she's naked on the stool, her back against the bar, her legs spread open for me, just for me, in the restaurant owned by her ex.

She glances around, and a flush creeps up her neck, like she's only now realizing how fucking dirty and hot this is.

I take off my shirt and toss it on top of the bar. "Nervous?"

She bites down on her lip. "This is so wrong. What if we get caught?"

I reach behind her and take the elastic out of her hair, admiring how it settles around her face. She looks like a fucking angel. "We're not going to get caught, but I think a part of you likes the thrill." My hand slides over her chest and down to her pussy, finding it wet. "This part right here.

You're dripping, baby." I pinch her clit and then rub it in tight circles, making her pant and squirm. "Do you want my cock inside your little pussy? Is it weeping for me?"

Her head lolls to one side. "Yes. God, *yes*."

I keep rubbing her as I undo my jeans, pushing my boxers out of the way and letting my cock spring out. When I fish a condom out from my pocket, she glances at it. Swallows.

"Do you always use those?"

"Yeah."

Her teeth dig into her bottom lip. "I can't believe I'm saying this," she murmurs, "but I'm on birth control."

I press my forehead against hers. "You want me to fuck you raw?"

She swallows again and then nods.

A surge of satisfaction rushes through me at the fact that she trusts me enough to do this with me, followed by a wave of heat. "Fuck. I can't wait to fill up your sweet little cunt." I'm harder than ever, so fucking desperate for her.

She curls her hand around me and guides me to her swollen, throbbing pussy.

The moment I sink into her, a groan tumbles past my lips.

Wet. Warm. *Mine*.

I pull out slowly and then push back in, stuffing her full of me. Her legs wrap around my hips while I bracket her with my arms against the edge of the bar. It's hard to hold back, hard to keep it slow, but she doesn't want it slow. She pulls me into her, digging her heels into the backs of my thighs, and begs me, "Faster. Harder."

I fuck her like I'll never get a chance to fuck her again. We're no better than two animals in heat, scratching, tugging, pulling. My teeth dig into her full bottom lip, and she carves my back with her nails, her moans spilling into the air.

"So good," she whines. "God, that's so good."

And then I feel her clench around me. It's enough to make my balls tighten, enough to push me over the edge. I groan and dig my fingers into her hips. She milks my orgasm with her perfect cunt, her face slack with pleasure, her eyes hazy with lust.

The silence of the restaurant is broken only by our ragged, panting breaths, and I wrap my hands around her narrow waist and lift her to sit back on top of the bar.

"Spread your legs, baby," I say in a voice that's no more than a rasp. "I want to watch my cum drip out of you onto that bar."

She licks her lips and then parts her thighs, showing me what I want to see.

"Good girl."

Seeing me leaking out of her calls to the most primal part of me. I'm entranced. I can't look away. I drag my thumb over my bottom lip and imprint the image into my memory.

She tips her head back, watching me with hooded eyes. "Did you get your money's worth?"

I let out a rough breath. "Sunshine, it was by far the best money I've ever spent."

CHAPTER 32

BLAKE

My first day back to work, I walk into Frostbite with a dazed smile on my face and a delicious ache between my legs.

The restaurant is still closed, and the dining room is empty.

"Hello?" I call out. The schedule said Carly would be opening with me today.

My eyes widen when I spot the bottle of Buffalo Trace still out on the bar from last night. I hurry over and put it back on the shelf, ignoring the little thrill that goes through me.

Truth is, I was surprised to get the schedule in my inbox a few days ago. After what happened at the mayor's party, I wasn't sure if Brett would want me back here.

I don't really want to be back here, but money's money, and no matter what Rowan says, I'm not going to take his.

He offered last night, and then again this morning right as I was leaving.

His insistence is surprising, but I'm trying not to read into it. I already know he's generous, so his generosity isn't a reflection of how he feels about me. If he was serious about me, wouldn't he have asked me about my plans to leave by now?

He hasn't. Which means he accepts I'll be gone soon, and he's fine with it.

He just doesn't want me around Brett. I get it. Rowan is protective. But I'm a lot less nervous about being around Brett at work where there are plenty of other people to keep him in check.

Footsteps sound, and the door to the back swings open to reveal Frank.

My grin widens. I jog over to him and pull him into a hug.

He laughs at my enthusiasm. "Hey, darlin'. We missed you these past two weeks."

Two weeks? My God. It's hard to believe it's only been two weeks since the fire, and since I agreed to Rowan's offer. The offer itself seems like something that happened in a parallel universe.

"I missed you too. How's it been?"

"Busy. The boss's been in a mood the whole time you've been gone. We all guessed why after we heard about your new boyfriend." He adjusts the cap on his head. "Looks like Brett's finally going to have to come to terms with you movin' on."

"It's about time, isn't it?" I spent five months telling Brett it was over and that we weren't getting back together. His stubborn insistence that he wasn't going to give up on us never made much sense to me, but after the charity auction, I finally understand.

He thinks he's entitled to me. He felt insulted that I would leave him. *Me*, a nobody. He thought I'd forgive any and all of his mistakes if it meant keeping him as my boyfriend, but he underestimated me.

"I'm not saying I deserve the world, but I sure as hell deserve better than him."

Frank grins. "That's the spirit, darlin'. Let's get this place up and running. Carly should be here any minute." He claps me on the back before disappearing into the kitchen, leaving me standing alone in the empty dining room.

My phone buzzes in my pocket. *"Can't wait to see you tonight."*

My heart flutters at Rowan's message, and a familiar warmth spreads through my chest.

"Me too," I say and type back quickly before tucking my phone away.

As I start setting up the tables for the day, Carly breezes in with her usual energy, her blond hair pulled back into a ponytail. She gives me a quick hug before grabbing an apron.

"You look good," she says with a wink. "I have to admit, I was a bit worried about you when I heard you and Miller moved in together, but I know how it is sometimes. My sister's husband proposed to her after only a month. I have to admit, I'm a bit jealous you get to wake up beside that fine piece of ass."

I chuckle, feeling a blush creep up my neck. "It was definitely hard to get out of bed this morning."

She plugs her fingers into her ears. "I'm way too single to be hearing that. Don't torture me like that."

I laugh, and we fall into an easy rhythm of setting up the restaurant together. As we finish arranging the last table, the doors to Frostbite swing open, and Brett strides in with a scowl on his face. Carly shoots me a concerned look, but I give her a smile. I can handle Brett. I've handled much worse.

He walks up to me until he's no more than a foot away. "Blake."

"Morning."

"Can I talk to you?"

"Sure." If he's decided he's going to fire me after all, it's better he does it now instead of making me wonder about it all day.

I follow him into his office, and he shuts the door. It's messy in here, with paperwork in haphazard piles and his laptop at the center of the desk. Photographs of Brett's family line one of the bookshelves. One is of him, his brother, and his dad at a ribbon-cutting ceremony for the new library. Another one is of his whole family at their cottage.

And the third photo is of us.

My gut clenches.

Did he look at it while he was having sex with Melissa? Or did he at least have the decency to put it away when they did it in here?

My skin crawls. I don't want to spend a second longer here than I have to.

Brett stops by his desk and turns to me. "I want to apologize. I was out of line at the party. I'd been drinking and said things I shouldn't have."

For the first time, I notice the bags under his eyes, and there's a desperate edge to his voice, like he's finally starting to realize he fucked up.

Amazing that it took him this long.

My lips purse into a tight line. The old me would have accepted his apology, but this new version, the version that won't accept being hurt over and over again, refuses to make his life easy for him. So I just say, "Okay. Is there anything else?"

He touches his fingertips to his desk. "Have you thought about what I showed you at the Christmas party?"

Is he talking about that background check he did on Rowan? I briefly considered telling Rowan about it, but it was so ridiculous and out of pocket that I decided to spare him. He doesn't need to concern himself with Brett's tantrums. What does it matter if there's no record of him being in New York? I'm sure it's just some kind of a mistake, or there's a perfectly reasonable explanation. "Not at all."

His expression darkens. "Why are you so determined to turn a blind eye to—"

"To *what*, Brett? Trust me, I know Rowan isn't perfect. But unlike you, he's been unfailingly honest with me, and it's a lot easier to see past a person's flaws when they're honest."

He slams his fist against his desk. "Goddamn it, Blake. He hasn't been honest with you. That's what I'm trying to tell you!"

"You've got no real proof of anything. You're just trying to start shit."

"What proof do you need that he's a scumbag? Tell me, and I'll get it for you."

Doesn't Brett understand that the more he attacks Rowan, the more I feel the urge to defend him?

"That's not how things work. You don't get to accuse a person of a crime based on absolutely nothing and then try to find evidence that fits."

"Him and that friend of his appeared out of nowhere with enough cash to buy a business. And then he bought the Jackson house too. Don't you think it's suspicious? Where did he get all that money?"

I have no idea. But that's none of my business. "You're not the only person with money in the world, Brett."

"If things were going so well for him wherever he was before he came here, why move to Darkwater Hollow?"

"He wanted a fresh start. Who am I to judge that? If I'd managed to sell my house before it burned down, I would have done the same thing."

Surprise colors Brett's expression. "Hold on. You were trying to sell your house?"

Shit. Why did I say that? I didn't want him to know about my plans. What if he tells Uncle Lyle?

I wait for the panic to hit. It doesn't. What can Brett or my godfather do to me if Rowan's got my back?

I trust Rowan to protect me. The realization spreads warmth through my chest.

I meet Brett's gaze head-on and cross my arms. "Yes. I even had an offer. I wanted to leave this town so that I could start a life somewhere where I don't have to work with my ex-boyfriend."

Brett takes a step toward me. "What happened to the offer?"

"It was withdrawn when they heard about the fire."

"Did Rowan know about this?"

"About what?"

"The fact that you wanted to leave."

"Yes, he knew."

"Was he in your house in the days prior?"

My lungs expand on a disbelieving breath. Jesus Christ. Is he getting at what I think he's getting at? "Yes, he was. Drop the detective act, Brett. Tell me what you're really thinking."

"I'm thinking everything seems to be working out very conveniently for him as far as you're concerned."

I shake my head. "That's enough. You're out of your mind."

"I heard he's the one working on your house. It wouldn't take a huge stretch of imagination to see how your house burning down could benefit him in more ways than one."

Anger burns through me. "Rowan is fixing up my house for me at *no cost*. Not a damn penny. In the meantime, you cut my shifts when you knew I needed the money. Instead of genuinely trying to help me, you spent your time trying to find non-existent dirt on Rowan and coming up with unhinged theories."

Brett swipes his tongue over his teeth. "You're not listening to me."

"I don't *want* to listen to you. I don't believe a word you say, Brett. Not a *word*. Can I get back to work, or do you just want to fire me right now and put me out of my misery?"

His scowl makes another appearance, but there's a triumphant glint in his eyes I really don't like. "As long as you need this job, you have it."

I turn on my heel to leave, but as I walk out the door, I hear him call out to me. "Think about what I said, Blake."

CHAPTER 33

NERO

The moment Blake comes home from work on Monday, I'm on her. She barely makes it through the front door before my lips crash against hers.

What has she done to me? Now that I've had her, I only want her more. Did I really think at one point that she'd stop invading my thoughts after I managed to sleep with her?

I want to laugh at that past version of myself. What a fucking fool.

She's in my head all the time, tempting me, taunting me, teasing me, and she's got no idea.

I pull her out of her winter coat while she kicks off her boots. Her eyes dance with lust and warmth as I lift her up into my arms and carry her into the bedroom.

My hand slips under her shirt, then under her bra. When I swipe my thumb over her nipple, she moans and reaches for my belt.

"I've been thinking about this pussy all day," I mutter against her ear, cupping her over her jeans as she works my zipper open. "Are you wet for me, Sunshine? Did you daydream about my cock filling your tight little hole while you were working?" I slide my hand inside her jeans, past her panties, past her sopping-wet folds.

"Yes," she whines. Her small hand wraps around my erection, and she gives it a few careful strokes, but they're enough to wreck me. I work her jeans down over her hips just enough on her thighs to give me access to her panties, and then I toss her on the bed. I prop her ankles over my shoulder, hold her wrists above her head, and pull her panties aside, thrusting in with one smooth stroke.

We both groan at the same time. It feels like coming home.

She lets me hold her down, lets me use her. Her climax comes first, a rough, rippling thing that sucks me deeper and deeper until I can't fight it anymore.

"Fuck. Here it comes," I growl.

She's still pulsating, still milking me as I spurt inside her tight, wet cunt, and it's the kind of feeling that obliterates all thought. I don't know how long I pump into her. I'm barely aware of pulling out and collapsing on the bed beside her. Minutes blur. The only hint at the passage of time is our ragged breathing.

Eventually, we manage to get our jeans untangled from our limbs. She curls into me, wraps herself against my overheated body, and starts to trace my tattoos with the tips of her fingers.

"What does this one mean?" she asks softly.

I crack open my tired eyes and glance down at the spot she's pointing to on my ribs. It's a fish with a man's face coming out of its mouth.

It means silence. It means loyalty. It means brotherhood.

But I can't tell her that, and I don't want to lie to her, so I do what seems to be my new default. I try to distract her when I don't have an answer to give her.

I roll on top of her, making her yelp, and I slide down her body. She's so fucking soft everywhere. My tongue darts out to circle her nipple and then I move lower and lower until my lips touch her inner thigh, just inches away from her pussy.

My cum is dripping out of her, and the sight of it drives me insane. I push it back inside with my fingers and suck on her clit. Her hips buck against my face, she tugs on my hair, and then she explodes.

She doesn't ask about the tattoo again.

When her body finally goes limp, I tuck her under my arm and drag my knuckles over her spine. "How was your first day back to work?"

She buries her face against the side of my neck and groans. "Terrible."

"What happened?"

Her palm slides up my chest, and she props her chin on top of her hand, her eyes meeting mine. Worry swirls within.

"Brett insisted on talking to me. He's obsessed with you, Rowan. First, he apologized about what he said at the party, but then told me this nutso theory that you had something to do with the fire."

I keep my body still and my expression neutral, but can she feel the way my heart's suddenly picked up speed?

"Where did he get that idea?"

"He dug it up from the dark confines of his messed-up brain." Blake sighs. "I told him he's insane."

Insane or perhaps smarter than I thought he was. But it can't be more than a vague suspicion on his part. No one saw me. I made sure of it. It was the middle of the night, and there was no one around to see me picking Blake's lock and sneaking into her house.

"I just hope he doesn't go around causing trouble for you and your business." Her stunning eyes are warm and tinged with concern. "I know he's just making things up, but I worry that others might believe him. The night of the mayor's party, he showed me a background check. New York wasn't listed on it, and so he tried to make it seem like that was proof you lied about coming from there."

A cold, hard stone appears in the pit of my belly. What the fuck? Brett's digging into my past?

My anger swells. I should give him a warning, the kind he won't be able to ignore. A conversation on the outskirts of the town should do it.

Then I remember myself.

That's what Nero would have done, but Rowan doesn't operate like that. Brett doesn't have anything real. He has no idea who I am. He's fishing, and he won't find anything about Rowan Miller, so all I have to do is simply let him waste his time.

"Rowan?" Blake asks softly. "You look upset."

"I'm not. I'm just thinking about what you've said." I let out a low breath. "He can run as many background checks on me as he wants. I've got nothing to hide. And if my clients believe some stupid rumor that's not backed up by any evidence, they're not the kind of clients I want to have."

She watches me, concern flashing in her eyes. "Are you sure?"

"I'm sure. But I don't like that you have to deal with him, Sunshine."

"I know. But I managed to do it for months. I can do it for a few more until I get everything sorted with the house."

My heart stills. "A few more months? And then what?"

She blinks at me. "Once the house is repaired, I'm going to try selling it again. And when I do..." She shrugs. "I'll leave."

I sit up. "Hold on a sec."

Whatever she sees in my eyes makes her get off the bed and pull on her robe. "Why do you look so surprised? That's always been the plan."

"That was before. This is after." She can't possibly still think about leaving. I mean, I know we haven't talked about it yet, but I thought it was obvious she'd stay given what's been happening with us.

"After what?"

"After *us*. I thought this was going well," I say, doing my best to ignore my rising panic.

She folds her lips over her teeth. "It is going well. But we both know it's not forever."

"We do?"

Her expression turns forlorn. "You'll get bored of me eventually, and maybe it makes me selfish to want to leave before that happens, but that's what I want. I don't want to wait for the day when you'll lose interest."

Anger surges through me. She doesn't get it. She doesn't see how I've fallen for her. The words have been there, on the tip of my tongue, but I've held them back because I wanted to be sure she was right there with me. And now I see that I was right to do so, because we're clearly on two different pages when it comes to us. "So all this time, you haven't been giving us a real chance?"

She exhales. "Rowan, I like you. A lot. But you said yourself that you're not interested in anything serious."

"I wasn't talking about you," I growl. "I thought I made it clear you're different, Blake."

"And I want to believe you, but I just can't. The last time I believed something that seemed too good to be real, I got burned." There's a sheen to her eyes now. "I can't go through that again." She turns and walks out of the bedroom.

I drag my palms over my face.

God, I'd love to kill Brett. This is all his handiwork. He hurt her so badly that she doesn't want to risk giving herself to anyone again.

But I'm not him. I want her, and I'd never hurt her.

Words won't be enough to convince her to stay. I have to show her that I mean it.

How? When the repairs to her house are finished, she'll put it back up on the market. I could delay the repair work, but I don't want to lie to her any more than I already have.

So I have a month, maybe two.

I need to figure something out.

THE NEXT DAY, after we wrap up our site visits, I drag Sandro to Riverbend Mall. It's the closest shopping center around here, and since Christmas is in just over a week, it's bursting with decorations. We walk by a guy in a Santa suit sitting by a gingerbread house and a long line of kids eager for a photo.

"What are we doing here again?" Sandro asks, glancing around the place.

"I need a Christmas gift for Blake." It's not much, but it's a start. If I've got somewhere between six and eight weeks to prove to her I'm boyfriend material, I'm going to take every opportunity I have to show her that I'm serious about her.

I have to get her something meaningful. Something that'll show her I've been paying attention and not just trying to get her into bed with me. This isn't a fucking fling. I'm not going to get bored of her.

Just the memory of her words sends a rush of annoyance through me. She really doesn't get it. I guess I can't blame her. She has no idea what my state of mind was before she waltzed into my life and changed everything. She has no idea how she's saved me.

"What does she like?" Sandro asks.

"Books. I've already thought about replacing the ones she lost in the fire, but she has nowhere to put them at the moment. I also don't have a list of the ones she had. If I ask, it won't be a surprise, and I want this to be a surprise."

"I took a picture when we came over."

I turn to look at Sandro. "You took a picture of the books?"

"Yeah. She had them all organized by color, I thought it looked neat." He fishes his phone out of his pocket and pulls up the image.

I squint. "The spines are a bit hard to make out."

Sandro zooms in on the photo. "Yeah. But maybe if you take it to a bookstore they can help you find the right ones."

"Send it to me."

I'm about to start searching for the closest bookstore, one of those big ones that could help me find even the special editions Blake was so passionate about, but then my steps halt.

Hold on. What's *that*?

I stop in front of an empty storefront. There's a sign hanging in the glass window saying it's for lease. It's a small shop with intricate metalwork adorning the window, a heavy wooden door, and checkerboard tile on the floor.

I step up to the glass and peer deeper inside. Shelves line the walls. It takes me a moment to process what I'm seeing.

When I do, a grin spreads over my face. "Forget about the books. This is better."

Sandro steps up beside me. "Huh?"

"This storefront. It's perfect. Do you remember what Blake told us when we came over for Thanksgiving? She's always dreamed of opening her own bookstore." And she's mentioned it to me a few times since then. Fuck, she's going to lose it. There's no way she'll want to leave Darkwater Hollow after I get her this. She can quit her job at Frostbite and start her own business right here.

"Dude, you started dating her less than a month ago." Sandro sounds aghast. "Fake dating, to be clear. I'm still not totally sure when it became real. Get her some heart-shaped earrings or something."

I turn to Sandro and grab his shoulders. When he sees the wide grin on my face, he pales. I probably look like a lunatic. "I'm getting her that store. I'll lease it for her. You're going to contact the mall's leasing office and get an agreement drafted."

"Wait, hold on—"

"This just became your top priority."

He groans and shrugs my hands off him. "I'm not sure what's worse, you burning down her house to get her to move in with you, or this. What the hell is it about this girl that makes you do this insane shit?"

"I like her, all right?"

"So it's getting serious?"

"More serious than anything I've ever had before."

313

Sandro throws his hands up and walks in a circle before coming back to me. "Tell me you haven't spilled your secrets to her."

His tone dampens my spirits. "I haven't, damn it."

"So what if this keeps getting more and more serious? Are you going to keep lying to her indefinitely?"

"If that's what I have to do."

His eyes narrow. "Does it bother you that she'll never know who she's really dating?"

"If she knew who I was, she wouldn't be dating me, so no. It doesn't bother me."

It's only after I say it that I realize it's a lie. It does bother me. It bothers me that she will never know my past, the past that made me who I am. The family, the friends, the enemies. The good times and the bad.

It shouldn't, because I know revealing the truth to her would end us, but there's a twinge of sadness in my chest at realizing she'll never truly understand me. She'll never see the darkness that's fueled me for so long, the darkness that I don't think will ever fully go away.

Even now that I have her, I still feel it pulsing deep inside my ribcage. Buried but not completely extinguished.

I don't want any secrets between us, but there's no way around it.

If the only way I can keep her is by keeping secrets, then that is my cross to bear.

I lift my gaze to Sandro. He's watching me with troubled eyes. "How do you know she wouldn't date you if she found out?"

"Her dad was in a gang. She hated him and everyone like him. She despises men who are criminals."

I can tell he doesn't miss the note of longing that slips into my tone. "You still miss it? The life we left behind?"

"Sometimes. Not as much anymore. Not since Blake."

Some tension disappears from his shoulders. "I see."

"Do you miss it?"

He gives me a sad smile. "Parts of it, sure. The thrill of breaking rules and getting away with it. The respect that everyone gave me when I said who I worked for. We had fun, didn't we?"

I think back to Rafe's wedding. To his wife's birthday party —the last one I attended. To the nights when we pulled off impossible heists or negotiated deals that made us millions. "Yeah, we did."

He runs his long fingers through his curly hair. "But I don't mind going straight. At least I'm sure I'll live a hell of a lot longer now than I would have if I'd stayed in New York. I met a girl the other day, you know?"

That's big news. "Who?"

He grins. "She's from Kansas City. Found her on one of the dating apps. Her name's Kelly, and we kinda hit it off right away. We talked, and she's the kind of person who skips right over the small talk and gets to the deep stuff, you know?"

"Sure."

"Well, she was talking about how she wants a family one day. A girl and a boy. And it got me thinking that out here, my future wife won't have to worry every day about whether I will or won't come home from work in one piece. I won't have to wonder if someone's put out a hit on my family. It's not as exciting, but it's good in its own way, you know?"

I swipe my hand over my beard. "Yeah, I see your point. You think that's enough for you?"

He lets out a breath. "I'm not sure. But I think so."

I'm not sure either.

We let the silence sit for a long moment. Then Sandro takes out his phone and snaps a picture of the phone number under the For Lease sign. "I'll give them a call."

CHAPTER 34

NERO

It's Blake's day off, and we're on the couch watching a movie.

Or at least we were some time ago, but it's been a while since either of us looked at the TV.

The couch groans beneath us. My body covers hers, but I'm careful not to put my full weight on her.

I wrap my palm around her breast and pinch a nipple. "You make me fucking crazy."

Her back arches as she presses her tit into my hand. It's a good thing she didn't have any plans today, because after having her work evening shifts for five days straight, I'm not planning on sharing her with anyone.

"Hellooooo... Fuck."

My gaze snaps up.

Blake yelps and cranes her neck to look over the sofa.

Sandro. He's standing at the threshold of the living room, his face beet red. He spins around. "Sorry! The front door was unlocked."

With a growl, I grab my discarded shirt off the back of the couch and drape it over Blake. He better not have seen anything he wasn't supposed to, or this is going to be an unpleasant conversation. "Just because the door's unlocked doesn't mean you can walk in here without knocking."

"Sorry, sorry, sorry! I had something urgent to talk to you about," Sandro says, his back still to us.

I get off Blake, help her put on the T-shirt she's still wrestling with, and pick up my jeans. "Go wait outside while we get dressed."

There's a beat. "It's snowing outside."

My jaw clenches with irritation. "Sam, get out!"

Sandro sighs audibly and shuffles out of the room with another mumbled apology.

Blake looks mortified, but when she sees the look on my face, she lets out a hysterical giggle.

I shake my head. "It's not funny."

"It's kind of funny. He looked like he'd burst a blood vessel."

"I don't like the idea of another man's eyes on you."

Her cheeks turn even redder than they already are. She gets on her tiptoes to give me a kiss. "I don't think he saw anything except for his life flashing in front of his eyes when he heard the sound you made."

That's probably true, given I was hovering above her. Still, I feel a caveman-like urge to tell Sandro off for waltzing in on us like that.

"Go talk to him. It's cold out. Do you think everything is okay?"

I nod. "Yeah. He's just working on an important project for me." I reach over and smooth her hair out of her face. "Don't go far. I'll be right back."

I step out onto the porch and cast my gaze at Sandro, who's sulking in a corner.

"Don't do that again," I snap.

"I didn't see anything."

"There'd be consequences if you had. What was so urgent that you're here without giving me a call?"

"I called. You didn't pick up. Now I know why." He leans against the wooden railing that wraps around the porch and crosses his arms over his chest. "So the leasing agent refused to hand over the keys."

I frown. "I thought we already signed the documents and sent him the deposit."

"We did." Sandro pats his jacket. "I've got our copy of the lease right here. We're supposed to take possession today."

"Then what the fuck?"

"I don't know. He said management told him not to give us the keys."

"Who's management?"

"He didn't say, but a quick Google search revealed that the leasing company is owned by Lewis & Co."

"The mayor's company?"

Sandro nods. "If I had to guess, I'd put money on your girl-friend's ex having something to do with it."

You've got to be kidding me.

"They have no legal right to stop us from taking possession."

"Yeah, so we can sue. But it'll take a while to get sorted, because the courts are closed for the holiday now. We're going to have to wait until January."

January? I don't have until January. This is supposed to be Blake's Christmas present.

A vacuum of anger opens up inside me. I'm so fucking tired of that prick causing Blake and me problems. I've tried to be patient. I've tried to take the high road. But with some men, there's only one way to make them learn.

I have to deal with that prick. There's no way around it anymore.

And yeah, that's Nero talking. The Nero I promised I'd keep leashed. But I'm going to let him out just this once.

"We're not suing shit. We're going to go talk to him and do this the old-fashioned way."

Sandro's eyes widen. "What is that supposed to—"

I leave him on the porch and go inside to grab my jacket.

"Blake, I'll be back in an hour," I call out. "Got to take care of something with Sam."

Her voice comes from the bedroom. "Okay! See you soon."

When I come back out, Sandro's wearing a determined expression on his face, like he's planning on talking me out of this. "Hold on—"

I cross the front lawn to my truck and unlock it. The gun inside the glove compartment is freezing to the touch. I slip it behind my waistband and wince at the cold, but something inside my chest clicks into place, like a missing puzzle piece.

A hand clenches my shoulder. "Dude. Can you slow down for a second?"

I turn around and face Sandro.

"I'm going to deal with this once and for all. You can come with me, or you can stay here. Your choice."

Frostbite's parking lot is busy enough, but it takes me only seconds to spot a familiar red BMW.

Sandro drove us here in his car. I reach to open the passenger door so I can get out, but he clicks the lock into place.

"We need to talk about this." His knee is bouncing.

I open my palm. "You got the lease?"

"Fuck the lease. You've got a gun tucked in your waistband, and I want to know what the hell you're planning on doing in there."

"I told you to stay home if you didn't want to be here for this."

"I want to be here for this, but what exactly is *this*?"

"This fucker's getting out of hand," I growl. "It's one thing to be a raging idiot, it's another to fuck us on a deal. I'm going to make it clear his actions have consequences."

"You can't kill him."

"I'm not going to kill him." But I am going to scare him into leaving Blake and me the fuck alone. "Promise."

Sandro seems reluctantly satisfied with that. He reaches into his jacket and takes out the lease. "Here," he mutters.

"Hold onto it for me for a while longer. You've got another copy somewhere?"

"Yeah. It's digitally signed."

"Good. Watch and learn."

We get out of the car. I hold the large wooden door open for a woman with a stroller as she comes out of the restaurant, and then we go inside.

The hostess looks familiar, but I don't remember her name until I spot it on the name tag. "Hey, Carly. Your boss around today?"

She smiles. "Sure. He's in his office."

"Got a question for him, mind showing me to it?"

"No problem, follow me."

She leads us through the restaurant and to the back before stopping in front of a door. "This is it."

"Thanks." I give her a ten-dollar bill. She shoots me a smile before going back out front.

My closed fist taps on the door. Once. Twice.

While I wait for Brett, I adjust my sleeves, tugging them back in place. It's been a fucking nightmare finding clothes that fit me around here, but this jacket is perfect. Smooth, supple leather, well-sewn lining, and a layer of wool inside that keeps me warm even when it drops below freezing.

There's a shuffling sound on the other side of the door, and then the lock clicks open.

I smile. "How you doing, Brett?"

Blake's ex doesn't look too surprised to see us, but he still asks, "What are you doing here?"

"Mind if we chat inside?" I don't give him a chance to answer before I press in on him, forcing him backward into his office.

He stumbles, his gaze narrowing. "What the fuck?"

"I should be asking you that question. Where are the keys to the storefront Sam and I leased yesterday?"

"I've got no idea what you're talking about."

"Don't you?" My smile grows wider. "No problem. I'll refresh your memory."

I grab him by the neck and slam him against the wall. He wheezes, clawing at my arm.

I glance over my shoulder. "Sam, come here."

Sandro appears by my side, his lips pressed into a thin line.

"Give me our signed lease, please."

Sandro slaps it into my open palm. I shake it until the papers unfold and show it to Brett. "This look familiar?"

I loosen my grip just enough for him to answer.

"Let go of me!" His nails drag against the leather.

I glance down. Fuck, he left a scratch.

"This is my favorite jacket," I warn. "Get your fucking hands off it or you might make me mad."

I guess there's a brain cell or two left in his thick head, because he does as he's told.

"Good boy."

I move my palm from his neck to his jaw and force it open. Then I show him the lease again. "You sure you haven't seen this before?"

The idiot shakes his head.

"Wrong answer." His eyes bulge as I ball up the papers in my palm and shove them into his mouth. "You owe us the fucking key." I push it farther and farther past his teeth until he's gagging on the paper, and then just as he looks like he's about to throw up, I shove him to the ground.

He coughs for a good minute. When he finally catches his breath, he lifts his gaze to me from where he's huddled on the floor, and it's pure, unadulterated hatred. "Fuck you. The agent shouldn't have signed that. I refuse to have my family's company do business with you."

"Does your father even know you pulled this move? Or is this you showing initiative?"

When he doesn't answer, I click my tongue. "I think if I went to your daddy and told him all about how I'm planning to sue your company for this, he'd fold pretty fucking fast." I tip my head sideways. "But where's the fun in that?"

Fear zigzags across his face before he can mask it. "Get out."

"Nah, don't think I will." I grab him by his shirt and throw him up against the wall.

And then I reach behind me, take out my gun, and press it right below his chin.

Sandro, who's been staying out of this for now, sucks in a harsh breath behind me. "Rowan."

Brett stills, his eyes growing wide. "What do you think you're—"

I click off the safety. "Shut the fuck up."

His jaw snaps shut. It looks like he's finally getting the message.

"I want the keys, right now. Do you understand? Nod once if you do."

A second passes before he does.

"Does the leasing agent have them, or do you?"

A flick of his eyes toward his desk tells me the answer.

"Sam, check his desk. Ought to be there."

A moment later, I hear Sandro rummaging through the desk drawers.

"Got 'em," he calls out.

Brett mutters a curse, but I press my gun harder against his chin to shut him up.

"Now, I want you to listen to me very carefully. You're going to stop talking to Blake unless it's required for her job. No more private office conversations. No more begging or apologies. She's mine, Brett. *Mine*. And the sooner you accept that and move on, the better things will go for you."

Impotent fury simmers inside his eyes. "Who the hell are you?"

"If you don't leave her alone, I promise you that I'll be your worst nightmare."

"Rowan, let's go," Sandro mutters.

I take a step from Brett and slide my gun back under my jacket. "Are we clear?"

"Clear," Brett spits.

I give him a vicious grin. "Nice talking to you."

"I DON'T THINK that was smart."

I adjust my sleeves as Frostbite disappears in the rearview mirror. "There's a time for diplomacy, and there's a time for force."

"You didn't have to pull out your gun."

"I didn't want to leave any ambiguity. I want him to know I'm serious."

Sandro runs his fingers through his hair. "I'm just now starting to feel settled in here. Business is good. You've got your girl. Let's not fuck it all up."

"We won't fuck it up."

"You're grinning."

He's right. I'm in a great mood. I feel like myself, my old self, for the first time since we got here.

"We're not in New York anymore," Sandro grumbles, as if I need a reminder.

Annoyance inches along my skin. Sandro's nothing but a buzzkill. It's bad enough I have to act like a fucking choirboy most of the time, but this was one fucking opportunity to flex an old muscle, and he won't even let me enjoy it.

"I'm well aware."

He glances at me, probably picking up on the change in my tone. That knee of his starts bouncing again. "I'm just making sure."

I tamp down my frustration. Sandro's just trying to watch out for me the way he promised Rafe he would.

"Give me the keys," I tell Sandro.

He hands them over. The keys to the storefront. Blake's future bookshop.

And the keys to my future here.

A future where maybe one day I'll be able to let go of my past.

CHAPTER 35

NERO

By the time Sandro drops me off at the house, I'm still buzzing.

I can't believe how fucking good that felt—like slipping into a pair of perfectly broken-in leather shoes.

People who've lived their lives following the arbitrary rules society imposes on them have no idea how good it feels to say *fuck the rules*. They're too scared to go against the grain. Too scared to risk being rejected by those around them.

But what they don't understand is that as long as they conform, they will never know true power. It comes from being your own fucking person and doing whatever the fuck you want.

Back at Frostbite, that power pulsed through me, but it's already fading.

When I was in New York, I felt it rushing through my veins all the damn time. It's stronger than any drug you can possibly imagine.

I stop on the porch, press my palms against the railing, and look out at the neighborhood. I can hear the distant sound of a dog barking, a car driving by, the soft rustle of some animal moving through the trees behind the house. It's a familiar scene, one that I was starting to get used to. But now, after tasting that freedom, that raw power, everything else seems dull and lifeless.

I close my eyes and give my head a shake, trying to rid myself of that insatiable feeling.

Just once. That's what I promised myself. I'd let Nero out *just once*.

Yes, it felt exhilarating to slip into old habits, but I can't be that guy here if I want to keep Blake.

And I want that more than anything. Even more than the thrill of my old life.

I push away from the railing and walk across the porch toward the front door.

As soon as I step inside, I call Blake's name. No answer.

I see her outside through the living room window. She's bundled up in her coat, getting something from the shed on the edge of her backyard.

The gun's still tucked inside my waistband, pressed against my back, and I need to put it away before she comes inside.

I'm about to go back out to put it back in the car, but something stops me. Better to keep it closer in case anything happens. Brett's not going to retaliate, he's too much of a pussy for that, but there's no harm in being cautious.

Upstairs, in one of the unfinished bedrooms, there's a built-in closet that should do the trick. I jiggle the drawer, trying to open it, but the damn thing's stuck.

Maybe it's a sign I should just put the gun back in the car.

"Rowan?"

I whip around and find Blake standing at the threshold of the room still in her winter coat and boots.

My stomach drops. "Jesus, you scared me."

"I just came in to get some scissors, but then I heard noise coming from up here and thought I'd take a look..." Her eyes widen. "Why do you have a gun?"

Fuck.

Great. This is just fucking great. I say the first explanation that comes to mind. "I thought I'd get one as a precaution in case your godfather starts coming by more often."

"Uncle Lyle?" A notch appears between her brows. "I haven't seen him since he came by here that one day."

I shift on my feet. "I know, but I've been thinking about it, and you were right. He's dangerous, and I shouldn't have been so cavalier about it. I don't want to be in a situation where I can't defend you."

A flicker of apprehension appears in her gaze. She doesn't like my answer.

I hold my breath, waiting for her to call me out on my lie. But after a long moment, her expression softens, and she gives me a small nod.

"Okay, yeah, you're right. We should be prepared."

I let out a silent breath of relief and turn back to the drawer. A few hard tugs finally get it to open up. I stash the gun away and close it firmly.

Blake watches me the entire time, her bottom lip between her teeth.

"It's going to stay right here, okay? If anything happens while you're home alone, you'll know where to find it."

She shakes her head. "I don't want to touch that. I wouldn't know how to use it anyway." A line appears between her brows. "Do you?"

Taking a few steps closer, I stop in front of her. "I took a class a long time ago. But I don't want you to worry. It's just a precaution."

Blake studies me, her eyes searching mine. Does she suspect I'm lying? Fuck, I should have been more careful. I'm still amped up from confronting Brett.

I hold my breath, waiting for her next move, praying she doesn't push further. After what feels like an eternity, her tense posture relaxes. She closes the space between us and wraps her arms around my waist, pressing her cheek against my chest.

"Okay. I trust your judgment. Just...be careful, okay?"

I smooth my palm down her back. "Of course."

"Did you just buy it at the store? Is that why you left?"

"Yeah. After the errand I had to run with Sam."

She pulls back to look at me. "What did he need to talk to you about?"

"Just a client being difficult."

"You know, I never asked how the two of you met."

"Sam and I?" Fuck, what was the story Sandro and I came up with?

"You said you worked together in Vegas. Is that where you met?" Her perceptive eyes scan over me, and I know she's still spooked by that gun.

"Yeah, we did. We met at work, at that construction company I told you about. We were on a project together, and we got along. He's a good kid. Smart. Hard-working. I could see us going into business together, and so we did."

"Does he have any family?"

"No. Just him."

"What happened to them?"

"I don't know. He doesn't like to talk about it, but you could ask if you're curious."

She shakes her head. "I wouldn't want to pry. Trust me, I get not wanting to talk about family. I hate telling people about my dad. I remember one time, he came to pick me up from a birthday party, and he showed up in his leathers with a gun strapped to his belt. Why would he do that? It was a nine-year-old's party, for God's sake. But he liked to show off. To intimidate people just for the sake of it."

An uncomfortable shiver slides down my spine.

Her hands find mine. "Seeing that gun... I guess it brought back a lot of bad memories."

"I'm sorry."

"You don't need to apologize. But I want you to know where my mind jumped to when I saw it. Why it freaked me out so much. I know it's not fair to compare you to my dad when you're nothing like him. You're generous and kind and good, even if you try to pretend otherwise on occasion." Blake gives me a wry smile.

Good?

There isn't a good bone in my body.

But Blake's oblivious to what's running through my head. "We should invite Sam over for Christmas. He's been amazing with getting the renovation of my place going. I don't want him to spend the holiday alone."

I squeeze her hands. "Good idea, Sunshine. Although judging by today, he probably already plans on just showing up."

She laughs softly and goes up on her tiptoes to give me a kiss.

I've never seen eyes as blue as hers. They calm me. They make me feel like all of this might just work out after all.

They also remind me that she deserves someone so much fucking better than me.

A man she doesn't even know.

A man who's definitely not good enough to ever let her go.

CHAPTER 36

BLAKE

Christmas Eve.

Sam, Rowan, and I are in the kitchen working on a dinner that's shaping up to be a real Italian feast.

Rowan's on pasta duty, stirring lamb ragù in a giant stainless steel pot. Sam's arranging the cheese and cold cuts he got from some specialty store in Kansas City on a wooden board and layering fresh mozzarella on top of the caprese salad. I've been put in charge of the garlic bread.

Christmas tunes filter in from the speaker in the living room. We even got a tree this morning and hung up some of the old decorations I found in my shed the other day.

I slice the baguette, careful not to cut all the way through, and spread a generous mixture of butter, garlic, and herbs in between each slice. I pop it into the oven to bake, and the warm scent of garlic fills the kitchen, mingling with the fragrant aroma of Rowan's lamb ragù simmering on the stove.

"More wine?" Sam asks, lifting one of the bottles of red he brought over.

"Sure."

He refills my glass and then tops off his own. "How's it been this week at work?"

"Not bad, actually. Brett's been out the past couple of days, which helps a lot." Carly told me he's visiting someone in Kansas City. He has a bunch of friends there from his college days. I'm not looking forward to seeing him when I go back to work the day after Christmas.

"I went over to take a look at the house this morning. Your guys are making good progress."

Sam smiles. "I wanted them to get as much done as they could before the holidays."

I place my hand on his arm, overcome with gratefulness. "Thank you. I really appreciate everything you and Rowan are doing for me."

Some color appears on Sam's cheeks. "Of course. Happy to help."

The tiramisu Rowan and I prepared yesterday is sitting in the fridge, so I take it out and bring it out to the new dining table in the living room. I've gotten used to eating on the sofa with him, but with Sam coming over, we've had to upgrade.

We? Careful.

I swallow, some apprehension appearing low inside my belly. There is no *we*. There's Rowan, and there's me. Over the last week, it's been getting harder and harder to remember that.

Outside the window, snow is falling softly, coating the world in a blanket of white. The lights on the Christmas tree twinkle, casting a warm glow over the living room.

It's almost too perfect. I don't think I've ever had a Christmas like this. Mom did her best, but it was the one holiday Dad never skipped, and I was always on pins and needles whenever he was around.

And the last few years with just my mom were difficult. I couldn't help but wonder if every year was the last one we'd celebrate together, and I'd usually be overcome with anger at Maxton for not coming again. We'd finish dinner, and I'd help her get into bed, and then all I used to want to do was pass out and forget about the day.

But right now, I don't want this day to ever end.

Truthfully, I don't want *any* of this to end.

Which means my control is slipping. How much longer can I keep denying what's brewing between Rowan and I?

God. This isn't a story I can stop by simply closing the book. This is my life, and if I don't rein in my feelings for Rowan, I'm setting myself up to get hurt.

I hear the guys laughing in the kitchen. A moment later, Rowan comes out with the ragù and puts it on the cork trivet in the middle of the table.

I walk over and peek inside the pot. "Smells incredible."

Rowan grins, looking pleased at the compliment. "It better be. It's been cooking for hours. Hope you guys are hungry."

"Fuck!"

Sam's shout makes Rowan and me rush back to the kitchen. We find him hopping from one foot to the other, wrestling with his wet shirt.

"What happened?" Rowan asks.

"The pasta water went all over me when I went to dump it out."

I gasp. "That water was boiling. Here, let me help you. Rowan, can you bring him something to wear?"

Rowan nods and leaves the kitchen. I quickly turn off the stove and grab a towel to help him dry off the scalding water.

"Damn, that looks like it hurts," I say, wincing as I see the red spreading across Sam's chest and arms.

He chuckles, though it's more of a grimace. "Should have been more careful. I don't spend much time in the kitchen at home."

I wet the towel with cold water and gently dab at the reddened patches on his chest. Sam inhales sharply. He's also got a few tattoos on his torso. Not as many as Rowan, but—

Wait, that looks familiar. It's a fish with a man's face coming out of its mouth.

I move the wet towel out of the way.

"That tattoo..." I frown. "Rowan has the same one."

Sam freezes.

Rowan returns and hands a clean shirt to Sam, who hastily puts it on, his eyes darting back to me. "Uh, yeah, he does."

"What are you talking about?" Rowan asks.

I gesture at Sam's chest. "Your matching tattoos."

A flicker of unease crosses Rowan's features. "What about them?"

I give him a befuddled look. Isn't it obvious I want to know the story? "How come you got them?"

They exchange a quick look, and there's something uneasy about it. "It's nothing, really," Sam says. "Just something we got together a while back."

Rowan rubs the back of his head. "It's kind of embarrassing."

"Yeah. We were drunk. Like really drunk."

I plant my hands on my hips, getting a weird vibe from both of them. "And you got a tattoo of a strange *fish*? Why?"

Rowan drags his tongue over his teeth. "It's stupid."

"Why are you being so cagey? I mean, what could possibly be so embarrassing—"

"We got them when we decided to leave Las Vegas," Rowan says. "The fish symbolizes our rebirth. The beginning of a new life. It's sappy, okay? But we wanted to do something to commemorate our decision to work on our own business together."

I frown. So leaving Vegas was a big deal for them, but Rowan's always been tight-lipped about what it was that caused them to leave. Why the secrecy?

"Why did you two decide to leave?"

Rowan drags his palm over his chin. There's something tense about his posture, something weird about this whole conversation, but I can't quite put a finger on it. Are they really that embarrassed by the tattoos, or is there more to it?

Brett's warnings come to mind, but I shove them away, refusing to let that asshole poison my thoughts about Rowan.

In fact, he's probably why I'm suddenly feeling so on edge. He managed to plant a tiny seed of doubt in my head, despite me knowing he's full of shit.

No. I'm not going to let a bad man manipulate my thoughts about a good man like Rowan. I just need to give Rowan a chance to explain.

"The owner of the company fucked up on a project, but he put the blame on the two of us. We might have gotten... arrested if we stuck around."

Shock crackles through me. "What?"

"He said we were stealing from the business. Taking materials from the construction site but charging the client for it. I was a manager, and Sam worked for me, but we weren't stealing anything. The owner was."

Rowan? A thief? He's the most generous man I've ever met. Just the thought of it is ridiculous. "Of course you weren't."

"We left quickly and not on the best of terms. It's not my proudest moment, but we didn't have a choice. Sticking around would have meant getting sucked into more problems."

Indignation rises inside me. "Well, I know what it's like to have an insane boss. I can't believe yours tried to pin that on you. You should have gone to the police."

"You're probably right, but we just wanted to get away from the whole situation."

"I get it." And I do. How many times have I kept my mouth shut around Brett just to minimize our interactions?

I sigh, feeling ridiculous for getting so suspicious earlier. "I'm sorry for grilling you."

Rowan smiles. "Don't be. I get why you wanted to know."

"Anyway, I think the tattoos are cool. You shouldn't be embarrassed by them."

Rowan wraps his palm around the side of my head and kisses my temple. "C'mon. Let's go eat."

I still feel a bit guilty for pressing them so hard on the tattoos, but the whole incident is forgotten as soon as we sit down.

Rowan serves the pasta, spooning the ragù on top of the noodles and then grating fresh parmesan cheese over it. Sam cracks open another bottle of wine and fills our glasses, and I remember the garlic bread at the very last second, somehow saving it from being burned.

Sam and Rowan chat about random things—work, upcoming plans, funny anecdotes from their past. I listen, content to just be in their presence. I wish Del could have come for Christmas, but she took a trip to visit her grand-parents in Florida. I think she would like Sam. I'll have to introduce the two of them the next time she's in town.

When Rowan tries to give me a second serving of pasta, I stop him. "I have to stop eating or I won't have any room for dessert."

Sam gets to his feet. "I'm going to grab some plates for the tiramisu."

"Make some tea, will you?" Rowan asks.

"Sure."

Rowan watches Sam walk out of the room before leveling his gaze on me. "How do you feel about getting your Christmas present early?"

A flutter appears inside my belly. I have no idea if he'll like the gift I hid under the bed. But I definitely can't give it to him while Sam's around. "You didn't have to get me anything, you know."

He gets out of his seat and pulls an envelope out from under the tablecloth. He must have stashed it there earlier. "I sure as hell did. What kind of a shitty boyfriend would I be if I didn't get you a gift?"

My pulse picks up speed. Boyfriend? "Rowan..."

He comes around the table, sits in the chair beside mine, and hands me the envelope. "Merry Christmas, Sunshine."

I turn it over in my clammy hands. There's nothing on it except for my name written on one side. "What is this?"

"Open it."

I tear along the seam and pull out a few folded papers. It takes me a few moments to decipher what I'm reading.

It's a lease agreement.

The address is a unit in Riverbend Mall.

I look at Rowan in confusion. "I don't understand."

His eyes are filled with so much warmth that it takes my breath away. "It's for your new bookstore."

"What?" My voice is no more than a weak whisper.

"Sam and I saw an empty storefront at the mall that would be perfect for a bookshop. You said you've always wanted to open one, right? Well, this has shelves installed, and I could help you renovate the interior if—"

My surroundings go blank, and my heartbeat's thundering inside my ears.

He got me a space for a *bookstore*?

The papers fall out of my hand, and a flock of butterflies invades my stomach.

He stops midsentence and frowns. "You don't like it?"

"No." I'm out of my chair, climbing onto his lap and kissing him with everything I've got. He wraps his arms around me and kisses me back, and I can feel him smile against my lips.

"I love it," I say when we break for air. There are tears in my eyes. "I can't decide if you're the craziest or the best man I've ever met."

Rowan gives me a crooked grin. "Why not both?" He brushes his fingers through my hair, pushing it away from my face. "I don't want you to leave, Sunshine. I want you to stay with me in Darkwater and give us a chance. Can't you see how good we are together?"

My breath hitches.

I've wanted to leave Darkwater Hollow behind for so long. I was convinced there was nothing for me here and that I would never be accepted, but that's not true. Rowan's changed all that.

He's given me plenty of reasons to stay. And maybe I don't need anyone else's acceptance, as long as I have his.

I press a kiss to his lips. "I'll stay."

CHAPTER 37

BLAKE

The day after Christmas, I walk into Frostbite knowing I'm about to quit, and damn if it doesn't feel good.

I'm practically floating. I can't wait to give Brett my resignation and say goodbye to this place. Riverbend Mall was closed for Christmas Day, but it's open today, so after I'm done with work, Rowan and I are going to go take a look at the space he leased. I'm so excited, I want to break out into a happy dance.

Rowan, Sam, and I spent most of yesterday putting together a rough business plan for the bookstore, and I'm so damn grateful for their help. There's a never-ending list of things that need to get done before I can open the store to the public. It's overwhelming, but in the best way.

My lifelong dream is starting to feel real.

I bite down on my smile, remembering Rowan's reaction two nights ago when I gave him his Christmas gift. After we finished our dinner and Sam left, I changed in the bedroom and walked out in a skimpy light-blue lingerie set I splurged on at the mall.

It made Rowan drop his wineglass. We didn't get much sleep that night, or the following.

While we lay in bed last night, our limbs tangled together and my cheek pressed against his chest, I felt like I wanted to tell him something.

Something that made me terrified.

I'm falling for you.

I rehearsed saying the words in my head a dozen times, but no matter how I tried, I couldn't get myself to say them out loud. After Brett, I wasn't sure I'd ever say them again.

Old fears are holding me back, even if they no longer make any sense given everything that's happened between Rowan and me.

He asked me to stay with him. He got me a freaking bookstore, for God's sake. That's not something a guy who's only looking for something casual would do.

He's proving to me time and time again that he's not the womanizer he was when we first met. He's changed. And he wants me as much as I want him.

Now I just need to work up my courage to tell him how I feel.

I'll tell him tonight when we go to see the bookstore.

A grin pulls on my lips as I go to the back to put my purse away. This was without a doubt the best Christmas I've ever had.

When I walk by Brett's office, it's silent. He's probably not in yet. That's okay, I was planning on working all day today anyway. As much as I can't wait to be out of here, I'm not going to just walk out of this place and leave all the other employees scrambling. I'll offer to do my two weeks so that Brett can find someone to replace me.

"What's got you smiling so big?" Frank asks when I come around to say hello.

I lean against the counter, twirling a lock of hair around my finger. "Just had a great holiday, I guess." I'm trying to play it cool, but I'm feeling too giddy inside to succeed.

Frank chuckles and gives me a knowing look. "That boy treatin' ya well?"

"Better than anyone ever has," I admit. I slide my hands into my pockets and take a deep breath. "I've got something to tell you, but it's a secret, okay? At least for the next few hours."

Frank turns, giving me his full attention. "I can keep a secret."

"Rowan leased a space in Riverbend Mall for me. I'm going to open up my own bookstore. Today, I'm giving Brett my two-week notice." I've probably looked at that lease a dozen times since Rowan gave it to me. Who would have thought a legal document could give me so much joy?

Frank's eyes widen. "You're kiddin'."

I bite down on my lip and shake my head.

Slowly, a giant grin spreads over his face, and he scoops me into a hug. "I'm so happy for you, darlin'. Congratulations. That's fantastic news."

I hug him back, my cheeks hurting from all the smiling I've been doing recently.

As we pull apart, Frank looks at me with fondness in his eyes. "I always knew you were destined for bigger things than this place."

"I can't wait," I admit. "I'm so excited to get to work on it. I haven't seen the space in person yet, but I'm supposed to go with Rowan after work today."

"I'll be your very first customer. Stock some thrillers for me."

"Give me the names of all your favorite authors, and I'll make sure I have them."

When Carly arrives, I share the news with her too. She's even more enthusiastic about it than Frank, picking me up and spinning me around until I beg her to put me down. The lunch customers give us weird looks before going back to their meals.

All day, I'm bursting with energy. It's the best day at work I've had in a long time, which is ironic given I'm about to quit.

Brett walks in during the late afternoon and gives me a wave as he moves past the bar, but he doesn't linger. Nerves buzz beneath my skin.

Carly shoots me a look as she loads a few drinks onto her tray. "Does he know already?"

"Not yet."

"He's not going to be happy."

She's right. Brett's not going to take me quitting well, but I just have to get it done. It's the last thing I have to get through before I can throw myself into my new business.

A half hour before my shift wraps up, I walk into Brett's office.

His eyes snap up to me as I close the door. "Blake." He pushes aside the papers he'd been poring over.

"Can we talk?" I ask.

"Of course. Have a seat." His tone is light and friendly. A bit too much so.

The look he gives me makes me uneasy, but I straighten my back and push through. "I'm giving you my two-week notice."

A second passes. Then another. He doesn't say anything, doesn't react until a small, barely there smirk appears on his face.

"You know, I finally figured out who Rowan is," he says quietly.

I blink at him. "Did you hear what I said?"

He opens his desk, pulls out a manila envelope, and slides it toward me. "See if you still want to resign after you take a look at what's inside."

Anger creeps through my body. Another envelope. Another lie. "I don't care what's inside."

"Indulge me."

"Why should I?"

"Because that's the truth about your boyfriend right there." He taps his index finger against the envelope. "Are you too afraid to find out what it is?"

"I'm so damn tired of your ridiculous allegations."

He shakes his head. "No allegations. Just cold, hard facts." Something flickers inside his gaze that sends a chill down my spine. "If you're so convinced it's not real, why not take a look?"

There's no need for me to sit here for this. I gave him my resignation. I should just stand up and leave.

But something holds me back. Something makes me reach for that envelope.

When I see what's inside, it feels like the ground has opened up beneath me.

It's photos of Rowan, Sam, and Brett. Photos taken in this office.

Brett's back is pressed against the wall.

And Rowan's holding a gun to his chin.

I blink. This can't be real. This is photoshopped. How dare Brett?

I throw the photos back down on the desk. "Enough. I'm not interested in seeing your experiments in photo editing."

Brett scoops up the photos before sliding them back to me. "It's not photoshopped. They're screenshots of a video I have. Look again. If you want, I can show you the video too."

"You really want me to believe Rowan walked in here and threatened you with a gun? Why would he do that?"

"Because of the store in the mall."

My stomach drops. Brett knows about the bookstore? How? Did he hear me talking to Frank? To Carly?

No, he wasn't here when I told them.

Then, how...

Brett's eyes flash with triumph. "My dad's company owns the leasing firm, and when I heard Miller signed a lease for that store, I told the agent not to give him the keys."

"Why would you do that?"

"Because I wanted to see how he'd react."

I pick up one of the photos. The picture is taken from some-where slightly above, as if the camera was placed on...

I glance behind me. That shelf. The one that's right above the photos of Brett's family. The picture frame with the photo of Brett and me has been moved from where it was to that top shelf.

"I hid the camera just behind the photo of us." Brett's voice is soft.

I turn back to face him. The photo in my hands is shaking. "Rowan would never do this."

"You have no idea who Rowan is." He gets out of his chair and walks around the desk toward me. "He's a dangerous man."

I stand up, and the chair skids against the floor. Panic wraps around my lungs. "Don't come any closer."

"I'll tell you everything about him, Blake. I've learned a lot in the past few days. But first, I want you to understand that ultimately, I want to put all of this behind us as quickly as possible. I'm tired of playing games."

"Why is it so hard for you to accept that I've moved on from you?"

His eyes darken. "You should be grateful I'm showing this to you. You should be grateful I still want you back."

"*Why?* Why do you still want me?"

"Because I put everything on the line when I started dating you. Do you know how my family warned me against you? What they told me about your father? Your mother? I probably know more about your family's crimes than you do."

My vision blurs. "My mother? Leave her out of this."

"Your mother is not as innocent as you think. She helped your father."

"What are you talking about?"

"When she was pregnant with you, she'd pretend her car broke down and lure innocent people to help her so that your dad could steal their shit. Your mother was an accomplice. And your father... Well, I won't even get started on him."

The office starts to spin. "You're full of shit," I choke out.

Brett steps closer. "I'm not. Every word I've said is true. My family warned me against you, and I ignored them all because I was in love with you. I liked the way you weren't like the other girls. How you weren't impressed with my wealth, even though you didn't have any money, and how you always had your head screwed on straight. I told my father I want a woman like you as a mother to my children. I still do. I'm going to prove my family wrong about you."

Hate runs through my veins like fire. "All of this is about preserving your pride? About saving face?"

Anger morphs his expression into something horrible. "What is wrong with you? You'd rather be with a criminal than me?"

"Rowan is not a criminal," I snap, squeezing my fingers around the photo I'm still holding. "I'm leaving."

"Don't you want to hear everything I found out about him?" he calls after me.

But I let the door slam behind me and walk out of Frostbite for what I know is the very last time.

CHAPTER 38

NERO

I prop my feet on the coffee table and pick up my book.

La Vita Nuova by Dante.

I've read the thing more than a dozen times throughout my life, but every time I read it, I pick up on something new. It's the kind of book that never gets old.

And now, as I read about Dante first meeting Beatrice, a woman he perceived as being more divine than human, his words hit me even more profoundly.

"Here is a deity stronger than I who comes to rule over me."

I get it, buddy.

The house doesn't feel right without Blake here.

Is it pathetic that I've done nothing all day but watch the time pass and wait for her shift to be over? Sandro and I gave the company the rest of the week off, and I'm regretting that decision.

I run my fingers through my hair. Whenever I'm around her, I'm fine. Happy even. But whenever I'm alone, that empty feeling reappears somewhere deep inside my chest.

I can't very well demand Blake never leaves my side, although she seemed happy enough to spend all of yesterday in bed with me.

During our breaks, she'd traced the tattoos on my chest and asked me about what they all meant. I tried to be as truthful as I could, but I still ended up feeding her a slew of lies.

That fucking fish. It's a tattoo many in the Cosa Nostra have to show we know how to keep our mouths shut. In the mob, no one gets a tattoo screaming their allegiance to any given family unless they're an idiot, but symbolic images are common.

She traced the fish again and again. Lingering on it. Making me worry that she didn't quite buy the story I told her.

My last job required me to know how to read people, and what I'm reading from Blake is that there's still something deep inside her that seems to know to not trust me fully.

I should be grateful she has that instinct. After all, it's correct.

How can I expect her full trust if there's a part of me that will never be accessible to her? A part she will never know?

It shouldn't matter, but it does.

But if that sting of loneliness is something I have to bear for the rest of my life to keep her in it, then so be it.

I read a few more pages, but even Dante's not doing it for me right now. I'm antsy to see Blake.

Fuck it.

I get to my feet and pull on my jacket. We were supposed to meet at the bookstore after her shift, but I'll just pick her up from work, and we can go there together. When I showed her some pictures the agent sent me, she squealed in excitement. She was more animated than I've ever seen her, her eyes shining with emotion.

My chest swells. When did I go from wanting things from her to wanting to give her everything? I don't know. But seeing her happy was even better than putting Brett in his place.

It's snowing lightly as I drive to Frostbite, and flurries land on the windshield. I get a text from Sandro saying he's dropping off some wallpaper I ordered for the bigger bedroom upstairs, the one I'm planning on moving Blake and me into. The view's better, and there's more light in the mornings, which Blake likes.

I send him a quick voice message letting him know I'm out, and that he can let himself in with his key.

Frostbite comes into view. I pull into the parking lot and glance around.

Blake's car isn't here. Did I miss her? She shouldn't be off for another ten minutes. Maybe she parked at the back.

As I get out of the truck, a familiar silhouette catches my eye, but it's not Blake.

Brett is standing by the entrance of the restaurant, smoking a cigarette. His posture is relaxed, but his eyes track my every move with a sharp intensity that sets me on edge.

I walk up to him. "Is Blake inside?"

Brett puffs on his cigarette. "You just missed her."

A feeling of unease settles in the pit of my stomach. Something about the way he looks at me, the way he speaks, sets off warning bells in my mind.

I should have just called Blake instead of trying to surprise her. I turn to leave.

"Rowan, hold up."

There's a weird lilt to his voice. And when I turn around, he's got a smile on his face that doesn't look quite right.

He takes a drag of his cigarette. "I always knew there was something off about you. When you bought Handy Heroes, I wondered who is that guy, and where did he get all that money?"

My fists clench. Where is he going with this? Fuck, this guy just doesn't know when to quit.

He sniffs. "You've got no roots in Darkwater Hollow, and you clearly had enough money to settle down anywhere you wanted. So why here? It never made a lot of sense."

"Is there a point to your rambling? If so, spit it the fuck out. I don't have all day," I growl.

His eyes narrow. "You made a big mistake, you know?"

"Oh yeah?"

"Shouldn't have pulled a gun on me."

Something's wrong. I can't explain it, but I've got this sudden urge to get the fuck out of here and find Blake.

I turn around and start walking back to my car.

"Hey, we're not done talking," Brett calls out, but I ignore him.

I've got nothing to say to him.

"Nero!"

I freeze. Goosebumps erupt over my skin.

What the fuck?

I haven't heard that name spoken out loud since Sandro and I left New York.

I whip around. "What did you say?"

Brett takes a step closer, the cigarette dangling from his lips. His eyes narrow, and there's a sinister gleam in them. "I said, *Nero*. That's your name, right? Your real name."

Fuck!

How does he know that?

How much does he know?

"Like I said, you made a mistake, wise guy. You think I didn't know you'd come to me when you didn't get the keys from the agent? I was prepared. Had a camera installed. Got a video of you pointing a gun at me."

I take a step closer. "If I were you, I'd be really careful about what you do with that video."

"Blake's already seen the still images." He makes a mocking grimace. "If I were you, I'd start thinking about how you're going to explain them to her."

My thoughts race. "What do you want?"

"I want you to leave Darkwater and never come back."

"Like hell. You going to go to the police with this video?"

"The police?" He chuckles. "No. If you refuse to leave, I'm going to set someone much worse on you."

"Oh yeah?" I take another step toward him. Fear skates across his face before he manages to hide it. "If you really know who I am, then you should know there aren't a lot of people worse than me."

"Blake's godfather has seen the video too. He's the one who helped me figure out this entire puzzle. Nero De Luca. He thought some people might be interested in knowing you're still alive."

My gut twists. Inside my chest, something shatters. "You fucking idiot. Do you know what you've done?"

Brett tosses the cigarette away and pushes off the wall. "I've put you in your fucking place."

The Iron Raptors know my identity. And now they know I should be dead.

Since I'm not... There's someone who'll pay good money for that information.

I've got to get ahead of this. If I still can. What if they've already contacted the Ferraros? What if the Ferraros already sent someone this way? Does Rafe know I've been discovered?

Fuck!

Blake's in danger.

And I might already be too late.

CHAPTER 39

BLAKE

My head is spinning the entire drive back home. It's snowing enough that I shouldn't speed, but every time I check the dashboard, I've somehow managed to be going ten miles over the speed limit.

The things Brett said about my mom can't be true. My mom wasn't like that.

Yeah, she might have made excuses for my dad and the life he chose, but she always taught Maxton and me the difference between right and wrong. One time, Maxton got caught trying to steal a bag of chips from a convenience store when he was about ten, and Mom wouldn't let him hear the end of it.

She'd never knowingly help my dad. She wouldn't entrap innocent people.

But she loved him more than she loved herself.

I give my head a shake. There were limits to what she'd do, even for my father. There's no way.

Brett lied to me about her, the same way he lied to me about Rowan.

The more I think about the photos Brett showed me, the more I'm convinced they must be doctored.

I glance down at the photo I took, the one that's now lying on the passenger seat. Rowan wouldn't pull a gun on someone like that. He's not violent. Sure, he's got a hell of a glare, and he can be intimidating, but he's never been aggressive. Even if Brett interfered with the lease and refused to give Rowan the keys, Rowan wouldn't threaten him.

But what's nagging at me is that the gun Rowan is holding in the photo looks just like the gun I saw him stashing away upstairs.

Or does it? I don't know enough about guns to know if it's a common model. I try to conjure up a clear image of the gun I saw in Rowan's hand, but my memory is fuzzy.

I'm too amped up to think straight. I just need to stay calm until I can talk to Rowan. I'm sure there's an explanation.

Finally, I turn onto our street.

Rowan's truck isn't in the driveway.

I park and let out a groan. He's probably already left for the mall where we're supposed to meet after my shift. My God, I'm so rattled I didn't think to just drive straight there.

I'm about to get back on the road when an idea comes to me.

It wouldn't hurt to check...

I hop out of the car and run inside, straight upstairs to the closet where the gun was.

The drawer's stuck, and it takes me some time to get it open, but when I do, the gun's right there, untouched.

When did I see him put it there? It was three days before Christmas Eve. No, four. I walked in on him putting it away right after he came home from going somewhere with Sam.

I look down at the photo I took with me.

It has a date in the corner.

The twentieth of December.

My heart's banging around inside my chest. So what if the dates match up? It could be a coincidence.

But a flicker of doubt appears. Could Rowan and Sam have gone to Frostbite that day?

My phone rings. Rowan's name pops up on the screen. My index finger hovers over the screen.

Buzz. Buzz. Buzz.

I let it ring. That day, Sam came here and said to Rowan that something urgent had come up. A work emergency. A difficult client.

And when Rowan came back, he had a gun with him. A gun he hid.

He said it was to protect us from Uncle Lyle, but what if he lied?

The buzzing stops, but another sound grabs my attention.

Did someone just open the front door? It can't be Rowan. He's waiting for me at the mall.

I freeze. The sound of footsteps echoes through the hallway downstairs, slow and deliberate. My heart thunders in my chest as I dip my hand into the drawer and grab the gun. I inch out of the bedroom and toward the stairs, my palm sweaty around the cool metal. Adrenaline courses through my veins, and I can hear the blood pounding in my ears.

"Hello?" Sam appears at the bottom of the stairs, a long package tucked under his arm.

I slump against the wall. "Oh my God."

Sam's eyes widen as he takes in the sight of me clutching the gun. "What's going on?"

"I don't know." What is wrong with me? I'm spiraling. "What are you doing here?"

"I just needed to drop off some wallpaper for Rowan. He told me to use my key."

I shut my eyes and take a deep breath. I need to calm down.

Sam props the package against the wall and climbs the stairs until he reaches me. "What's up?" He sounds concerned. He's probably worried I'm having a nervous breakdown. "Why do you have a gun?"

I look down at the weapon. "It's Rowan's. I just heard someone coming in, and I got spooked, so I grabbed it."

"Okay...why don't you give that to me?"

I hand him the gun and let out a long breath. "I need to talk to you, Sam."

"You okay?"

"Not really. Can we go downstairs?"

His brows are furrowed. "Sure."

I walk into the living room and sink down on the couch.

Sam sits down beside me and puts the gun on the coffee table. "What happened, Blake?"

I look at him. "I have to ask you something."

"Okay. Anything."

"You have to promise me you'll be honest."

"Of course."

I watch his expression for any tell that he's about to lie to me, but he seems more confused than anything. "That day you walked in on us on the couch...you know..."

Sam nods. "I remember."

"Where did you and Rowan go?"

"We had to go see a client."

"So you didn't go to Frostbite and threaten Brett?"

The line between his brows deepens. "Where is this coming from?"

"I saw photos of you two. Brett showed me a photo of Rowan pointing a gun at him. He had it pressed just under Brett's chin, and you were there too." I dig out the rumpled photo from my pocket and hand it to Sam.

He pales.

He fucking pales.

The world around me dims. "Sam, you promised to tell me the truth. Did you go there with Rowan? Is this photo real?"

He swallows. "You should talk to Rowan."

I jump to my feet. "I'm talking to *you*!"

"Look, I don't know what to say—"

"The truth! Where did you really go that day?"

"Look, Blake—"

Outside, an engine rumbles. It's that distinct revving sound that always alerted me of my father's arrival.

I interrupt Sam midsentence. "Do you hear that?"

He frowns, listening. "Sounds like a motorbike."

"It's my godfather," I whisper.

Something shifts in Sam's face. All traces of emotion disappear as he picks the gun off the coffee table. "Stay here."

My eyes widen. "What are you doing?"

"I'm going to go see what they want."

"Sam, they're dangerous. They're—"

"In a gang. I know. Rowan told me." He's already up and moving toward the door. When he gets halfway down the hall, he pauses and glances back at me. "Grab a knife. Just in case. If anyone comes in, use it."

My blood runs cold. I get to my feet and run, blocking him from going outside. "Let me talk to him. He might just be checking on me."

Sam pushes past me and walks over to the window by the front door. He pulls back the curtain. "There's at least four of them. Armed. Three on motorcycles and one in a van. There might be more men in there."

Panic crawls up my throat. "Let me call the police."

"There's no time," Sam mutters. "Lock the door and call Rowan."

And then, before I can stop him, he steps outside and slams the door behind him.

I turn the lock and run to the kitchen and grab a knife like he told me.

By the time I return to the window with my phone clutched in my hand, Sam's already talking to the leader of the four men.

My godfather.

I dial Rowan with shaking fingers and wait for him to pick up.

I can't hear what the men outside are saying, but their body language is easy enough to read. They're not chatting about the weather.

What does Uncle Lyle want? Fear zips through me.

"Blake?"

I readjust my grip on the phone. "Rowan, where are you? Uncle Lyle is here. He's brought men with him."

"Fuck. Lock the door and stay inside."

"Sam's talking to them. He told me to call you."

"I'm on my way. Less than ten minutes."

"Hurry."

Uncle Lyle says something to Sam, his expression a menacing scowl. Sam shakes his head. Uncle Lyle spits on the ground. Says something else. Sam shakes his head again.

And that's when it happens. Everyone draws their guns.

A gasp escapes past my lips.

"Blake?" Rowan's voice feels as if it's coming from far away.

Four against one. Those aren't good odds.

Two of the men pounce on Sam, disarming him within seconds.

"They're fighting."

"Shit. Okay, don't hang up. Stay with me."

I've never heard Rowan sound so scared.

"They're hurting him." My face is wet. The two men are kicking Sam. He's trying to fight back, but he's outnumbered. Uncle Lyle watches his men beat Sam for a few moments before his gaze slides toward the house.

"He's coming here," I breathe.

"Blake, I'm five minutes away."

Five minutes is too long, because only seconds later, the doorknob rattles.

I take a step back. Then another.

Something hard slams against the door. Again. And again. Until it bursts open.

My phone falls out of my hand.

Uncle Lyle walks in, his men trailing behind him, two of them dragging Sam. He's got blood dripping down his face.

"Blakey girl." My godfather smiles at me. It's the most disturbing thing I've ever seen.

That's when I remember I'm holding a knife.

I don't think as I run toward Uncle Lyle, slashing my knife at him, but before I know what's happening, I'm on my back and pain is exploding through the back of my skull.

Sam screams something. I go in and out, my vision blurry.

One blink, I'm on the floor.

The next one, I'm on my knees beside Sam right in the middle of the hallway. My arms are bound.

"Blake?"

I moan in response, trying to keep my body from falling back down. I can't seem to hold onto a thought.

Sam's shoulder bumps against mine. He slides something into my hands—his car keys.

Does he want me to try to run to his car? I can't. There's no way for me to get past my godfather's men. They're blocking the door.

I slide the keys into the back pocket of my jeans.

"You okay?" he asks hoarsely.

I glance at him. His lip is gushing blood onto his T-shirt, and there's a horribly resigned look in his eyes.

There's a hard slap against my cheek, and it knocks me off-balance. The only thing that prevents me from falling over is Sam's shoulder digging into my upper chest. "Keep them with you," he whispers into my ear.

"You ran with a fucking knife at me?" my godfather hisses.

When I meet his gaze, it's pure darkness. His eyes are dark pits, devoid of all light.

My blood is loud inside my ears. "What do you want?"

He grabs my chin. "We'll have plenty of time to talk later. We need to get going."

"What do we do with him?" one of his men asks, gesturing at Sam.

"He's not important. Get rid of him."

Horror floods through me. "No. Please, Uncle Lyle. No! Just tell me what you want, and we'll—"

The gun goes off.

Beside me, Sam jerks.

"Sam! No, Sam!"

His body falls backward. There's a bullet hole in the center of his forehead.

I shriek so loud I can't believe that sound is coming out of me.

And then everything goes black.

CHAPTER 40

NERO

The sound of a gunshot rattles inside my skull. I can feel the vibration travel down my spine, sending shivers through my body. Time seems to slow down.

"Hello? Hello?" I shout into the phone, but the only thing I hear back is Blake's stomach-curdling scream. And then the call drops.

I toss the phone on the passenger seat and slam my foot on the gas, running through a red light.

I speed down the street, dodging traffic, my heart pounding in my chest.

What am I going to find when I get back home? Did they shoot Blake? Is she already dead?

The thought makes me gasp for breath, but I push it away, focusing on the road.

Finally, I screech to a halt outside my house. Without even turning off the engine, I jump out of the car and race up to the porch. Blake's car is in the driveway, and so is Sandro's.

The door to the house is open.

I sprint inside, my heart in my throat. Fuck, fuck, *fuck*! How did this happen? If they hurt a hair on Blake's head, I'm going to fucking destroy them.

I barge inside, and the first thing I see freezes me in my tracks. The house is deathly quiet.

And I see him.

Sandro. My partner. My friend.

His body's in a pool of blood. There's a hole in his forehead.

"No," I say even though there's no one to hear me. "Fuck. *No!*"

A torrent of emotions swirls inside my chest, but I don't have time to indulge them, so I lock them all away.

I need to find Blake.

Her phone lies discarded a few feet away from Sandro. The screen's shattered as if someone stepped on it.

I search the house, looking for any trace of her, but there's none.

Back in the hallway, I slide Blake's broken phone into my pocket and sink to my knees beside Sandro. Pressure builds behind my eyes. When I touch him, he's still warm.

They killed him in front of her just minutes ago. This is why she screamed.

If I'd just stayed put, I might have still been home when she came back.

I could have protected her and Sandro.

His eyes are open. I reach over and close them.

I've killed many men and watched even more get killed. But this death feels different. It feels *wrong*. We came to Darkwater Hollow so that we could live.

And Sandro did *live*. He had an entire fucking life here. He was seeing someone. He wanted a family.

I get to my feet with a pained groan. It feels like it comes from the very depths of me.

They will pay for this. I won't rest until I remove every single man responsible for this from the face of the earth.

I'll find Blake. And then I'll kill them all.

My phone rings. It's an unknown number, but somehow, I just know who it is.

The man who'll soon regret every single one of the choices that led him to this moment.

"How do you feel about road trips?" Lyle's voice crackles over the line.

"If you touch a hair on her head, I will rip out your throat with my bare hands."

Lyle chuckles. "Blake's ex wouldn't leave me alone until I showed your photo around. He's an annoying prick, but he's got good instincts, I'll give him that. He said your background check came back empty, and his contact in the police wouldn't agree to run your photo through their facial-recognition system, so he came to us. We don't take orders from guys like him, but when we saw that video of you pointing a gun at him, our curiosity was piqued. He mentioned you said you came from New York, so I showed your photo to someone I know who rides around those parts. A member of the Black Talons. He recognized you right away."

I clench my jaw. Fuck. I know the Black Talons. We've worked with them in the past.

"If you want Blake to live, you're going to do exactly as I say."

"Let me talk to her," I demand.

"She passed out when we shot your friend. Still hasn't come around. Her skin's so fucking soft, like a baby's ass."

Anger blurs my vision. "If you know who I am, you should realize taunting me is not a good idea. Or are you just that fucking stupid?"

"Yeah, I know who you are. That's why we took her. We don't want a confrontation with you, Nero. We want this to be a civilized affair. If you follow my instructions, Blake will be just fine."

I pace the hall. "What do you want?"

"You're going to drive yourself to New York and meet us there. You're coming home, Nero. How does Staten Island sound?"

That's Ferraro's territory. "When?"

"Take your time. Bury your friend. We'll see you there in two days. December twenty-eighth, at noon. I'll call you that morning with the exact address."

Two days? Fuck that. "I'll come to you now. Wherever you are."

"You're not listening to me, and you need to if you want Blake to survive. You're going to drive yourself to Staten Island, and that's where we'll meet."

They don't want to transport me there themselves. Why would they? It's risky. Lyle's right to be afraid of me, so he wants me to deliver myself straight to the man who'll pay Lyle his finder's fee. "She doesn't need to be involved in this. I'll go there whether you hold her hostage or not."

"They said you're a smooth talker, but I don't know about that. It feels like you're feeding me shit. We both know that if I let her go, you'll take her and run."

And kill him and all the men he's managed to involve in this suicide mission.

"Whatever they're offering to pay you, I'll pay you more."

"Ho ho ho." He laughs. "Is that right?"

"Name your price."

"Three million."

"Done."

He laughs again. "I'm just fucking with you. I don't want your money. I see this as only the beginning of a fruitful relationship."

"Ferraro will never work with you. He doesn't—"

"This conversation's getting boring. Goodbye, Nero. Drive safe." He hangs up.

Squeezing the phone inside my hand, I resist the urge to throw it through window.

I need to figure out their route and intercept them before they get to New York. If I don't, Ferraro will kill me, and Uncle Lyle will get to keep Blake, and that's not a fucking option.

I pull up the map on my phone and try to figure out their most likely route.

They want to meet in two days. The most direct route would take twenty hours, so they've got plenty of time to spare. If they're smart, they'll probably hide somewhere during the day and drive during the night to minimize the chance of anyone seeing their hostage.

There are a hundred cheap motels they could stop at, and I've got no way of determining which ones to check.

Rage and frustration pulse against my temples. I need to figure this out, but how?

I walk outside and glance around the street. The neighbors on the other side of the road aren't home. Their driveways are empty, which means no witnesses.

How the fuck am I supposed to track Blake down?

Desperation starts to build inside my gut.

I brought this onto her.

I was so fucking sure my past wouldn't catch up to me that I got careless. Stupid. I put her in danger.

I clench my jaw, my vision narrowing. I need to focus.

This is what I used to do. Solve problems. Fix shit when everything goes wrong. I might be out of practice, but it's in my blood.

First things first, I've got to bury Sandro. I can't just leave him here. He deserves a burial.

Ten minutes later, I'm digging a grave at the far end of my backyard. The soil is stubborn and iced over, but I force my shovel through it until I have a shallow grave.

Back inside, I empty out Sandro's pockets. Wallet, phone, some change, his business cards. The business cards make my vision go blurry. He was so fucking happy when he got the damned things that he drove over to show them to me.

I let out a heavy breath.

Hold on.

He drove here… Where are his car keys?

I check his pockets again, but they're empty.

Maybe he left them in his car?

I go to check, but they're not there either. I search the front lawn, the porch, the living room… Nothing.

There's an AirTag on them. I remember because he bought me one too, but I never put it on. I grab his phone, hover it over his face to unlock it, and then pull up the locator app.

There they are. *Car keys.*

They're all the way out on the I-44, moving toward St. Louis.

The fuck?

And then it dawns on me.

Blake's got the keys.

CHAPTER 41

BLAKE

"Try him again. We've gotta get in touch with those fucking Italians in the next twenty-four hours for this to work."

"Maybe we should have waited until we talked to them."

"Did I ask for your fucking opinion?"

A groan escapes my lips. My head's pounding, and my throat is bone dry. Suddenly, my body bounces, and pain shoots up my spine. I'm in a vehicle.

"You awake, Blakey girl?" That's Uncle Lyle. I crack my eyes open and see his face hovering over me. "Thirsty?"

I nod, my thoughts struggling to coalesce into coherence.

A hand slides under my head and lifts me a few inches off the ground. Lukewarm water that tastes like plastic drips past my lips, but I'm so parched I don't care. I drink greedily, my palms pressing against the rough carpet stretched over the floor of the van.

Uncle Lyle watches me closely. "You're a bit banged up. Hit your head against the floor when you passed out."

It's like a light suddenly turns on. Memories come flooding back, and I choke on the water, spitting it all down my front.

Sam!

"Oh my God, Sam... Sam's—"

Uncle Lyle shushes me and pulls me against his chest. "He's dead, Blakey. That boy's dead."

Adrenaline surges through me. I fight him, claw at him, scream. This is a nightmare. This isn't real.

An arm appears around my throat, then a hand presses to my lips. I smell cigarette smoke and gasoline. My eyes roll to the back of my head as the reality of my situation crashes into me.

"Stop fighting, girl. You're only going to make this worse for yourself. You want me to tie you up?"

I go slack in his arms. A few seconds pass before his grip on me loosens and he turns me around to face him.

His eyes are pools of pure darkness. I'm trembling. Crying. Begging.

He just smiles. "I told your daddy I'd take care of you, but I haven't been doing my job very well. Until now." He slides his palms down my arms, brushing against the sides of my breasts and lingering there for a moment too long. "After all of this is over, you'll be staying with me."

I feel like I'm about to pass out again, so I bite on my tongue, hard enough to draw blood. I've got to keep my wits about me. "I don't understand. Where are you taking me?"

"You're bait." He brushes my hair out of my face, and I recoil from him. I want him to stop touching me.

His eyes narrow. "Behave yourself."

"Bait?" I choke out.

"Your boyfriend's gonna come for you. Save us the trouble of trying to transport a demon like him across six states."

Nothing makes sense. "I don't understand. What do you want with Rowan?"

"Lyle, he picked up," someone calls out from the front of the van. "You want to talk to him?"

Uncle Lyle grins at me, clearly pleased. He reaches over to take the phone from one of the men.

"Took you long enough," he says to whoever is on the other end of the line.

I scan my surroundings for anything that could help me escape. The van is moving at a steady pace along the highway, the barren landscape flashing by in a blur of muted colors. It's dark out, but there are enough cars around us to make me think it's not that late yet.

Shifting my position, I feel something dig into my butt cheek. I slide two fingers into the back pocket of my jeans and remember Sam's keys.

Grief pangs through me, mixed with a healthy dose of disbelief. I can't believe he's dead. He died trying to protect me.

Tears blur my vision.

He knew they were going to kill him. I saw it in his eyes. So why did he use his last seconds to give me his keys? Can I use them as a weapon? I won't know until I can take a closer look at them.

He told me to keep them on me, so for now, I'll just have to do that.

"What more evidence?" Uncle Lyle growls into the phone. "You got the photos, didn't you? The video? That's the fucking evidence."

Who is he talking to? He wants to lure Rowan to somewhere. What for?

"Good. We need to discuss compensation."

I try to make out what the person on the other end of the line is saying, but it's impossible to hear over the hum of the vehicle.

Uncle Lyle laughs sardonically. "Why do I get the sense you're not taking this seriously?" A pause. "I see. Well, it's your lucky week, because this is the real deal, but we're not bringing him over until I've got a guarantee I'll get paid." A longer pause this time. "Fine. Good. Like I said, two days. We'll be there." He hangs up and slaps his palm against the driver's shoulder. "We're good, boys. Told you it would work out in the end. Now focus on the driving. Not a mile above the speed limit. We don't want any attention on us." He turns to look at me. "And you're going to be a good girl and do exactly as I say, understand?"

I nod, even though I understand nothing. Who were they talking to? What do they want with Rowan?

When I shift my position, my bladder whines in protest. "I need to use the bathroom," I whisper.

Uncle Lyle drags his gaze down my body in a way that makes my blood chill. "Let's stop in Wilmington, boys. Gotta rest up and eat something before we get back on the road later tonight." He sits down beside me and pulls me against him. I start shaking again.

"Shhh, Blakey girl," he whispers, his dry lips pressing against my ear. "Don't you worry. I'll take care of you."

He doesn't let go of me until we come to a stop what feels like fifteen minutes later. Outside the tinted window is a motel with peeling yellow walls. Two women who look like prostitutes loiter by the vending machine.

Something tells me I'm not going to find much help here. I have to try to run.

As soon as we get out of the van, I jerk out of Lyle's grip and with everything I have, force my half-numb legs to move.

Faster, faster.

My feet pound against the cement. There's a road with cars driving down it. If I reach it, I can try to flag one of them down. Maybe someone will stop. I'll throw myself into the middle of traffic if I have to. I'll—

Something collides against my back.

I land on my elbows, my long-sleeved sweater ripping against the rough concrete.

Rough hands turn me over, a weight lands on my belly, and then there's a hard slap against my cheek.

I start crying. It's instinctive.

"You stupid girl," Uncle Lyle seethes, his spittle landing on my face. "Didn't I tell you to behave?"

"Why are you doing this?" I plead through my tears.

He hauls me up, his palm wrapped around my arm like an iron coil. "Shut up."

"What do you want with Rowan?"

"Don't play dumb," he mutters. "You fucking know who he is."

One of the other Iron Raptors comes over, looking at me with contempt while he hands Uncle Lyle a key. The thought of being locked inside a room with Uncle Lyle weakens my knees, but he just drags me along and pushes me inside one of the units.

The door slams shut behind us.

Another sharp slap lands against my stinging cheek. "Don't ever do that again."

I cradle my burning flesh, blinking at him through my tears. "I don't understand why you're doing this. Whoever you think Rowan is, you're wrong."

Uncle Lyle rears his hand back again.

I raise my arms to protect myself. "No, please!"

He stops, hand in the air. Realization flashes in his eyes. "You really don't know who Rowan is?"

I shake my head.

He stares at me for a long moment, and then he starts to laugh. It's cruel and ugly, and it makes me so fucking scared.

Dread fills my stomach, thick and heavy. I take deep breaths, trying to calm down. I won't get anywhere if I keep acting out of panic.

"You stupid girl," he says through his laughter. "He pulled one on you." His eyes darken. "This is exactly why you're going to stay with me from now on. You can't take care of yourself, can you? You've been sleeping with a New York gangster for the last few weeks, and you had no idea?"

A New York gangster?

Brett's office. Those photos. I'd forgotten about them in all the chaos, but they come back to me now. "What?"

"He was high up. And he's got quite the reputation." Uncle Lyle's sick smile disappears. For a split second, I think I see a hint of fear in his eyes. "They call him the Angel of Death."

I blink at him. "You're lying."

"Don't worry, I'll make sure you see us hand him over to the people who are going to pay us a lot of money for finding him. He's got a big bounty on him."

"Who wants him?"

"The Ferraro family. You ever heard of 'em?"

I shake my head.

"They're one of the mob families in New York. Your 'Rowan' killed one of their family members and then faked his own death. He's been hiding like a fucking rat."

He's got it all wrong. He has no idea what he's talking about. Someone lied to him, and now he's going to ruin my life and Rowan's over that lie. Was it Brett? "Rowan will call the police. They're going to find us, and you're going to go to jail."

He chuckles. "So naive. Your boyfriend's got a record twice as long as mine. Before he disappeared, he worked for

Rafaele Messero. Of course, you've got no idea who that is either. Messero's the head of a very powerful mob family."

My head swims.

"You really trusted him, didn't you?" He leans forward and grabs me by the chin. "Well, then it won't be so hard for you to trust me."

Rowan, a gangster in hiding? The whole story is insane, but Uncle Lyle thinks he's telling me the truth. Either someone's managed to fool him or...

Or...

He drops his hand. "I'm going to leave you alone for a bit now. Got some calls to make. But don't get any ideas. One of my guys will be just outside the door."

He waits for me to acknowledge that I heard him with a nod, and then he walks out the door.

I slump against the wall, my heart racing. Then I remember Sam's keys still lodged in my back pocket.

I fish them out and hold them in front of my face. Looking for... I don't know what.

Then I see it.

An AirTag.

Relief expands inside my chest like a balloon. Rowan has a way to track me. Assuming he figures it out, but I have to believe that he will.

And then it hits me that Sam spent his last moments thinking of a way to save me. He knew they were going to kill him, and he still tried to protect me.

A tear slides down my cheek, but I wipe it away. I have to be strong. Strong like Sam. Losing my shit again isn't going to help me, but staying aware of my surroundings and being ready for when Rowan comes will.

The motel room is small and bare-bones. It takes me only fifteen minutes to search every nook and cranny for something I can use as a weapon. But there's nothing at all. Not even a phone to call reception. I do have Sam's keys...

I take the AirTag off the key ring, slip it into the tiny pocket nestled inside the bigger pocket of my jeans, and keep the keys clutched in my hand.

Soon enough, Uncle Lyle comes back. He comes in holding a greasy paper bag in one hand. "Got you some food."

I get to my feet from where I'm sitting on the bed. "I'm not hungry."

He closes the door and drops the bag on the small table by the window. "Suit yourself, but don't complain when you're hungry later. We're not making any unplanned stops."

My gaze tracks his movements. "Okay."

He takes off his leathers and hangs them on the back of a chair. "You should get some sleep. We'll be back on the road in three hours."

Sleep? It would take an elephant tranquilizer to get my adrenaline levels anywhere low enough for me to sleep.

When I don't say anything, his eyes skate down my body, lingering on the outline of my breasts. "If you don't want to sleep, there's something else we could do. Something I've been thinking about for a very long time."

I take a step back.

He gives me a sickening grin and walks closer.

I start to move around the bed, trying to keep some distance between us, but then he leaps forward, and he's right there, pushing me up against the wall.

I scream, and he puts his palm over my mouth.

"Quiet," he hisses. "You don't want to make me angry, Blake. If you behave, I can make this good for you."

My body grows very still as my brain goes into overdrive. I can't fight him. He's stronger, and he'll overpower me in seconds. Maybe if I go along with it and strike him when he least expects it... If I can catch him off guard, maybe I can get away.

I have no idea if he's still got one of his guys outside the door, or if he told them to leave when he returned. I just have to hope the guard left. It's a risk, but I don't have any other choice.

"Can I remove my palm?"

I nod.

He drops his hand and steps closer, pressing his body into me. "Even at fifteen, you were already a beauty." His dry lips drag over my cheek. "The perfect mix of innocence and temptation." He slides his hands under my shirt, and then his hands are on my breasts, squeezing painfully.

I readjust my grip on the keys, pushing them through the gaps between my fingers.

He kisses me, and I nearly gag. He pushes his tongue between my lips, tasting like ash, smelling like stale sweat. His fingers pinch my nipple.

You have to kiss him back. Make him believe it.

It takes everything in me to force my lips to move. As soon as they do, he groans and rubs himself against my thigh.

My vision blurs. I've never felt more sick.

Because I'm not confident my stomach can survive more of this, I shove at his chest. He breaks the kiss and takes a step back, sliding his hands out from under my shirt. His expression starts to turn angry once again.

"I have to tell you something," I rush to say.

The anger halts. Just like I thought it would. "What?"

"You're right." I take a deep breath. "I think I've gotten myself into a lot of trouble."

He arches a brow.

"I've been so lost on my own." I swallow hard, the keys gripped tightly in my hand. "And Brett was never any help."

Uncle Lyle's eyes flash. "That boy's an idiot. You need a real man, Blake."

"Maybe I do."

A self-satisfied smirk starts to bloom across his face. "I told you—"

And that's when I strike. I slash the keys over his face, trying to get his eyes. I think I manage to do it, because he yelps in pain and staggers backward.

I don't waste a second. I run toward the door and grab the lock, trying to turn it.

Fuck, it's stuck.

It's stuck.

Oh God.

And then it isn't stuck anymore, and I fling the door open. One foot manages to make it out.

Just one.

Before something rams into my head, and I pass out.

When I regain consciousness, there are hands all over me and a tongue inside my mouth. I scream.

Uncle Lyle jerks away from me, his bloody face coming into focus. There are two bloody gashes running from his forehead to his cheek. I missed the eyes after all.

His expression is a twisted snarl. "You lying cunt. You really fucked up now."

His level of anger is enough for me to deduce that little time has passed. I must have been out for less than a minute.

He pins my hands above my head, his blood dripping onto my face, and starts to undo my jeans.

I buck against him, fighting him with all my strength.

He slaps me hard, and the taste of copper fills my mouth. "You want to do this the hard way, then? After the move you just pulled, I think I'll enjoy making you scream."

He tears open the zipper and starts pulling down my jeans. I'm thrashing like a captured animal, but he's so much stronger that it's no use. He squeezes my wrists with his hand until I think he's about to break them, and he shoves his other hand inside my panties. He probes me painfully, his nails scratching me as he forces two fingers inside me.

I scream again, but it's not as loud anymore. My voice is hoarse. Defeated. I can feel myself losing, my will breaking.

BANG.

The door flies open.

Uncle Lyle roars, pulling his digits out of me, scrambling off the bed. He pulls a gun from behind his waistband and points it at the person in the doorway.

My vision blurred with tears, I stare at the silhouette standing in the doorway.

It's Rowan.

CHAPTER 42

BLAKE

One look at Rowan is all it takes. Relief floods through my body.

Everything will be okay. He's here. He's found me. He figured out Sam's plan.

The cops must be near too. They'll come bursting through any moment now. They'll lock up Uncle Lyle and the other men who kidnapped me.

But instead of keeping the door open, Rowan walks in and closes it behind him. Deadbolts it.

What is he doing?

His expression is colder than I've ever seen it as he stares down the barrel Uncle Lyle is pointing at him.

When his gaze moves to me, skating over my hunched form, his eyes flare with fury and then narrow. Our eye contact lasts for only a moment, but in that split second, I see a hurricane unravel inside his hazel gaze.

Fear claws up my insides.

What now? What's his plan?

Uncle Lyle isn't going to let us go without a fight. Can Rowan fight back if he has to? Where are the damn cops?

And what about the other Iron Raptors outside?

I tighten my arms around myself.

Uncle Lyle sneers. "Look, let's calm down." His fingers are white around the gun. He sounds...scared.

Ignoring the gun pointing at him, Rowan takes two steps closer to Uncle Lyle.

"Stay the fuck back," Uncle Lyle spits. "I'll shoot you if you take one step closer."

"We both know that's a lie. You won't get paid if I'm dead."

My stomach hollows out. What?

Oh...fuck. Fuck, fuck, fuck.

Does that mean there really is someone out to get Rowan?

A shadow passes over Uncle Lyle's face. "How the hell did you find us?"

A humorless smirk graces Rowan's face. I can barely recognize him like this. He looks bigger, broader, taller. And he's not scared.

There's a man pointing a gun at him, and *he's not scared*.

"The question you should be asking is what will I do now?" Rowan's voice is low and deadly.

Uncle Lyle's throat bobs on a swallow. "Even you can't take down me and my guys."

Rowan just smirks.

The silence is so thick, so tense, it clogs my throat.

"Blake?" Rowan asks without taking his eyes off Uncle Lyle.

"Yeah?" My voice is a horse whisper.

"Did he hurt you?"

I bite my lip and shift on the bed. My breasts ache, and there's a lingering pain between my legs. "Yes."

Rowan still doesn't look at me, but his expressionless face morphs into a mask of fury.

And everything suddenly moves very quickly.

Rowan is fast. He tackles my godfather, and both of them crash to the ground. The gun Uncle Lyle is holding slips out of his hand. They wrestle on the floor, swinging punches and throwing kicks, but Rowan's got the clear advantage. Within seconds, he's got my uncle beneath him.

Rowan reaches behind him, takes out his own gun, and presses it against Uncle Lyle's forehead.

"Stop," Uncle Lyle pleads. "Hold on! Jesus, fuck. Take her and go."

Rowan laughs, and it sounds all wrong. It doesn't sound like him at all.

Uncle Lyle's eyes dart between Rowan and me. "Blakey, tell him to stand down. He won. He can take you and lea—"

"You're lucky I don't have time to stick around and rip you apart piece by piece," Rowan growls.

The gun goes off.

He shoots him point-blank in the exact same spot Uncle Lyle shot Sam.

Blood bursts out of my godfather's head and starts leaking onto the floor, seeping out from beneath his body.

The walls of the room spin, and I slide off the bed, needing to feel solid ground beneath me.

This can't be real. I feel like I'm unraveling, the seams that hold my body disintegrating. My palms wrap around my head. I rock back and forth, back and forth.

Sam is dead.

Uncle Lyle is dead.

Rowan is a killer.

Dull footsteps approach me. Familiar leather boots. But when I lower my hands from my face to look at my savior, the edges of him blur.

He crouches down and steadies me, his gaze finally meeting mine, his eyes softening.

"Rowan," I whisper. "What did you do? You should have called the police—"

He tucks his gun away and interrupts me by cupping my cheeks with both of his hands. "Are you okay?"

My lips wobble. "I don't know."

Guilt crisscrosses his expression. He pulls me into him and presses his lips against mine again and again. His kisses are gentle but underscored with desperation. "I'm sorry. I'm so sorry."

"I don't understand what's happening."

His jaw tightens. He's not saying what he's thinking, and that terrifies me.

"I want to get out of here."

He tucks me against him, his palm cradling the back of my head. "We will. Stay here. I just need to take care of something first."

I nod against his chest, numb. "Okay."

He pulls away from me. "Don't look out the window."

Confusion strums through me. "What?"

"Promise me you won't look out the window."

I swallow. "Okay."

He gives me one final long look and leaves.

Some seconds pass. At first, I have no intention of getting off the ground. I'm not even sure I have the strength to do so. But when I hear the sound of fighting, adrenaline drips into my bloodstream, and I hobble up to my feet.

Don't look out the window.

The curtains are blackout, but the sound insulation sucks. Shouts reach my ears. The sound of a scuffle.

What if Rowan needs help?

I don't have a phone, but Uncle Lyle does. When I look back at his body, the pool of blood has grown, and I have to glance away. If Rowan hasn't called the police, I should do it, but instead, I find myself moving closer to the window.

Don't look out the window.

There's a gunshot. A scream.

393

My fingers curl over the edge of the curtain. I peel it back a few inches, just enough to see the parking lot outside.

Rowan is fighting two of my godfather's men. Another two lie on the ground, passed out.

Or...dead?

It's too dark to see them clearly. The parking lot is illuminated by a single lamppost. I can see Rowan though. I watch as he holds his own, each punch and kick landing with precision. His body moves fluidly, a blur of dark ink and shadow.

One of the men lands a punch, and a gasp spills past my lips.

Don't look out the window.

But I keep looking. I watch as Rowan keeps fighting. I can't tear my eyes away. It's horrible and beautiful at the same time.

When did he learn how to fight like that?

Maybe it's just the adrenaline. No, it's not just that.

He's confident and in control. Like he's fought like this countless times. Like he's been trained.

Uncle Lyle's words swirl inside my head.

You've been sleeping with a New York gangster for the last few weeks.

Rowan kicks out one of the men's legs and then rams his angled palm against the other's nose. I shut my eyes when the man's face bursts with blood. But a second later, I'm looking out again. Both of the men are on the ground now, and Rowan's pummeling one of their faces with his fists until the body goes limp.

The second man gets back on his feet and then falters. He spots a discarded gun and dashes toward it, but as he reaches for it, another dull shot rings through the air.

The man yelps and falls to the ground.

The bullet went through his hand. It's now a bloodied mess.

I gag, pressing my palm to my mouth.

Rowan walks to him slowly. He stops right before the man. Even through the glass, I can hear the man pleading for his life, just like Uncle Lyle did.

Rowan kneels beside him, pushes the gun between his lips, and pulls the trigger.

They call him the Angel of Death.

I let go of the curtain and back away from the window.

He just killed him.

He just killed five men like it was nothing.

I stumble over something. Uncle Lyle's feet. My hands are shaking, and I can't make sense of what I just saw.

Rowan saved me, but I don't feel safe. I feel like I've been seeing everything through a veil, and it's just been lifted.

The door swings open. Rowan's covered in blood, but most of it isn't his own.

He extends his hand toward me. "Let's go."

I'm frozen still. I can't move. His fingers are stained red.

He glances down, grimaces, and disappears into the bathroom. I hear the water running. I should run, save myself from whoever this is, because this man isn't Rowan. I have no idea who he is.

By the time I manage to suck in a shaky breath, he's back.

"You're safe now. I won't let anything happen to you. I promise." His eyes are burning with a lingering fury that still hasn't subsided. He grabs my hand and pulls me out the door.

My heart hammers inside my chest. I wish I could trust him, but how can I when the truth is finally clear to me?

Rowan's been lying to me.

He saved me from Uncle Lyle, but who's going to keep me safe from him?

CHAPTER 43

BLAKE

I don't fight Rowan as he walks me to his truck, but on the inside, I'm spiraling. An atomic bomb's been dropped, decimating everything I thought I understood.

Rowan murdered those men in cold blood. At least some of what Uncle Lyle told me must be true, if not all of it.

What if it's all true?

My knees buckle, but Rowan holds me tightly to his side.

When he opens the passenger door, I whirl around, my shock slowly turning into something darker, colder. "Who are you?"

His gaze shutters. "Get inside."

I shake my head. "Rowan, who the fuck are you? You just *killed* those men. Why did you do that? Why didn't you call the police?"

I'm screaming, my grip on reality coming undone. It feels like I'm disassociating, like I'm looking down at Rowan and me from above.

"Get. In. The. Car." He wraps his hand around my elbow and nearly lifts me inside. "I'll explain everything, but right now, we have to leave. We have to get out of here before the cops come. Someone must have already placed the call."

Someone. Not him. As in, he's running from the cops, not hoping they'll arrive to help.

"What is wrong with you?" I whisper harshly.

He stares at me for a long moment and then slams the door shut.

We get on the road. He's driving fast, but there's nothing frantic about him. He's cool and in control.

Someone who's just killed a person for the first time wouldn't behave like this.

He's done this before.

Bile rises up my throat. "Start talking."

"My name is Nero De Luca. I was the consigliere of one of the five New York mob families until I had to fake my own death."

The words feel like sharp stabs right through my chest. I gasp for breath.

It's...true.

Everything Uncle Lyle said was true.

"My boss's name was Rafaele Messero. His wife was taken, and I was supposed to get her back, but I didn't know

398

Rafaele asked one of his allies, the Ferraros, to provide backup. When their guys arrived, I thought they were there to fight us, not help us, and I killed one of them. It was a clusterfuck. The Ferraros wanted me dead. Rafe felt that wasn't fair, but he couldn't risk starting a war with them, so he sent me away. Gave me a new identity. Told me to start over."

He delivers all of this so calmly, as if he's completely oblivious to the way he's destroying me.

"You're a criminal," I whisper.

His jaw clenches. "I am."

"You've been lying to me the whole time I've known you."

"I've been lying to everyone."

He hasn't just been lying. He *is* a lie.

The Rowan I thought I knew—the Rowan I thought I *loved* —never existed.

He played me for a fool.

All the signs are so obvious now. That dark look he got in his eyes when he looked at Brett. The way he was never scared of Uncle Lyle. Why would he be when they're both cut from the same cloth?

The fucking gun he brought home?

The cufflinks. *NDL.*

It was all right there. Staring me in the face.

I was so determined not to let Brett manipulate me that I turned a blind eye to all the signs, to the man who was doing most of the manipulating.

My heart trembles, cracks, and shatters. He betrayed me.

I clutch at my chest, because the pain feels entirely too real.

How did I make the same mistake again? What is wrong with me? How could I allow myself to get so taken in?

I blink against the stinging in my eyes. "And Sam…"

"Sam's real name is—" He swallows. "Was. His real name was Sandro. And he was sent away with me."

Just when I think the pain can't get any worse, it does. "Sam was part of it too?"

The fish tattoo. Their matching fucking tattoos. They fed me nonsense. Lies.

How was I so oblivious?

"He was one of our drivers. He was sent to keep an eye on me. Make sure I didn't do anything stupid like try to go home or draw attention to myself by getting involved in things I shouldn't."

"Did you?"

"No. I didn't."

"But you did threaten Brett. He showed me photos of you pointing a gun at him. I told him they must have been doctored, but they were real, weren't they?"

"They were real."

Then a thought comes to me. Brett suggested something else too. Something that sounded crazy. Something that I was quick to dismiss…

"Rowan, did you start the fire in my house?" My voice is barely a whisper.

When he doesn't answer, my gaze snaps to him.

His throat bobs with a swallow. "Yes."

Time stops. The fury leaks out of me until there's nothing left. I'm empty. Numb. *Cold.*

Slowly, I turn away from him, my unfocused eyes landing on the road. "Why would you do that?"

"I couldn't let you leave. I wanted you."

"*Why?*"

"Because!" he snaps. "Because I loved my old life, and it was taken from me with no warning. Rafe sent me away to save my life, but the moment I left New York, I became a dead man. I felt fucking dead, Blake."

"You missed being a criminal?" There's no inflection in my voice.

"I did. And then I saw you, and something about you eased the pain. And the more time I spent around you, the less it hurt. So I wanted you. I couldn't let you leave."

He wanted me, so he burned down my home?

He destroyed my chance at getting out of Darkwater Hollow?

He convinced me to live with him, date him, give myself to him?

What kind of psychopath does that?

If it weren't for him, I wouldn't be here now. I wouldn't have been nearly raped by Uncle Lyle. I wouldn't have seen all those men killed in cold blood right in front of me.

I need to get out of here. I need to get away from him.

At the next light, I grab the door handle and rattle it as hard as I can.

He reaches over, wraps his palm around my forearm, and rips me away from the handle. "Enough."

"L-let me go. I don't want to be with you anymore. I want to go home."

"We can't go back to Darkwater."

"Let go of me!"

He does, but I still can't breathe. I don't want to be in this car. Don't want to sit beside him and share air with him. "You're a monster."

"Slap whatever label you want on me," he growls. "But I'm not letting you go home."

"Why not?"

He takes a deep breath, and when he starts talking to me, his voice is low and soothing, like I'm a wild animal he's trying to tame. "The Ferraros would find us."

"Us? What do I have to do with any of this?"

"You're mine. They know you're mine. Your godfather most likely told them he was using you to get to me. They will kill me, and they will kill you, Blake."

"I'm not yours. I don't want *anything* to do with you."

"It doesn't matter what you want," he says. "I'm trying to save your life."

I stare out the window, watching the side of the road pass by in a blur. The world outside feels distant, like a dream. How did I get here? How did I become entangled in all of this?

My gut told me not to trust him the day he moved in.

But again, I didn't listen. And now I'm going to have to pay for that mistake.

CHAPTER 44

NERO

She's looking at me like she's never seen me before. And the truth is that she hasn't.

What she saw before was a mask.

And now that the mask is gone, she has no desire for the man behind it.

It's not surprising. I knew she'd never accept Nero, but what I didn't know is how much her rejection would decimate me.

This morning, I woke up happy in the knowledge that she would stay with me, that she was going to try to have a life with me.

But now that it's dark outside, that happiness is no more than a distant memory. My mind is a vortex of bleak, joyless thoughts.

Sandro's not the only person I lost today.

"Where are you taking me?"

I don't answer, because I don't know. I need to think.

When she talks, her voice shakes. She's scared of me. Petrified.

Of course she is. She just saw me kill a bunch of men.

I don't regret killing them, but I hate that she thinks I'd ever hurt her. That she fears me.

My heart throbs like an open wound. I want to kiss her, to give her comfort, to tell her everything will be okay, but she doesn't want any of that from me, and she doesn't need more lies.

Whatever we had between us... It's over.

Maybe I was an idiot to think it would ever work between us. A criminal like me, and a pure soul like her.

I squeeze the wheel between my hands. *Fuck.*

If I hadn't pulled a gun on Brett, he wouldn't have had enough evidence to convince those bikers to look into me.

I made a mistake. A terrible fucking mistake.

Why did I do that? So that I could feel powerful? So that I could be Nero again?

Well, I've gotten my wish.

The air thickens inside my lungs. I messed up, and this time, I've got no one to blame but me.

Blake's been quiet for the last few minutes. I glance at her. There are silent tears slipping down her cheeks, and the sight makes me feel like the world's most wretched man.

How could I do this to her?

She notices me looking and meets my gaze. "Just let me go. I'll take care of myself."

It's impossible. She can't go back to Darkwater Hollow. Someone from the Iron Raptors will take her as soon as they discover she's back. She'll pay for their deaths. "It's not safe there for you anymore. That life is over."

"My house is there. What about your company? We can't just disappear."

"If we go back, we'll be killed. We have to leave everything behind."

She's silent for a beat, and when she speaks again, her voice is no more than a weak whisper. "So what do we do? Where are we going?"

There really is only one option.

A city I thought I'd never see again.

I have to go back to New York. And she has to come with me.

The Ferraros know I'm alive. Lyle must have talked to someone on their side. He was confident he was going to get paid for delivering me. That means when we don't show up at the meeting spot two days from now, we'll be tracked down, hunted, and killed.

My cover's blown. My new identity's done.

I don't have a way to get new documents for me and Blake. Not without reaching out to my old friends, and if I do that, I'll only get them in trouble and probably die anyway.

Truth is, I'm tired of pretending. I'm tired of running, lying, and living a life that isn't mine.

There's a clean way out of this.

I can face the consequences.

Give myself up to the Ferraros.

Let them kill me.

But I have to find a way to protect Blake first. I need to be sure that even after I'm gone, she'll be safe.

Think, Nero. *Think.*

The Ferraros won't grant me any favors. If they know she's important to me, they might just kill her as punishment before they kill me.

Maybe I can find a way to talk to Rafe before I give myself up to them. I can ask for his help.

But I know my old boss, and he won't put his relationship with the Ferraros in jeopardy. If the Ferraros decide to kill her after I'm gone, they could do it. She's a nobody to Rafe. He wouldn't try to stop them.

She's not family. If she were, things would be different. The don must protect the family of his made men. That's law. That's something the don swears to all of us when we become made.

I stop at a red light.

Hold on.

That's it. I can *make* her family.

Then Rafe won't be able to refuse me. And then, no matter what happens to me, she'll be safe.

"I asked where we're going?" she says.

I turn to her, taking in her glistening blue eyes. "We're going to get married."

Nero and Blake's story continues in When He Takes, part 2 of the Fallen God duet:

PREORDER WHEN HE TAKES

Coming August 2024

DELETED SCENE

Want to read a deleted scene from When He Desires in which Rowan does a bit of not-so-innocent spying on his new neighbor?

Just scan the QR code to get "The Voyeur":

JOIN GABRIELLE'S GALS

Talk about When He Desires with other readers and get access to exclusive content in Gabrielle's reader group!

www.ingramcontent.com/pod-product-compliance
Ingram Content Group UK Ltd.
Pitfield, Milton Keynes, MK11 3LW, UK
UKHW041317130325
4982UKWH00025B/109